tara sullivan was born in India

and spent her childhood living in Bangladesh, Ecuador, Bolivia, and the Dominican Republic with her parents, who were international aid workers. She received a BA in Spanish literature and cognitive science from the University of Virginia, and a MA in Latin American studies and an MPA in nonprofit management from Indiana University. To research *Golden Boy*, Tara traveled to Tanzania, where she interviewed those working to rescue and educate Tanzanian people with albinism. She currently teaches high school Spanish and lives in Malden, Massachusetts. *Golden Boy* is her first novel.

GOLDEN BOY

GOLDEN BOY

tara sullivan

G. P. PUTNAM'S SONS
AN IMPRINT OF PENGUIN GROUP (USA) INC.

G. P. PUTNAM'S SONS

An imprint of Penguin Young Readers Group.

Published by The Penguin Group.

Penguin Group (USA) Inc., 375 Hudson Street, New York, NY 10014, USA.

Penguin Group (Canada), 90 Eglinton Avenue East, Suite 700, Toronto,
Ontario M4P 2Y3, Canada (a division of Pearson Penguin Canada Inc.).

Penguin Books Ltd, 80 Strand, London WC2R 0RL, England.

Penguin Ireland, 25 St. Stephen's Green, Dublin 2, Ireland (a division of Penguin Books Ltd).

Penguin Group (Australia), 707 Collins Street, Melbourne, Victoria 3008, Australia
(a division of Pearson Australia Group Pty Ltd).

Penguin Books India Pvt Ltd, 11 Community Centre, Panchsheel Park, New Delhi–110 017, India.

Penguin Group (NZ), 67 Apollo Drive, Rosedale, Auckland 0632, New Zealand
(a division of Pearson New Zealand Ltd).

Penguin Books South Africa, Rosebank Office Park, 181 Jan Smuts Avenue,
Parktown North 2193, South Africa.

Penguin China, B7 Jiaming Center, 27 East Third Ring Road North,
Chaoyang District, Beijing 100020, China.

Penguin Books Ltd, Registered Offices: 80 Strand, London WC2R 0RL, England.

Published simultaneously in Canada. Printed in the United States of America.
Design by Ryan Thomann. Text set in Chaparral.

Library of Congress Cataloging-in-Publication Data is available upon request.
ISBN 978-0-399-16112-4

1 3 5 7 9 10 8 6 4 2

To Nick,
for making this, and all my successes, possible.

MAP TO COME

1.

I AM SITTING under the acacia tree on the ridge when I first see them: three men, in nice clothes, coming toward our house. Their shoulders are straight and their fat bellies strain against their belts when they walk. They are the image of power.

I wish I could see their faces, but my eyes aren't good enough for that at this distance. I peel off my long-sleeved shirt and my floppy hat with the cloth sewn onto the back and crawl to the edge of the ridge in nothing but my long pants. My skin burns so easily that I could never do this in the middle of the day, no matter how hot it was, but now that the sun is setting I can enjoy the feeling of the wind whispering over me. Our goats mill around me, eating their dinner; the breeze carries the smells of the evening meal my mother and sister are preparing up the slope. The three men walk to our door.

"Hodi hodi!" the first man bellows.

Mother appears in the doorway. After a moment, Asu joins her. Beside the big men, my mother and sister look weak and small. Mother bows her head respectfully and invites them into the house. The men walk in, and now I can't see them anymore, can't hear what's going on. Curiosity crawls over me like army ants.

I toss my long clothes over my shoulder and grab the horns of the lead goat, pulling her down the hill toward the three-sided pen set into the wall of our house. She digs in her hooves and bleats angrily at me, but I push her in anyway.

"I'll make it up to you later," I promise, and shove the other goats in behind her. Pulling the gate shut, I sneak around the wall toward our front door. I rest my hand against the mud wall; its heat warms my fingers. For a moment I feel happy about my cleverness. But as I hunch there, listening, that feeling bleeds out of me, until soon it's as if it had never been.

I'm not sure how long I crouch there, but it's long enough. Long enough to hear that the men are the tax collector, the seed provider, and the landlord. Long enough to hear my mother and sister beg. Long enough to hear what the men say in return: No.

No, you cannot have three more months to pay your taxes.

No, you cannot have more seed if you cannot pay.

No, you cannot stay here anymore.

The men leave, closing the door behind them—*thump*. My mother and sister don't come out with them. There are no more sounds of dinner-making. Instead the hollow sound of sadness fills the house.

When I stand up, my knees creak like an old man's. I don't go in. Instead I go to the goat pen because I can't think of anything better to do. And that's why I'm the first to see the hole in the side of the enclosure where the goats have kicked and butted and chewed their way to freedom and the dinner I didn't let them finish. They're nowhere to be seen.

I need to get the goats!

I toss my crumpled clothes toward the house and scramble up the side of the hill separating our farm from the rest of the village. No goats. I race off into the brush under the trees. No goats. I call and shout, hoping against hope that they will return to the pen at the sound of my voice. I run home: still no goats. But my brothers, Enzi and Chui, have arrived from working in the coffee fields, and they're standing by the hole in the goat pen with Mother and Asu, waiting for me. The instant I see the four of them there, I know I'm in trouble.

"Habo!" my eldest brother, Enzi, calls out to me, his voice low and angry. "Where are the goats?"

I stop where I am and look down at my feet.

"Well?" Enzi stomps across the space between us until the shadows from his broad shoulders completely cover me.

"Gone," I mumble.

"What?" Enzi is shouting now, which really isn't necessary. My ears are the one part of my strange body that work just fine.

"They got out," I say.

Enzi looms over me. His hands fist at his sides, making his upper arms strain against the thin material of his shirt.

"And just where were you when they got out, hmm?" he asks.

I don't want to admit what I heard. I dart a glance toward Mother, but she is staring off in the direction of Arusha city and doesn't see me look at her. In the pause I hear Chui grumble to Enzi, "He looks like a ghost and he does as little work as a ghost. I bet he was sleeping."

I hate Chui for saying it, but it gives me the lie I was looking for.

"I guess I must have dozed off."

I don't see Enzi raise his hand, but the force of his slap sends me staggering into the wall of our house. Small clumps of mud break off and fall to the ground from the impact of my shoulders. When my head snaps back, I bite my lip and my mouth fills with the taste of my own blood. Mother's head whips toward me at the sound, but she doesn't say anything. Enzi is twenty, and man-grown, and has been in charge since my father left. She rarely questions what he does.

Asu is a different story.

"Enzi!" she says with a gasp. "What did you do that for?" She runs over to me and dabs at my bleeding lip with the edge of her *khanga*, her pretty face all crunched up in concern. Mother looks away over the hills again, her dark eyes strangely empty, her face as smooth as the sky.

"That stupid ghost boy lost our goats!" Enzi points at me when he says this, the muscles of his arms standing out, tense.

"And how is hitting him going to bring them back?" Asu snaps. She stands facing Enzi, her frown pulling her headscarf low over her eyes, hands on hips. She has dropped her hem again and I can see my bloodstain peek in and out of the folds at her ankles.

Enzi throws up his hands and stalks into the house, head low between his shoulders.

"You always defend him," mutters Chui to Asu. His round face twists deeper into a scowl. He kicks a rock by his feet and it goes skittering off into the bush.

Asu turns away from Chui. She pushes the heels of her hands into her eyes, seeming suddenly tired. "Well, none of you ever do," she answers. But she says it so quietly that I don't think anyone else hears her.

As if released from a spell, Mother starts moving again. She wipes her dry face, as though to remind herself that she exists. Her fingers trace the wrinkles around her eyes and mouth. Then she straightens her hair scarf and turns to Chui. "Pack," she says to him. Over her shoulder, to me, she adds, "Go find the goats."

"Why do I need to pack?" asks Chui as the three of them head into the house.

Face still stinging from Enzi's slap, I leave to look for the goats, grateful that I have a reason not to be there when Mother tells Enzi and Chui we have to leave.

❉

I hunt for the goats for hours: until my face is red and sweaty, until my feet are sore and my lungs burn. The darkness soothes my skin, but my bad eyes are worse than useless. It's luck more than skill that sends me tripping into a gully where

I land right on top of the goats, who have huddled together for warmth. Not sure whether I want to kick them for running off and scaring me or hug them for still being alive, I tie them together with the length of sisal twine I brought with me and lead them home.

When I get to the front door, I'm not sure what to do since I can't put them into their broken pen. I decide to bring them inside with me. They're still hobbled to one another and they start to walk around the small interior of our house, bleating and getting tangled in people's legs. Mother *tsks* in annoyance and strides out the door with a big burlap sack over her shoulder, pushing the goats to one side with her hips when they get in her way.

"I found the goats," I say unnecessarily. Chui shoves his hands into his shorts pockets and glares at me. When he scowls his eyes become angry little slits in his face. Enzi glares at me, too, from where he's folding his clothes. Asu looks up from sorting the kitchen goods and laughs softly.

"I can see that, Golden Boy. But did you have to bring them into the house?"

"Well, their pen is kind of broken." I smile at her.

"Hobble them outside by the door, then" she says, "and pack up your things. We have to leave tonight."

I pull the goats outside and hobble them with the twine. I tie the horns of the lead goat to the side of the pen too, for good measure. Then I head back inside.

Even though I know the answer, I ask the question so Asu won't know I heard what happened. "Why do we have to leave?"

Chui's head snaps up. "Because of you!" he snarls.

"Chui," Asu warns softly.

"It's true!" he shouts at her, waving his raggedy-finger-nailed hands around to make his point. "We used to be fine here, fine! Enzi says that Father was able to keep the farm running through worse droughts than this. If he hadn't left because of that stupid ghost, none of this would be happening!"

"*Chui!*" Asu's voice is no longer soft. Chui stops talking and continues shoving things into his pack. His neck is stiff and his movements are choppy. His face is tight and hard.

There's an awkward silence. I move over to the corner I sleep in and start piling my clothes into the middle of my blanket with my white hands. Not black and strong like Enzi's. Not black and slender like Asu's. Not black and stumpy like Chui's. Not black and calloused like Mother's. Milk white. Bone white. Ghost white.

Mother comes back in and her sack is bulging at irregular angles. I see the outlines of tools. She unpacks them and sets them against the wall, for whoever will have our house next, I suppose.

"Aren't we bringing those with us?" asks Chui.

"No, my dear," says Mother absently as she joins Asu near the food stores.

"Where are we going?" I ask her. If we're not bringing the tools with us, that means that Mother doesn't think we'll be farming anymore.

"To Mwanza," she says, tying an aggressive knot in a large

bundle of cornmeal and dried pigeon peas. "My sister lives there. We'll have to stay with her until I figure out what to do next."

"Where is Mwanza?" I ask.

"Far away." Her voice is a tired sigh. "We'll have to catch a bus from Arusha. Even so, it will be many, many hours before we get there."

"What's it like to take a bus for the whole day?" asks Chui.

"Oh, ask Enzi and Asu," says Mother distractedly. "We used to go up every year to visit when they were small. Before . . ."

She trails off, never saying before what. But Chui shoots me a poisoned look anyway. We all know what "before" means. Before I was born. Before Father left.

Enzi looks up from where he is putting his machete and the last of his clothes into a plastic bucket.

"Ask Asu about the bus," he says to Chui. "I'm not going with you."

We all stare at him.

"What did you say?" Mother asks, suddenly very alert. Her hands clench and unclench by her sides. I don't think she knows she's doing it.

"We need the money," says Enzi, not looking at her. The light from the kerosene lamp throws shadows across his face, highlighting the jut of his cheekbones, hiding his eyes. "I can make ten thousand shillings a day picking coffee. It just doesn't make sense for me to leave until after the harvest is finished."

"No," says Mother. "No, I won't split the family. We're all

we have now."

Enzi moves to put an arm around her shoulder. She's swallowed by his shadow, and now I can see his face. His eyes are sad, but his jaw is rigid. He's not going to change his mind.

"You can't leave us now!" exclaims Asu, slapping her hand down on her bundle. "How will we be safe on the road without a man?"

"You'll be fine. Chui will be with you."

Asu narrows her eyes. "Mother and I are supposed to make it all the way across the country with a fifteen-year-old for protection?" Asu may be nineteen and old enough to be married, but she and Enzi fight like two children about how to run the family.

"Hey!" says Chui. "I help Enzi in the fields and get almost a man's wages. Why do you still think I'm just a little boy? Enzi thinks I can do it."

Asu doesn't respond and instead returns to packing. I can tell she's frustrated, though, because instead of folding things neatly, she's shoving them into the bags.

I'm only two years younger than Chui, but no one has mentioned that I might help on the road, too. Chui may not be a man, but I'm hardly a person. I finish tying off my bedroll and help Asu with the kitchen supplies, handing her things to pack. It slows her down enough that she isn't crushing things anymore. I know if I let her keep doing that she'd be angry at herself later. Chui has stopped packing entirely, staring at Enzi as if he could make him stay with us just using the power of his thoughts.

"You're going to abandon us, then?" Mother has started to cry onto Enzi's shoulder. Her hands make fists in the material of his shirt.

"Just because I'm staying here doesn't mean I'm abandoning you or breaking up the family," Enzi says softly, patting her on the back like you would a baby. "The money here is good. How am I going to make this much money on the road? In Mwanza? It's a fishing city. I don't know how to fish. We need the money I can make here." His hands are huge and calloused from working in the fields, but he holds her softly. He looks deeply into her eyes. "You need the money I can make here more than you need me on the bus with you. I'll come as soon as the harvest is done. I promise."

Mother lets go of Enzi and sinks down beside the packs. She rubs her fingers into her temples as if she's getting a headache. I want to go and put an arm around her like Enzi just did, but I don't think she would want that from me, so I stay where I am.

A vein on Enzi's forehead is throbbing up and down, up and down, casting a line of shadow across his face, but he doesn't say anything else. Asu wraps a wedge of *ugali*, the thick cornmeal porridge that's the basis of most of our meals, in a banana leaf and hands it to Enzi.

"For your breakfast," she says flatly, and reopens the bundle she just tied shut to leave some other food with him, too.

"Let me stay here with you. I can help!" insists Chui, breathing hard. He has always stuck close to Enzi. Maybe that's why there was never any room left near Enzi for me.

"No," says Enzi, reaching over and squeezing Chui's shoulder. I see Chui's shirt wrinkle under Enzi's fingers. "You need to go with the family. You'll be the oldest son until I join you again."

"But I can help!" Chui says. His eyes are big and shiny even though his hands are clenched by his sides. "We could work together."

"No," says Enzi firmly. "They can't go alone." He looks Chui directly in the eye as he says this, and after a pause, Chui nods at him, like a man. No one looks over at me. Enzi goes on: "I'll put you on the bus in the morning, but I'm going to stay here. I'll sell the goats and, at the end of the coffee season in December, I'll follow you to Mwanza."

Chui nods again, then stalks out into the night. "I'm going to check on the goats," he says over his shoulder.

I say nothing. Enzi is the closest thing to a father I've ever known. Even if he never really liked me, he was all that I had. Now he's staying behind. I want to say something, but I feel like I have no words. Even if I did, they probably wouldn't want to hear them from me, anyway. Other than the occasional bleat of a goat, it is so quiet in the house that I can hear the rustling of the grass outside and the whine of the cicadas and, when the wind changes direction, the muffled sound from over the hill of Chui crying.

❋

It takes us most of the night to organize ourselves: leaving

Enzi with the goats and the things he'll need and packing everything else into bundles we'll be able to carry on our heads.

When everything is packed we stand beside our bundles for a minute, looking at our house. Mother's hands rattle by her sides like dry palm fronds in a wind. Finally, Enzi says, "Let's go."

With the first step I feel a terrible shift in my chest. This leaving is not like leaving for the river or school. This leaving is the kind of leaving you do at a gravesite. It's a leaving that is also a giving up. Our home is no longer our home. Our farm is no longer our farm. I make the mistake of looking back one more time.

I hope that everyone will think I'm rubbing at my eyes because I can't see well in the dark. But tonight no one teases me, not even Chui.

2.

THE BUS TO MWANZA leaves from Arusha city at six in the morning, and we decide not to bother sleeping. My family plods, bored and tired, along the long path from our village to the city, but I crane my head around, wishing it was daytime so I could see.

I've never been to Arusha. The farthest I've been from home is our little village school and the places I wander when I'm grazing the goats. I know where I'm supposed to stay: in our house, in the shadows of the wall, in the shade of the trees. Out of the sun and out of sight. The scorched path of gray dust leading from our little village into Arusha is not my place. I learned this the day I tried to follow Asu as she left for secondary school in the city. I made it as far as the front yard when Mother grabbed me by the arm and hauled me inside.

"Don't even think about it, Habo!" she had said. *"Don't you dare think about shaming us in the city, too."*

I had stared up at her then, unable to say anything,

terrified by the intensity in her voice. Mother and I have always been like the two posts of a doorframe, unable to move closer or farther away, and the emptiness that sits between us is the shape of my missing father. He left right after I was born, when the whispers started that Raziya gave birth to a white son—not a good brown child like the three born before him, but white. White like *ugali* in the pot; white like the teeth in your face; white like a tourist who isn't where he should be. Why do I look like this when both my parents and my brothers and sister are a deep, warm brown? I don't know what to think. But whatever it was that my father thought, he thought it hard enough that he left and has never come back.

Was he a superstitious man? Did he believe, like the old women in our village, that I'm an evil spirit? Or was he a practical man? Did he believe a white man was my real father, not him? I've wondered that, too, though it's a dishonorable thought. I wonder it every time I hear people mention Americans or Europeans, the tourists that come to Arusha to go on *safaris*. I want to think the best of my mother, but I have no way to judge, because I've never seen a white person. When I look up in the sky I can see the silver flash of the airplanes that bring them here, and when I let the goats wander extra far toward the road I can see the clouds of dust kicked up by the boxy Land Rovers that are taking them to the parks, but I have never seen *them*. Perhaps they're trying to stay out of the sun, like I have to. Perhaps I'd be normal somewhere else.

No one in my family can tell me what I need to know. Chui tells me to shut up. I don't dare ask Mother or Enzi, and every time I've asked Asu, we have the same conversation:

What are they like? I ask.

Well, they're white, Habo, she replies.

White like me? I ask.

A little, she says.

I've tried to figure out what "a little" means, with no success.

Do they have yellow hair? I ask.

Sometimes, she says.

Do they have light eyes? I ask.

Some do, she says.

Do their eyes shake like mine? Do they have trouble seeing, too?

I don't know, Habo, I've never talked to one. Some wear glasses . . .

This goes on and on. All of which is no help at all. What I want to know, what I need to know, is *Are they like me? Am I like them?*

It's still dark when we arrive at the far outskirts of Arusha. We walk through neighborhoods where men stand just beyond the light of streetlamps and women with dead eyes lean in open doorways. Places where the smell of burnt cooking oil and urine is strong, and we have to step carefully around the trash and trickles of water in the street. I'm glad to leave those places quickly.

By the time the first light of dawn is streaking the sky, we're walking through better streets, full of the smells of people cooking *ugali* and women turning ears of corn on open braziers. Here, the concrete of the buildings has paint on it, and the little shops have their wares out on the side of the street for people to see: carved wooden bed frames, motorcycles lined up for repair, small hills of used tires. I stare and stare, but I don't see anyone who looks like me. I keep my head down, grateful it's July and lots of people are in long sleeves because of the dry season's cold nights. Otherwise, I'd stick out twice as much. As it is, I can feel the people's stares pulling at the sides of my face. I curl inward like a turtle and walk faster.

Soon, though, my pace is determined by others. Even though it's still early, the sidewalks of Arusha are becoming more crowded than I could ever imagine: Boys selling sunglasses on large trays dodge around women carrying black plastic market bags. Merchants are lining the broken sidewalks, laying out rows of shoes, or vegetables, or music discs to sell. On some blocks sewing machines take up half the sidewalk, waiting for their tailors to sit behind them; on others, men are folding down the scrap wood sides of little kiosks where they will fix and sell mobile phones and watches.

Enzi asks one of these stall boys what the time is, and when he tells us, everyone starts to walk a little faster. I'm following them closely, not wanting to get lost, when the sound of voices speaking a language I don't know and the metallic popping sound of a car trunk being opened make me turn my head. And I see them: Two women and three men are hefting their bags into a long white Land Rover, ready to go out on *safari.*

They are white people.

They are not like me.

Their hair ranges in color from corn-tassels to tea-with-milk and falls around their faces in soft waves. None of them has tight knots of yellow hair. Their eyes are a range of colors, too—sky blue, mud brown. One even has my light, bluish-color eyes, but none of their eyes shake from side to side, not even the one who is wearing glasses. And their skin, their skin is *not* white. It is pink, or eggshell-with-brown-spots, or the color of the inside of finely cured goat leather, but it is not white.

Then a woman with bright hair and sky eyes sees me, and her mouth goes round. She says a startled sentence to the man beside her, and he turns to stare, too. That's when I know for a fact that I'm the freak I've always been called. Even to the strangers, I am strange.

I turn away from their wide foreign eyes and their surprise that marks me as different and jog to catch up with my family.

❄

We get to the bus station with less than half an hour to spare before the bus leaves. Mother quickly finds a shop with a phone in it and pays the shop owner to make a call to Mwanza.

"Yes, Neema," Mother bellows into the phone receiver. Maybe you have to speak loudly to make your voice carry all the way to Mwanza. I don't know. I've never used a phone.

Who would I call? I have a brief mental picture of me calling our goats on the phone. *Get into your pen!* I would shout into the receiver. I smile to myself. Mother continues: "No, I don't know when we'll get there . . . We'll call you along the way if we can . . . *Kwaheri!*"

She hangs up the phone and Enzi leads us through the crowd, pushing with his elbows toward a long blue-and-yellow-painted bus. People jostle him, but he doesn't let them change his path. When we finally get to the bus, the news is not good. The cost is 25,000 shillings a person, no exceptions. And everyone has to pay 1,100 shillings for park fees, too, to get the bus through the gates of Ngorongoro and the Serengeti. Enzi argues with the bus driver, but there's no way to change the price.

Enzi scowls furiously as he and Asu step to one side to count our money. Mother doesn't help them, but I can tell from the way the lines on her face sag that she knows we don't have enough Not even close. Enzi looks grim as he grips the money. Asu goes up and quietly asks the driver if we can ride halfway for half the price. He agrees to that.

Enzi isn't happy that we won't make it all the way, but we can't stay here with no house or farm, and this makes it even clearer that we need the money he will make on the plantation, so there are no more arguments about his coming with us.

Once the price is agreed on, Enzi tosses our bundles onto the roof. Then he boosts Chui up, to make sure our packs don't fall off. The roof is like a second bus, piled dangerously

high with belongings and sacks of mangoes and millet, all
tied to the thin guardrail running around the edge. Like Chui,
boys of all ages sit on the sacks or balance up near the front.
It looks like a lot of fun. At just thirteen, I'm the youngest and
that should have been my job, but of course I have to stay inside, in the shade, useless as always. Chui's words come back
to me: *You look like a ghost and you do as little work as a ghost.*

Enzi gives Mother one last hug, pokes Asu in the belly,
making her yell at him, waves to Chui and me, and then walks
away, standing tall. I try to keep him in sight as long as possible, but soon my bad eyes cannot tell his head from the others in the crowd, and I've lost him. I swallow hard against the
sudden tightness in my throat.

"Come on, Habo," says Asu. She puts her arm around me
and steers me into the bus.

As we walk down the aisle I can hear the hollow clanging of
boys' feet on the roof above us. I feel the vibration of it in my
feet. It's like living in a drum. Asu sits by the window in the
very last row of the bus, and I sit between her and Mother. I
don't want to sit so near the window, but I don't have a choice.
I bet no one but my family would be willing to sit beside me.

All the windows of the bus are open, and the early morning sun sits on my lap like a hostile cat. I can get sunburned
no matter what time of year it is. I lean awkwardly to line up
my arm with the thin stripe of shade cast by the window bar
and sit on my hands.

Staring out the window, I see boys and young men with
baskets of fruit and trays of sweets. They mob the sides of the

bus, holding up their wares and shouting. Some of them have no shirts on in spite of the cool morning air and, warm from running, their sweating chests and shoulders glisten like roasted coffee beans. I tuck my hands deeper underneath myself and imagine that I'm one of them, slapping deep brown hands against the dirty metal, smiling with perfect dark eyes at the people on the bus. Everyone would smile back.

Just then, one of the boys sees me staring at him. He lets out a cry of surprise and grabs his friend's arm to get his attention. I turn my head away and let the floppy brim of my hat cover me as much as it can before I can see them all start to stare at me. But I still hear them.

"Hey, white boy!" they call. "Hey!"

I feel Mother stiffen beside me on the seat, but she keeps her eyes focused forward, not acknowledging them. I don't answer, either. The boys clap their hands to get my attention and keep calling out. Asu leans out the window.

"Go away," she snaps.

"Who's that white boy?"

"He's my brother."

"No, he's not!" I can hear them laughing as the heat creeps up my neck. Mother reaches over and picks up my hand. I glance up at her quickly, surprised. We rarely touch. She doesn't look at me, so from anyone else's point of view it would seem like she was ignoring both me and the boys, but her warm fingers curl around mine and give a little squeeze. I squeeze back and square my shoulders.

"*Ndiyo*, he is," Asu says angrily. "What do you know? Go

away!"

"Why does he look like that, if he's your brother?"

Asu pulls her head inside, ignoring the question.

I hear a chorus of guesses from the boys below. "He's sick!" "He was born in a cave!" "He's really an animal!" "His father's a white man!"

I feel Mother's fingers begin to tremble in mine, but she doesn't let go. The boys' voices, used to shouting bargains, carry a long way. They've all forgotten that they're supposed to be selling oranges and cigarettes. I give up trying to be brave and shrink deeper into the seat, but it's too late. The creaks of springs and the sigh of protesting plastic tell me that everyone in the bus is turning around to see the family with the white-animal son. Mother lets go of my hand and I shrink away from the eyes.

I huddle into my long clothes and wait for the people to forget about me. Finally, over the sound of the boys outside our windows, I hear the clatter of the engine. The bus gives a great shudder, and a cloud of dark smoke pours in the rear windows. We're on our way to Mwanza.

As the bus travels I stare out the window, squirming to keep my exposed skin in the moving shade of the window frame. Every few kilometers, the sky is punctured by an enormous yellow Vodafone sign or red Airtel sign. I amuse myself trying to read them as we pass. Some of them have print big enough that even I can mostly read it. But after a few hours, my eyes feel grainy and my hair is crunchy under my fingers. The dust from the road gets so far into my lungs that even coughing doesn't clear it. For all that, though, I love the bus ride. Since I always had to stay hidden away at home, I've never been on a bus before. I stare out the window as village after village whisks by. I see children clustered around a water pump, joking while they fill their plastic containers; children carrying babies while running errands; children minding goats. I see Maasai boys leading long strings of humpbacked cattle across the dry fields to graze. It makes me smile to see that the cows wait for the boys' signal before they cross the road. I wonder how they trained them to do that. Our goats never listened to me.

Some towns are well off: rows of neat concrete houses with tin roofs. Others towns are small, thatched places that look like our home. When we take the turn onto the road that runs along the ridge of the Ngorongoro crater, we see only Maasai villages with their circular huts. The air up on the crater rim is cold and misty, and I shiver in my seat until we come down the other side.

I'm sorry when, hours later, I see the entrance to the Serengeti Park because I know the ride is over and we have to get out. I reach over and softly jostle Asu and Mother's shoulders, waking them up. They nod and, when the driver pulls over at the first village inside the gate and looks at us in his mirror, we file quietly out of the bus.

❋

The Maasai village just inside the Serengeti park gates is a small place, about ten circular mud houses clustered around a central cattle pen. When the bus pulls away, Mother, Asu, and Chui head into the village to buy some food. No one suggests I go along, not even Asu. In any village, strangers are unexpected enough. They don't need me there, stranger than strange.

I walk away from the village, just to make sure I don't complicate things for them. I find an umbrella acacia tree over a rise and I sit in its shade to wait. When I hear a rustling to my left and see a head duck quickly behind a bush, I realize I've been found by children from the village. They must be very young to not have chores or herding to do. I try not to let their muffled laughter bother me while I wait for them to go away again. Then a small rock flies out from behind the thorn bushes.

I can't believe it: They're throwing rocks at me for fun, like I'm a street dog. I want to shout at them to go away, but I remember my family inside the village, trying to buy things we need. I can't help them barter, but at least I won't turn the village against us, either. I cover my head with my arms and let the rocks bounce off. I begin to count in my head, slowly, to pass the time until they leave me alone.

Mmoja, mbili, tatu, I count. *Nne, tano, sita, saba.* I can feel myself starting to bruise. *Nane.*

I am at *thelathini*, thirty, when I finally realize that they are not planning to go away until they have made me do something. I'm sore and angry, and this makes me stupid. I pull off my hat and stand up. I let my eyes wave around without even trying to focus them. I make a wailing ghost noise in my throat.

"Oooh!" I say. "You've made me angry! Now I'm going to curse you and your families!" I start to walk toward the bushes.

The children drop their rocks and run toward the village so fast, they stumble going down the hill. I laugh a high and ugly laugh, making sure they hear me. For a brief second, I feel a flush of triumph. A minute later, I realize how much of an idiot I am.

Rumors of a witch-boy in the fields will make it impossible for us to stay here very long, maybe not even a night. I sigh and hunker down miserably to wait for my family.

3.

MOTHER COMES UP the hill with an armload of red and purple cloth and an unusual light in her eyes. The other two follow her. Asu looks disgusted, but Chui is smiling. I don't know what to think. I wasn't expecting them to buy clothing. Dumping it all in a heap, Mother pulls out one long piece of red-checked cloth and starts to wrap it around herself.

"I can't believe you're doing this!" Asu says to her. "You look ridiculous!"

Mother ignores Asu entirely. "Put some of these on," she says to me. The sides of her eyes crinkle as she says this.

I stare at her, baffled.

"Why?"

"Just put them on. You, too, Chui." She holds a piece of cloth out at arm's length. "Asu," she says warningly, "do as you're told."

Chui reaches into the pile and starts to drape a big purple

thing around himself. Asu grabs the cloth from Mother and glares at her.

"This is a terrible idea," she says, then turns her back on Mother and starts to wrap the cloth around herself, hiding the original color and drape of her *khanga* from home.

"*What* are we doing?" I ask again, although I, too, am following Mother's lead, dressing myself in a red cloth with thin purple stripes.

Asu sighs and looks over at me.

"Mother has decided that it would be a great idea for us to sneak through the Serengeti on foot."

"And hitch a ride if we can," adds Chui, nothing but a voice from the middle of a big purple mess.

I'm glad we're not going to stay here and try to earn bus fare, but this plan doesn't make sense to me.

"Why do we need new clothes to do that?"

Mother turns to me, that light I don't recognize in her eyes again. She clutches the red-checked cloth so tightly in her fingers, I can see her knucklebones popping out against her skin.

"We're disguising ourselves as Maasai," she says. Her voice is higher pitched and fuller than normal. "That way we can make it across the parklands without paying entry fees or being stopped by rangers." A smile darts across her face like an animal crossing a road: quickly, unsure of itself.

I finally puzzle out her tone. My mother is having fun. I layer on the unfamiliar clothes without another word.

Soon we're walking along the Serengeti road, a slightly-too-short Maasai family of four with all their worldly belongings balanced on their heads.

❋

Mother, Asu, Chui, and I walk late into the night, heading north. We stay on the road for safety and so that we don't get lost, but even after dark Mother insists we leave our Maasai robes on. I feel silly dressed up as something I'm not, but the extra layer of cloth does keep me a little warmer in the dark. Only when we're all stumbling from exhaustion does Mother lead us off the road a little to sleep under a tree. We take turns staying awake, holding a big stick, just in case any wild animals show up.

This seems like a great idea when it's my turn to sleep. But when it's my turn to sit there, squinting into the darkness with my bad eyes, holding nothing but a piece of wood and looking for animals with giant teeth and claws, I think it's really, really stupid.

Dawn finds us stiff and cranky. Since we didn't unpack last night, we just get on our feet and keep walking north, in the direction of my mother's people, away from Enzi and home.

By midday my throat is parched and the sun is blazing down on us. Even though it's the dry season, it still gets hot in the middle of the day. The land is grassy all around us now, with few trees. By the time we find one to shelter under during the hottest part of the day, I'm feeling dizzy from the heat. The backs of my hands and the tops of my sandaled feet are burnt, and even my face is pink under my hat. We all collapse in the shade, and soon the others have fallen asleep. But I can't sleep. I'm hot and miserable and there's nothing quite as lonely as being the only one left awake. When I can't stand it any longer, I lean over my sister and whisper her name.

"Asu!"

She stirs on the ground.

"What is it, Habo?"

"Will you tell me the story of when I was born?" I ask.

"Oh, Habo, not now! Go to sleep," she grouses.

"I can't sleep. I'm burned."

For a moment Asu is quiet, scowling sleepily up at me. The light and shadows of the leaves flicker over her high cheek-bones and highlight her dark brown eyes. I'm afraid she'll say no again. But instead, she pushes herself up on her elbows and opens her pack. She takes out a little gourd full of aloe and takes my burnt hands in hers.

"Fine," she grumbles, rubbing the sticky stuff into the angry red welts over my knuckles as she talks. "You were born on a hot, cloudy day, right before the long rains. Mother was inside the house with the *mkunga*, the midwife, and Father stood outside with us, waiting. Then that *mkunga* screamed so loudly that we all poured in through the door of our house to see what was the matter. I was only six at the time, but I remember it. You should have heard her, Habo—she shrieked like a baboon!"

I smile. The *mkunga* in our village is a cranky old lady, dried out like a banana skin left in the sun. "Where was I?" I ask, even though I've heard the story a hundred times before and know exactly where I was.

"You were lying on the floor, bellowing," says Asu.

"No one would pick me up." I got this detail from Chui, though he was only two and probably doesn't even really remember it.

Asu scowls. "*I* picked you up," she says, and scoops more aloe out of the gourd for my other hand, "and Mother wasn't awake, so you can't blame her, either. Just Father and the *mkunga*." She crinkles up her nose at me. "You're welcome to blame them."

The aloe is heaven on my hands. I sigh, content. Asu goes on.

"You'd be amazed, Habo, if you could remember it. Everyone was arguing about what you were. The old men thought you were a ghost of the ancestors. That stupid *mkunga* was wailing on about demons. I think Father figured you were the son of one of the white men who come to climb Mount Kilimanjaro or take a *safari*. All those people, arguing back and forth, and no one paying attention to the fact that you were acting just like any other newborn baby."

I look down at my white and red hands nested in her even brown ones. I wonder again, for the thousandth time, why I'm so different.

"And then I looked at your white skin, your yellow hair, and your light eyes, and I said to them, '*yeye ni mtoto dhahabo!*'"

"I was a golden child."

"*Ndiyo*, and so we called you *Dhahabo*, gold." Asu lets go of my hands, now shiny with aloe, and puts the gourd into her bag. "Now let me get some sleep, Golden Boy. We have a lot of walking ahead of us."

"*Asante*, Asu, for the aloe," I say.

"*Karibu*," she says, and lies down again.

We continue walking that evening, pushing as far as we can in the failing daylight. We all keep a lookout for the plume of dust that means a car is coming along the road that might be the park rangers. Any time we see one, we find a place to hide until it has passed us. We get so tired that everyone starts snapping at one another. Then we get so tired that everyone stops talking to one another altogether. When darkness falls, we settle down for another uncomfortable night. Tonight I can hear the animals—grunts and coughs in the distance, and from time to time the vibration of many hooves hitting the ground at once. We avoid the long grass and the trees and lie down on the road itself, in a line. It's uncomfortable to be on the packed earth. No matter how much I brush my palms over the surface, there are always little rocks I've missed that jab into me as soon as I try to lie down. I'm having trouble getting comfortable enough to fall asleep.

"I'd rather sleep in the grass," I grumble to no one in particular as I squirm.

"Cars have headlights," Chui whispers, "lions don't. Go to sleep, Habo."

That thought doesn't help me relax. No matter which way

I face, the waving grass is only a few feet away. The darkness plays tricks with my mind, and I keep thinking I see a whisker or a tail. It takes me a long time to fall asleep.

In my dreams I'm being stalked by a huge lion. I'm running down the never-ending road, alone, and I can hear the whisper of its movement through the grass as it stalks me. No matter how fast I run, I get no closer to the end of the road, and no farther from my hunter. With a great roar, the lion jumps onto the road behind me, its teeth bared, its eyes glowing brightly. As it pounces I think, foolishly, that this lion does have headlights. And then I wake up.

For a moment I'm not sure if I'm still dreaming, because I'm blinded by yellow light and there's a shadow looming over me. I cry out and put my hands up in front of my face.

"Easy!" says a man's voice. "Do you think I'm going to hurt you?"

I blink up at him in confusion. Then I look behind him and see the rest of my family gathering their belongings and pushing them into the back of a battered white Jeep. That's the source of the light that's hurting my eyes.

"You sleep like the dead, boy. Come on!" And a dark hand extends down out of the light and pulls me to my feet.

❋

By the time I'm awake enough to figure out what has happened, we're flying down the road, the headlights showing the world in swaying patches, the wind whisling in through the open sides of the Jeep and making my eyes water. It had been Asu's turn to stay awake and hold the stick when the Jeep came up the road. The driver had gotten out and asked her what she was doing on the road in the middle of the night. She told him that she and her family were traveling north and we had nowhere else to sleep. The man said he was driving north to a hunting base camp and offered to take us as far as he was going. From there it was a simple matter of packing the belongings, waking the boy who slept on even when the car's lights hit him in the face, and squeezing in between our things and the man's gear. It's uncomfortable, but it's so much better than walking that none of us complains. I watch the tall grass zip by on either side of us and think to my dream lion, *Take that! I'm ahead of you now!*

I'm just dozing off when laughter wakes me. Asu is talking to the man as he drives. Even Mother seems amused. "What?" I ask.

Asu turns to me with a smile. "We're in the car, at night, with the entire day!" Mother laughs again, but I still don't understand. The driver takes pity on my confusion.

"My name is Alasiri," he says, and waits for me to get the joke.

"I understand now," I say. *Alasiri* means "late afternoon" in Kiswahili. *Asubuhi,* my sister's name, means "morning."

Alasiri's white teeth shine in the darkness when he smiles. I'm not sure why, but I'm reminded of the lion in my dream with the shining face, and it makes me look away from him. But Asu turns toward him and smiles back.

I soon lose interest in their conversation, and I doze off again as we flash along the road like a metal fish swimming with the current of a dusty stream.

⁕

Dawn is still a few hours away when we pull off the main road and bump over the brush to reach Alasiri's camp. After a few jarring kilometers of driving where there's no road, we get there. It's not a fancy place. There are dust-colored tents circled around a smoldering campfire and stools and cooking supplies pushed over to one side. This tells me that other people must share this camp with Alasiri, but no one's here now.

"Sleep near the fire," he says. "The light and the smoke will keep away the animals."

We don't ask which animals he's talking about. I can see signs of relief on the faces of my family and, really, I'm glad to be here, too. The safety of a fire and a man makes everyone feel better than when we were sleeping on the road. Though it's only a few more hours until morning, we all lie down in the circle of orange light and sleep.

I wake up soon after sunrise. I pull myself to my feet, stiff after another night on the ground, and lift my arms high over my head to stretch out my shoulders. I kept the Maasai cloth on for warmpth overnight, but now I unwrap it and leave it on the ground next to my pack. I see that Asu, sitting over by the fire, is back in her usual clothes too. Now that it's daytime,

I'm expecting to see more of the men around, but it's still just Alasiri. I wonder where the others are. There are tents and supplies for at least five people.

I go behind the Jeep to pee and then walk over to where Asu and Alasiri are talking while she makes coffee in a pan over the fire. When I get there Alasiri is finishing a story. I think he's trying to impress her.

"So, what do you do when you're not in the cities?" she asks as she stirs the grounds in circles with a long ladle so they don't stick to the bottom. She's smiling at him. I sit between them, pretending this is only to be near the fire. But really I don't like the way she's smiling at him. Also I'm hoping that, being so close, I'll be able to get some coffee this morning, too. I prefer tea when I can get it, but in the middle of the wilderness here, I'll be happy with any warm drink.

"Some of this and some of that." Alasiri's smile gleams in his dark face. *Handsome face,* I admit grudgingly, noticing his clear brown eyes and high, thin cheekbones. I scowl down at my feet. "During the tourist season, I help with *safaris.* When there are no white people around, I find other work."

"That's interesting." Asu nods.

"And what about you?" Alasiri continues. "Why is such a pretty girl not married yet?"

Asu looks flustered and I know it's not just because of the flattery. It's embarrassing enough to be poor, to be dressed up as Maasai and sleeping in the road, but we're so poor that we'll probably never have enough money to get Asu a good husband. I can't tell if this man is teasing Asu or flirting with her, but either way the answer will embarrass her. I break into their conversation so that she doesn't have to answer him, and say the first thing that comes into my head.

"So what is it, exactly, that you do when you're not on *safari*?"

Alasiri's gaze eats my face.

"A white boy in a black family," he muses. "How odd. Where did you come from, white one?"

Now it is my turn to feel embarrassed, but I refuse to hang my head in front of this disrespectful man, and so I scowl at him instead.

"The same place everyone else did," I snap. This makes Alasiri laugh.

"Well, well, the little *zeruzeru* has teeth!"

This makes me dislike him even more. I hate it when people call me *zeruzeru*. The name means "zero-zero," "nothing." A *zeruzeru* is an unnatural thing, like a zombie. It's like calling me an animal.

"Don't call me that," I snap.

"Habo!" exclaims Asu, horrified. "Don't be so rude to Alasiri when he's gone out of his way to help us."

Now I'm mad at her, too. The only reason I got involved in this conversation in the first place was to defend her, and now she's defending him. Alasiri gives a small cough that could have been a laugh and changes the subject.

"Tell me, boy, why are you so interested in what I do?"

"I just am," I say, still bristling.

Alasiri strokes long fingers down his chin, considering.

Then, "Would you like to see for yourself?"

Asu and I both look up at him in surprise. I'm not entirely sure I want to do anything with this man. *Was he flirting with Asu? Was she flirting, too, by talking to him in the car and making him coffee? Or is she just being her usual nice self?* I can't decide. I want to tell him I don't feel like going anywhere with him, but he has a job and a car. If he's really trying to be Asu's boyfriend, I don't want my stupid temper to ruin her chances of a better future.

"*Ndiyo,*" I lie, deciding to play it safe for Asu's sake. "Very much. *Asante.*"

Alasiri chuckles softly. "Well. We'll see how much your curiosity likes what it gets once I finish my coffee."

"Here you go," says Asu, ladling a serving of coffee into a tin cup for Alasiri and a half serving into a clean jar for me. She's careful as she pours, but even so, as I sip at the steaming jar, I can feel the bitter gravel of the coffee grounds lodging in my teeth.

I wonder where Alasiri will take me when we're done.

4.

CHUI HAS NEVER wanted to be anywhere near me.

I learned this clearly six years ago on my first day of school. He even tried to talk Asu out of sending me to school entirely.

"Does Habo really have to go to school?" he had asked.

"Of course," Asu replied. "He's seven now, just like you were when you started school. Why wouldn't he go?"

"Well . . ." Chui glanced sideways at me. "Look at him."

I remember how Asu's eyes got hard when he said that. She turned to me.

"You're right," she said, "Let's double-check. Habo, reach your hand over your head and touch your other ear. Can you do that?"

I did. It was a little bit of a stretch at the end, but I was able to touch the end of my longest finger to the top of my opposite ear. This is how the teachers know you're over seven and old enough for school if you don't have a birth certificate.

I smiled a missing-tooth smile at her. She smiled back.

"Okay, Chui, I've looked at him, and it seems like he's old enough to go to school after all. That *is* what you meant, isn't it?" She looked him straight in the eye, her question an outstretched hand with a piece of broken glass in it.

Chui knew better than to grab it. He dropped his gaze.

"*Ndiyo*, Asu," he mumbled.

"Good. That's settled then. Off you go," and she'd pushed us out the door together.

Chui and I had set off on the tiny footpath that led from our family's small farm to our village. Since we were walking into the rising sun, I kept my head down so that the brim of my hat kept my face shaded. I was watching Chui's black ankles in front of me, comparing them to my own white toes, when suddenly the feet turned around. I looked up, squinting. Chui stood in front of me, with both arms crossed over his chest, blocking the path.

"Now listen," said Chui. "Just because you're my brother doesn't mean I have to walk with you." I stared at him. Hadn't he heard Asu's scolding?

"But I want to walk with you," I said finally.

"Sorry," said Chui, not sounding sorry at all, "but you don't have a choice. I'm going to walk in to school first. You'll come in after me."

"What if I'm late?"

"I don't care," said Chui, his sneaky eyes narrowed to make his point. He turned to leave.

I was furious. It was my first day at school. I knew my

brother didn't like me, but all brothers and sisters walked together. I had never seen a child walking anywhere alone, ever.

"Fine, go on!" I had shouted at him. "Run away, *Chuijoya!*" Chui's shoulders stiffened, but he just walked faster. *Chui* means "leopard" in Kiswahili, and Chui is proud of his strong name. *Chuijoya* means "paper leopard." It's a way to call him a coward, my little revenge for the way he calls me names when Asu isn't around to hear them.

I kicked at the dirt in the road until I couldn't see him anymore, then followed.

By the time I made it to the thatched three-wall schoolhouse in the village, I was late. Palms sweating, mind racing, I hovered by the mud wall listening to the hum of children's voices as they greeted one another. *You're not getting any earlier,* I finally told myself, and forced my feet to cross the threshold. When I entered, a hundred dark eyes swiveled around to stare at me. I had no one to go to, no one I knew who I could sit next to on the floor. I stood there, unable to move.

Then, like locusts coming in to destroy a year's crops, the whispers spread through the room. Among the general hiss, I distinctly heard Chui's voice whispering *"mtoto pepo"*—ghost boy. Burning with shame, I stood there alone and listened as the plague of whispers ate my hopes.

Even though it was six years ago, that memory still makes me angry. After that first day, I have never again tried to walk with Chui. Even if we're going somewhere at the same time, I leave some space between us.

Which is why I'm surprised when Chui insists on coming

with me and Alasiri. And I have to admit, though I never thought I would be grateful for Chui's company, I'm glad it won't be just the two of us for the day. For some reason, I can't shake my dream of the lion whenever I'm around our eerily cheerful guide, and it makes me uneasy.

"All right, boys! Grab those tarps and get in!"

Following Alasiri's directions, Chui and I haul four big squares of thick blue plastic out of the storage tent and heft them into the open back of the Jeep. The tarps smell the way our goat shed at home did after the nanny gave birth, and we both hold them at arm's length.

"Hop in and sit on them so they don't blow away," commands Alasiri, turning the key in the ignition.

I hesitate, and Chui clambers past me.

"Habo will do that," he says. "I'll sit up front here, if that's all right."

Alasiri laughs delightedly at Chui's forwardness, waving him to the empty front seat. I scowl and climb after him, sitting on the stinking tarps. I hunch into my long clothes to keep the sun off my skin and face backward, away from both of them.

As we drive away from the camp, I notice Asu standing with Mother, looking after us as if to memorize where we're going. I realize, from the way our tire tracks stretch away from the camp, that we're driving away from the road and out into the Serengeti.

When we're out of sight of the camp, Alasiri brings out a small radio. He talks into it in a low voice, then releases the button and waits through minutes of static. He has stopped smiling. When a voice answers him, he turns the wheel sharply to the left and begins to drive faster.

"Where are we going?" asks Chui, leaning forward and examining the buttons on the radio.

"Ah," says Alasiri, his smile in place again. "We're going hunting."

"Hunting?" asks Chui. His eyes are sparkling with excitement. But this time Alasiri doesn't answer.

Chui and Alasiri are sitting on padded seats with springs in them, but I bounce around every time we hit a rock or pothole. Which is all the time. The Serengeti seems so flat when you look at it—long tan fields of grass and slowly rolling green hills, dissolving away in the heat-haze of the distance—but when you're driving across the wildlife park the ground is full of animal tracks that have turned into dips and spikes when the mud dried, and the grass is full of stones and holes. I feel like someone is trying to shake my teeth into my brain and I'm having trouble keeping track of where we're going. That must be why I feel like we're going in circles.

The trip goes on and on. I'm now so jumbled around that I couldn't even tell you which way the camp is from here. I could ask Alasiri, but he is serious again, and his eyes shine as he talks into his radio, and I'm afraid. Chui looks at me over the shoulder of the front seat. Even though neither of us says anything, I think he's not so happy to be here anymore, either.

Finally, Alasiri lets out a little yelp and throws the car into park in the long grass on the side of a small hill, beside another battered-looking Jeep. For the first time in over an hour, his smile is back, and he turns to speak to us.

"Get out, boys! It's time to make yourselves useful."

Chui and I get out of the car gingerly. My vision sways a bit for a while even after I put my feet on the ground, though whether that's from the bumpy ride or my usual bad eyes, I'm not sure. All I can make out against the bright sky is an immense lump on the hill that Alasiri is pushing us toward. I haven't quite gotten my eyes to focus when I stumble and land heavily against the leathery side of the thing. It gives a little under my hands, and I pull away with a cry of surprise because it's slightly warm. I realize I'm leaning against an enormous animal carcass, but I can barely imagine that an animal could be so huge. My mind races through what it knows about big animals, trying to match what we've found. Rhino? Elephant? Hippopotamus?

Alasiri steers Chui around the corner of the carcass, bending out of my line of sight. I hear Alasiri calling out greetings, men's voices replying, and the sputtering of a small machine. The shape next to me is giving off the faint hay-and-earth smell that reminds me of the days when we could afford to keep a cow. There is also the hot, sticky smell of blood. I walk around to rejoin Chui and Alasiri, running my fingers along a spine with bones wider than my hand to steady myself as I go.

It's the ears, like great gray leaves, that finally let me identify the animal. It's the first time I've ever seen a real elephant.

There are three men up at the front of this elephant, and

Alasiri has joined them. The men are covered in blood, and bits of flesh hang off their arms and stick to their clothes. Two have machetes and one has a diesel chainsaw, and they're attacking the elephant's head the way a boy beats a bush with a stick when he's angry. But none of these men are angry; they smile at Alasiri and wave. The chainsaw makes a wet sound as it digs into the cheek and then a high whining sound when it hits the bone of the skull. Clouds of black diesel smoke blow over us. I feel a little like I want to vomit, but this reaction embarrasses me. At home we butchered meat with knives, not with chainsaws, but meat is meat and Alasiri did tell us we were going hunting. I should be glad that we'll all have dinner tonight, not upset by the sounds we make getting it. *And I'm not going to let Chui call me a coward!* But I don't like the expression on Alasiri's face. He's all lit up inside, a lamp burning excitement instead of kerosene. I'm sorry I ever agreed to come out here.

"Boys!" he shouts. "Go get the tarps!"

Chui and I walk to the Jeep, and I grab the first tarp my hand lands on, hauling it into my arms with all the force I can muster. It's heavy. *Soon,* I think, *soon we can leave.* I repeat this to myself as I begin to drag the folded tarp over to the dead elephant. Alasiri waves and shouts, but I can't make out what he's saying. He seems upset. Then the weight goes off my arms, and I see that Chui has picked up the other end of the tarp where it had been dragging on the ground. Alasiri stops shouting and waves us forward.

As we get closer, the smell of a butcher shop on a hot day

hits me again and the flies begin to land on my face. *Food is food*, I remind myself. I squint to keep the flies out of my eyes and keep trudging forward.

"Good, good!" Alasiri's voice is right in front of me now, so I must have made it all the way to where the men are standing. The keening of the chainsaw is just behind my left ear, but I refuse to turn and look at it. Instead I look at Alasiri. In his delight over the kill, all the lines of his face have shifted slightly. I no longer think he's handsome. "Not so curious now, eh?" He takes my face in his hands and grips it hard, then pushes my cheek away. "Go get the rest of the tarps, and be quick about it. We need to get out of here before any park rangers show up. Move!"

Chui and I trot to the Jeep, and then slowly, quickly, slowly, quickly we go, bringing the tarps to the elephant butchers. As we run I can feel the hot, slick imprint of Alasiri's hands on my face drying and flaking off, little pieces of elephant blood falling like dry tears onto the ground in my wake.

Keep going, I tell myself. *All you have to do is bring them these tarps, maybe help them cut up the meat, and then you're done. Just keep going.*

But instead of carving up the meat, the men are focusing entirely on the elephant's head, leaving the huge body to bloat in the sun. All they seem interested in is ripping the long horns out of the animal's face, though why they would do that is a mystery to me since you can't eat bone.

As soon as the men have cut the long, curved horns out of the elephant's face and have wrapped them in the tarps,

they load one into each vehicle. After talking a little with Alasiri, the three men drive away in their Jeep, trailing a cloud of
dust. Alasiri goes back to the elephant and picks more bits off
with a long hunting knife. Again, though none of us has eaten
lunch, he leaves the meat alone. He harvests the teeth and tail
and toenails and dumps all of this in the last tarp, which he
makes Chui and me carry to the Jeep. He helps us wedge the
tarp through the rear door and then hops in the front himself. He starts the engine.

For a split second I'm terrified that he's going to drive away
and leave us here. I don't know what it is that I fear, whether
that evil spirits will be attracted to such a spot or scavengers
with large teeth, but I know that I'm afraid to be there a moment longer.

Chui runs to get into the front seat again. But when he sits
down, he looks away from Alasiri, out the window. I scramble
in awkwardly, climbing over the pieces of elephant we have
wedged in it.

"*Bwana*, are we going to the camp now?" I ask.

"Oh, so now it's 'sir,' is it?" He laughs and wipes the sweat
out of his eyes, leaving a swatch of blood across his forehead.
It makes him look fierce. "*Ndiyo*, we're going back now."

Alasiri drives at a slightly slower pace, but I wish for the
bone-rattling speed of our first journey. Because all the way
to camp, I am sitting on a tarp-wrapped bundle, still warm
from the animal we have de ❄ ed, and my feet give me no
traction in the blood on the floor.

We are still far away when I hear Alasiri give an ugly chuckle. I pivot around, but all I can see is a blur of light in the distance, which at first I think is the setting sun, but Chui stands up in his seat and waves through the open top.

"What is it?" I ask him when he sits down.

"Mother and Asu have made a big fire," Chui whispers to me, "and they're standing in front of it, waiting for us. They're the only ones there. The other Jeep isn't here yet."

I'm surprised that he's willing to talk to me like this, but I guess he's decided he likes me more than he likes Alasiri. It puts a warm feeling in my chest, and it's hard right now to remind myself that I hate my brother.

When we get close enough that even I can see the outline of where Mother and Asu are standing, I raise my hand and wave, too. Alasiri pulls into camp in a spray of dust. I see Mother put down a heavy pan, and Asu returns a cleaver to the pile of cooking knives. I realize they were waiting for us, ready to fight Alasiri if he had left us behind or hurt us. This makes me feel warm inside, too. Alasiri puts on the parking brake and turns off the engine.

"*Habari gani, Bibi!*" he calls politely to Mother. "You can see that I've returned with both your sons in one piece." His tone is pleasant, but I feel cold because I know he saw what she and Asu did. I worry what he will do, but he does nothing more than sit down beside the fire and wait for them to serve us our meal. I sit down as well, but on the other side of the fire, not next to Alasiri. After only a tiny hesitation, Chui sits next to me.

"Uh! Is that blood?" asks Mother, coming up behind us with a pot of *ugali*. She leans forward to sniff at us and then pulls away again, wrinkling her nose. She points toward the water barrel on the other side of camp. "Go wash up immediately!"

Chui and I look at each other, taking in our gore-crusted arms and spattered clothes. I'm about to answer her, but Alasiri drowns me out with a huge laugh.

"*Ndiyo, Bibi*, it's blood! Today your little boys have become men! Hunters!"

A brief silence follows his statement as the women look us over. I know they can guess that there's more to the story than that. Asu passes us a plastic bowl full of water and a rag. I start to scrub my face and arms. When I'm done, I hand the now pink water to Chui. Asu cautiously breaks the silence.

"What did you hunt, boys?"

"Elephant," Chui mumbles, scraping the blood out from under his stumpy fingernails. He does not look like the man of the family as he says it. I know that I don't feel like a man, either. Hunching in the long shadows of late afternoon, I feel like a scavenger, taking from the dead.

"Well," Asu says, filling her voice with a fake cheerfulness to cover our lack of enthusiasm, "I've never had elephant before. Shall I cook it to go with our *ugali* now, or will we have it later?"

Mother and Asu glance around for the meat, but of course they don't see it because we haven't brought any home. Just the thought of eating that gigantic, bloated carcass makes me wonder whether I'm really hungry, after all.

"Ah, pretty one," says Alasiri, "we did not hunt today for meat."

Without realizing she's doing it, Asu reaches up and touches her cheek at his compliment. Then her hand falls into her lap and she gives him a puzzled frown as the rest of his words sink in. "What did you hunt for, then?" she asks. Alasiri gets up off the ground and walks over to the Jeep.

"We went . . . for this!" He whips back the top tarp with a flourish. The curving expanse of bone gleams in the sunset and the firelight.

"What's that?" asks Mother.

"That," he says, "is *ivory*! It is the special thing that an elephant's tusks are made of, and it's very valuable. I get more money from one tusk of ivory than from an entire season working for the tourists!"

"Then why do you work for the tourists at all?" asks Chui. I can see that he's getting interested in spite of himself. Chui is always interested in money.

"Because if I don't find out where the rangers take the white people, how would I know what areas to avoid when I'm hunting ivory, hmm?"

Chui has no answer to Alasiri's question and remains silent. Alasiri smiles at him, winks at Asu, and flips the tarp over the tusk again. He walks to his seat and continues eating the food Mother and Asu prepared while we were gone.

"Ivory is a very good thing for me," continues Alasiri, pinching off wedges of *ugali* and using it to smush the spiced pigeon peas into his mouth, "and it's a good thing for you too, because now I'll have to take it quickly and sell it, and that means that I will be driving straight across the game parks and can take you most, if not all, of the way to Mwanza." He bumps Chui playfully with his elbow.

It's only then that I notice that Chui has left me to go eat beside Alasiri. *I guess money makes it all okay*, I think bitterly. I look away from them both and pick at my food.

5.

MOTHER AND ASU join us around
the fire, satisfied with the explanation and with the offer of
another ride. But I feel like my stomach is a piece of cloth
that the women have washed in the river and are now twisting, twisting dry. I can't get past the image in my head of the
gigantic elephant, rotting out in the scrubland, not because
anyone needed to eat, but because little pieces of it could be
sold for a great deal of money.

The conversation moves on to other things. About an hour
later, when the second Jeep of men arrives, Mother and Asu
get food for the other men, too. I look over. Their Jeep is empty. They have already sold their piece of ivory. They brag to
Alasiri about this, and I see his face tighten with anger, even
though he laughs with them. I wouldn't tease him the way
they do. It's not wise to tease a wild animal, no matter how
big a stick you're holding.

They also tell him about a park ranger that they saw after

they completed their sale. Alasiri's face looks like a storm about to split open with lightning. He turns to us with a tight smile.

"*Bibi*, you're in luck. It appears I'm leaving right now and going in the direction of Mwanza. Would you like a ride?"

"Really?" asks Mother. "You can go straight across? At night? We were following the road and had to stay hidden all the time."

"*Ndiyo*. We will go north and west through the game reserves. I have to make a few stops on the way, but then I need to see a man in Mwanza city, and I can drop you off near the center of town."

Mother nods to acknowledge this information and starts clearing away the dinner things. Alasiri pauses beside me on the way to his tent.

"Pack quickly, ghost boy!" He puts his hand heavily on my head when he says this. I try not to flinch at his touch. I see Asu's eyes leave Alasiri's face and fall on his hand. A small line appears between her eyebrows.

"The white boy doesn't like me," Alasiri says to no one in particular. His fingers tighten on my temples. "Such a shame. Then again, it's one more reason to move on, isn't it? I wouldn't want the little white boy running out and telling anyone about the elephant. But you know better than to do that, don't you, boy?" He tips my head backward and looks me straight in the eyes. The other men chuckle darkly.

"Don't hold his head like that," says Asu. Then, when he looks at her, she adds, "Please." Alasiri looks down at me again.

"*Ndiyo, Bwana*," I mumble. "I know better." He releases me and his tent swallows him. I look hollowly across the fire at the rest of my family. Chui has already gotten up to find his bedroll, but Mother and Asu exchange a glance with each other and look at the tent flap, still quivering from where Alasiri has disappeared into it. It's the look that is the end of a long conversation that I didn't hear. Too tired to piece together what might have been said, I turn away and start to pack my belongings.

"Here," says Mother, walking over and handing me a rolled bundle of our blankets. "Go ahead and keep this in the back with you. "Asu and I will sit up front with him." Her thin face is serious, and there are dark circles under her eyes. She touches my arm just briefly as she hands the bundle to me. The unexpected touch makes me look at her more closely. She gives me a tight-lipped nod and walks away. I begin to think that this setup is not just because the women want the comfortable seats. I look over and see Asu talking quietly to Chui. She and Mother must have finished their conversation and come to the conclusion, like I have, that Alasiri is no good.

Chui says something to Asu and turns away, scowling. As he walks over, Mother heads around to the front of the Jeep and climbs in. Chui pushes past me and boosts himself into the rear, shoving the pack in ahead of him. He takes a seat high up on the tarps, away from the mess on the floor. I sigh and follow Chui. I wedge myself in uncomfortably between the tusk, our belongings, and Chui.

"One last bag!" says Alasiri, and he shoves a large duffel in at us. I catch it reflexively and set it by my feet. I center it in the pool of blood and watch with a smile as it soaks in. I hope all his clothes are ruined.

Alasiri calls a goodbye to the other men who are staying at the camp and he and Asu head around to the front. Chui is muttering to himself about being stuck in the worst seat, but I'm glad to be far away from that man and his predatory smile, even if it does mean sitting on pieces of a dead animal.

We drive out over the plains through the long dusk. Though the others chat, I keep quiet. Asu and Mother are up with Alasiri and, after he went to sit with Alasiri at dinner, I don't want to talk to Chui, either. So I fold myself into my long clothes and stare up at the bright stars beginning to dot the Serengeti sky above me and wish away the hours until we can leave this man and his wretched ivory behind.

We drive mostly north, bumping over wild grassland and dried creek beds. As Chui and I shiver in the open Jeep, vast stretches of the Serengeti whip past us. We drive out of our way twice on our trip to Mwanza city. The first time, just as it's darkening into night, we pass a village and Alasiri pulls over to the side of the road and tells us to wait in the car while he goes into a stand of trees. He's gone for an uncomfortable amount of time, and then returns with four men who tell Chui and I to get out. When we do, they unload the long, curved ivory from the Jeep before letting us climb in again with our bags. As we climb back in I see one man hand Alasiri a thick roll of money. I have no idea how much it is, but Chui whispers to me that it's in dollars, not Tanzanian shillings. This puts me over the edge.

"It's always about money with you, isn't it?" I hiss at him. I cross my arms and glare out of the moving car.

"What?" says Chui, caught off guard.

"You think Alasiri is so great just because he makes all this money. But really, he's only getting money because he's breaking the law."

"What do you know about money?" Chui's getting angry now, too. "You just sit around at home, relaxing in the shade, playing with the goats. You have no idea how hard Enzi and I work on the coffee plantation. You wouldn't know anything about money. You've never earned anything in your whole life."

I'm furious at him for having a point. He's right. No one would ever pay me to do anything, so instead of having odd jobs to help with the bills like most boys my age, I've had to stay home and do house chores. And only chores in the shade, at that. My guilt makes me even angrier.

"So that makes it all okay, then? It's okay to kill an elephant and take bits from it and leave all the meat to rot? And now we're sneaking around in the dark, hiding from the rangers. There's no way that what he's doing is legal. He should probably be in jail, and you *like* him."

Chui fixes me with a cold look of pure disdain.

"Do you know how much money he just got for a few hours' worth of work? Do you?" His voice is low and intense. He leans down to put his face closer to mine. "That was enough money to pay off all of our debts. To keep the farm. With two of those tusks I could have fixed the house for Mother, bought a second farm for Enzi to live on with that pretty girlfriend of his that none of you know about, given Asu enough to finish secondary school or get married, and still had enough left over to feed your worthless self. Or"—his eyes are big now, seeing all the things he could have had—"we could have left the farm and moved to Arusha and all lived there comfortably. Instead, here we are, stuffed into someone else's car, with no home and no money, heading toward being the charity of some relative I've never met."

There is a pause where Chui waits to see if I'll say anything. I don't. He leans away from me and stretches out on the packs.

"*Ndiyo*," he says, "to not be here right now and have all of that, I'm okay with killing one animal. To not be poor . . . yes, I would do what he does."

We sit there for a while in a prickly silence, each of us on our different sides of the car. Now that the large tusk is gone, there's much more room and it's more comfortable. I think about what Chui has said. It is an awful lot of money for just one animal. Would I do this again, if I knew that I would keep the money and it would save my family? I don't have an answer, and the question leaves a queasy feeling in my stomach. Then I realize something: Chui never said what he would spend the money on for himself.

"Chui," I ask, staring out over the dark grassland, not looking at him.

"What now, Habo?" He sounds tired, grown-up. The way

Enzi usually sounds if you ask him a question after work.

"If you were rich, what would *you* buy?"

For a moment, Chui considers whether or not to tell me. Finally, he says, "I'd pay the apprentice dues to be a mechanic and work on sports cars."

"A mechanic? Really?"

"What, you think it's stupid? Well, you're stupid!"

"No, no! I don't think it's stupid. I just never thought of you as a mechanic before . . ." I trail off. I've never really thought about Chui as anything really, except an annoyance. I try to think of what else Chui would be good at. Finally I find something. "I thought maybe you'd be a footballer. You're the best goal scorer in the school."

There's another pause, but this one is not as tense as the last one.

"Maybe I could work on sports cars during the day and then play football at night. That would be good."

"That would be good," I agree.

And when we both fall silent now, the silence is soft.

The second time we stop, the stars stretch bright and brittle over us and it's full night. We've been traveling along the Sirari-Mbeya Road for hours, and the others have started to comment on how close we're getting to Mwanza. We twist along a dusty path until we are some way from the road and Alasiri has found what he is looking for.

There's not much here, just a few huts clumped together and a smear of flickering lights that might be a village in the distance. Alasiri gets out of the Jeep and calls out.

"Hodi hodi!"

An old man emerges from the largest of the mud huts and walks slowly out to where we're waiting. At first it's hard to see him in the waving light of the lantern he's holding up over his head. When he gets close though, I can see what he is. The man is wearing ratty clothes and necklaces made of teeth. His hair floats out around his head, but the wildest thing about him are his eyes. I realize this man must be a *waganga,* and I slide down as far as I can.

Wagangas control great forces of spirits and luck. Luck is very important. Good luck brings you full harvests, strong sons, and a peaceful death. Bad luck gives you sickly animals, needy relatives, and lets everyone treat you badly, even Death. Really bad luck could curse you with a ghost boy. Freakish, weak, useless. Worse than a girl.

When any of us would get sick at home, Mother would take us to the *waganga wa tiba asili* in the village nearby. He was a not-so-old man, with a certificate from the government on the wall of his hut that allowed him to make home medicines. He would give us powders he made from plants and tell us ways to feel better. We respected him because he would use his power to help people.

But there are other kinds of *wagangas.* There are *waganga wa jadi* and *waganga wa kienyeji.* The first are born into the power and the second come into it later, but they both control magic. They use pieces of animals, and sometimes even the hair and nails of people, to make magic spells. They talk to spirits, and they can curse you as easily as cure you. Alasiri's *waganga* does not look like a simple village healer, and I'm almost certain he is a *waganga wa jadi*. At the look in his eyes, I'm afraid. It's like seeing a huge bull behind a twig fence. It's terrifying to think of that much power corralled by so little sanity.

The *waganga* takes the ears, toenails, and teeth that Alasiri took from the elephant. He doesn't give Alasiri any money, but instead spits on his head and mumbles over him. Then the old man gives Alasiri a small bag. Now it makes sense why Alasiri took the other pieces of the elephant, too, not just the ivory. He wanted luck medicine from the *waganga* and needed something to trade for it.

Alasiri is turning away when the *waganga* tips his lantern and looks at us. When he sees me, he lets out a small cry. His hand darts out and grabs Alasiri's arm. Deep shadows mark where the old man's thin fingers must be digging into Alasiri's skin, but Alasiri doesn't make any complaint. He simply leans his head down and listens as the old man whispers in his ear. Once, just for an instant, his eyes flash up to meet mine. Then he lowers his gaze and nods. The *waganga* releases him.

Alasiri gets in, and his smile is wider than ever. The *waganga*'s spit glistens in his hair, and he holds up the little bag.

"Luck!" he says, and starts the Jeep again. I tell myself it's the uneven road that is making me feel like vomiting, not the fact that the old man's eyes follow me, never blinking, until his lantern is only a dot in the distance and the dust clouds from our tires hide him from my sight.

We get onto the road to Mwanza again and continue west. Alasiri sings along loudly with the *Bongo Flava* playing on the radio and talks to Mother. He asks her about where Auntie lives and what we will do in Mwanza. Mother is polite and answers everything he asks, but her answers are vague and give little information. Asu is also no longer flirting with him, and I'm glad that they're both acting this way. I don't want Alasiri to know where we'll be. I don't want to ever see him again. I don't want to help him ever again. And though his Jeep eats the kilometers a hundred times faster than we could walk, I wish we were still on our own and had never met up with this luck hunter.

It's late when Alasiri pulls over to the side of the Sirari-Mbeya Road in the city. We're surrounded by dark houses and closed shops. I wish we had gotten here sooner so that I could have seen a bit of what the city looks like, but I'm content to finally have finished the trip with this man.

"So, this is where we part from each other," he says cheerfully. "All you have to do is keep walking this way along this road and you'll be at the center of the city. Then you can head to where your family lives. Come on! Get down."

We get out of the car and pull out our bundles. Mother and Asu thank him while Chui and I stand at a respectful distance.

Alasiri drives away, taking a hard right at the intersection. Asu helps Mother rearrange our belongings into travel packs we can balance on our heads. I know I should try to be useful, but instead I stare after Alasiri, just like the *waganga* stared after me. I stare until the red glow of his Jeep's lights dim away in the distance. I stare until I am certain he isn't coming back. Then I heft my bundle onto my head and join my family, walking through the dark along the final stretch of the long road to Mwanza.

6.

IT'S WELL PAST midnight by the time we arrive at Auntie's house in the Kirumba fishing neighborhood just north of Mwanza center. The road is a pale stripe, crowded by the hunched shadows of the fish market. To our left Lake Victoria shines dark and wet like a dog's eye. We turn away from the water and walk uphill, winding past houses and tall rocks that cut into the sky like broken teeth. Finally we get to a small house near the top of the hill. I can't see much, only that the walls are some pale color that glow a little in the moonlight. The dark doorway is set into the concrete-block wall.

"Hodi hodi!" Mother calls into the darkness. "Neema! Sister!"

There's the snap of a switch and I can see the glow of electric light leaking out between the pieces of wood in the door and around the edges of the shutters on the windows. The door is opened a crack and then flung wide. I can see vague shapes behind her that must be my cousins, but they can't get out because Auntie is so fat, she fills the doorway. I look at her jealously, thinking what it must be like to have that much to eat all the time. Maybe if my father had stayed, my mother and sister would be that fat. Instead, we all look like we have missed meals.

"Raziya!" Auntie gasps when she sees Mother. "Raziya, Raziya! You made it! Come inside." Mother is hauled forward in her sister's embrace, and the rest of us shuffle in too. Auntie is still talking as I shut the door softly behind us. "Oh my goodness, it's been so long since your phone call, I didn't know what to think! *Karibu! Karibu sana!* How was your trip? Are you all right? You're so skinny! Let me look at you!"

"Here we are, Neema, here we are." Mother is slightly breathless, caught between her sister's hug and her questions. "*Asante, asante sana.* We've had quite the journey! I will tell you all about it . . ."

But she doesn't get the chance to tell Auntie anything, because just then, Auntie sees me. Her eyes lock onto my face. Her mouth drops open.

I can imagine how I must look in the harsh light of the electric bulb hanging by its cord from the ceiling—like a blue goat: all the right shapes in all the wrong colors. I had hoped that meeting family would be less awful than meeting strangers, but I can hear my cousins whispering among themselves, and Auntie's eyebrows are so far up her forehead, they brush her head-wrap.

"Was he born like that?" she asks, pointing straight at me.

Mother sighs deeply. "*Ndiyo.* I don't know what made him

like that. He's not like the others." There is a small pause during which I move the dirt on the floor around in small circles with my big toe. I try to pretend that I can't feel their eyes on me like physical blows.

"Is he a . . ." Auntie seems to be struggling for words. "Have you really brought a *zeruzeru* into my house?"

I flush a dark red under my hat. *Why does everyone always have to pick on me?*

"What are you talking about?" Mother snaps. "Why are you calling him that? He may be unusual, but he is not an animal!"

In the middle of this whole awful evening, it makes me feel good to hear Mother defending me.

"Raziya!" Auntie snaps back. "I'm not insulting him! He *is* a *zeruzeru*, an albino. It's true that some call people like him demons or ghosts, and some say they're animals, but *zeruzeru* is only a term that means a person like him—all white and yellow where he should be dark. How could you not know this? Did that worthless farmer you married take you so far out into the country that you never heard any news at all?"

I see Mother stiffen at this description of Father, but she doesn't contradict her sister.

There is another pause where I feel the eyes on me again. They burn the edges of my mind, but they are nothing compared to the burn inside me now. Auntie used a word to describe me. *Albino.* There is a word for people like me. I'm not the only one.

Zeruzeru, the word I always thought referred to a type of

animal, really does refer to me. The knowledge swims around and around in my head like a fish trapped in a rock pool. No one in my family has ever known what to call me before. I have never known what to call myself. *Albino*. I test the word in my head, seeing how it feels. It doesn't feel comfortable and I decide to think about this more later.

I'm so deeply sunk in my thoughts that for a while I haven't heard anything said around me in Auntie's house. But now I look up and find that everyone in the room is shouting at one another at the tops of their voices. No one is pausing to let the other finish, and their voices cross and tangle like a badly woven basket.

Asu is shaking her finger at Auntie, who has turned almost purple with the effort of shouting at Mother. Mother is shouting right back, tears streaming over her cheeks. She gestures at us, at our bags stacked just inside the door.

"How can you ask us to leave?" Mother screams at Auntie. "You, my sister? My only living relative? How can you turn us out to starve on the streets when you have a house and strong sons and a husband? Look at my children! Look at them!" Her voice goes shrill. "They are too young to work anywhere that will pay us enough to live. What am I to do if you turn us away? What?"

The last word comes out as a loud sob, and Mother buries her face in her hands. Asu and Auntie stop yelling at each other and stare at Mother in silence. Asu reaches over and puts her arm around Mother's shoulders. From where I stand, backed up against the wall, I can see her elbow jump up and down with the force of Mother's crying. I don't know what to do. There is a short, awful silence. Then Auntie huffs out a sigh.

"I won't turn you out into the streets, Raziya." Her gaze wanders over to me, then flinches away again. "But you don't understand what you're asking. Come. I'll make some tea, and we'll talk."

Auntie puts a pot full of water on her gas stove and adds tea leaves and milk. Leaving it to boil together, she has us all sit down in the main room. Mother, Asu, Chui, and I untie our stools from our bundles and add them to the ones belonging to Auntie's family. We sit there quietly while we wait for the tea to boil, but the quiet is full, aggressive, the way the empty space around a hive is filled with the knowledge of wasps. I feel a growing fear of the words that will soon swarm out.

To distract myself, I look around the room at my cousins. There are five of them: The three oldest are tall and wide like Auntie, but the two youngest are slight with delicate faces. It makes me wonder what my uncle Adin looks like. The five of them throw glances at me while we wait, but only the littlest one meets my eyes. I look down at the ground between my feet. Finally the tea is ready, and Auntie pours it into a row of cups lined up on the counter. Other than the splash of hot liquid hitting the bottom of each cup, there is no sound even though there are ten of us in the room.

Auntie's oldest daughter hands everyone a cup. She puts mine on the floor in front of me. I bend forward, pick up the cup, and sip it slowly, blowing on the steam. The warm, deep feeling of tea with milk settles into my belly, and I tell myself to relax and enjoy it. Auntie lowers herself onto her stool with a sigh and finally starts talking.

"I don't know what life was like for you and your *zeruzeru* in Arusha province," Auntie begins, "but here in Mwanza, having an albino in your family is a dangerous thing."

I hunch my shoulders.

"Why?" asks Asu, leaning forward.

"Well," says Auntie, "times are difficult." This comment is greeted by silent nods from my family. We know times are difficult. We had to leave our home because of how difficult the times are. Auntie doesn't seem to notice. She is staring straight at Mother, talking as if the rest of us are not even in the room. "People are hungry and out of work. The drought is very bad." She waves her hand around, as if trying to scoop more problems out of the air. "In difficult times, people will do almost anything to get better luck. They visit the *wagangas* and ask them for spells and charms."

Mother nods.

"How does all this relate to Habo?" Asu asks.

"Well," Auntie says with a sigh, "here in Mwanza, people believe that albinos bring good luck."

I look up at her, startled. Usually I'm underfoot or unable to help. The idea that people might see me as lucky is a pleasant change. The idea is so exciting that I speak up for the first time since we entered Auntie's house.

"If I'm lucky, why did you say it's bad to have an albino in your family?"

Auntie looks at me, surprised, I suppose, to hear me speak. She holds my gaze for a minute, but then drops it. She looks down at the floor as she continues.

"Perhaps I misspoke. It is not that people consider albino *people* to be lucky. People consider albino *medicine* to be lucky."

There is a silence as we try to understand what she has just told us.

"Albino medicine?" prompts Asu finally. Auntie looks uncomfortable, and the silence stretches. Then she straightens her shoulders and looks Mother in the eye.

"The *wagangas* here in Mwanza kill people like your son and use the parts from their dead bodies to make luck." Auntie's words run together. She spits them at us like rotten fruit, quickly, as if she cannot wait to get them out of her mouth.

"No." A strangled gasp comes from Mother. If there were any other sound in the room, we would not have heard it. But there are no other sounds; it's as quiet as if everyone in the world has stopped breathing. "No, that's impossible!"

"It's not impossible!" Auntie snaps. "It happens all the time. Just last week, Charlie Ngeleja, an albino man who lives—lived—just on the outskirts of town, was having dinner with his wife when three men came out from the bushes with machetes. Charlie asked them to sit down and join in the meal, but the men said, 'We are here for something else.' And they killed him, Raziya, killed him just like that. His wife ran for help, but by the time she got back, it was over. They took Charlie's legs and his hands and his hair. They left the rest of him there like garbage." Auntie's voice is still strong, but there are tears making tracks to her chin. She goes on, softly: "The police did nothing, even though people knew who had killed Charlie. It is a terrible, terrible thing, Raziya. But it is not impossible."

She finishes to silence. I no longer know where to look. My gaze roves slowly around the circle of my cousins, looking for a single smile to tell me this is a joke. There are none. Instead, my cousins stare at me with wide eyes.

"They take body parts?" asks Asu with a note of hysteria in her voice. She is looking at me with wide eyes, too.

Auntie's smallest boy twists a length of fishing net in his hands. "They say if you tie an albino's hair into your nets, you'll always catch fish."

"The hands and the skin are for luck in business," adds the girl who gave me the tea.

"And if you put albino legs on either side of the entrance to a gold mine, you'll get rich very fast," the tall boy with the start of a mustache says.

"Even the children have heard of it," says Auntie, as if this means something special.

I put my cup of tea on the floor, no longer able to drink it. I hug my knees to my chest and put my head down onto them so I don't have to see anyone looking at me anymore.

"People will try to kill him?" Chui's whisper of disbelief fills the silence.

"Now you see, Raziya," Auntie continues, "why we didn't want you to stay. Charlie was a man who had grown up here. Everybody knew him. Everybody knew his parents, his wife, his children. And still they killed him. Nobody knows your boy. He will be too easy to take."

I look around. Mother is breathing in short, shallow breaths, and her eyes are unfocused. Beside me Asu is sitting very still. Chui is looking at me as if he's never seen me before.

Would it be worth it to kill me *if it's enough money to save the family, Chui?* I turn away, sickened.

"Really, Raziya," Auntie asks, "how could you not have heard of it? More than twenty albinos were attacked just this past year. There are speeches on the radio telling the whole nation how it must stop."

"We had to sell our radio five years ago," Asu says, her voice hollow.

"Well," says Auntie, "now you know."

Asu jerks to her feet. "We have to leave! Mama, we have to leave now and go somewhere else. We can't stay here. We can't let them kill Habo!"

"No," says Mother softly. "No, we can't."

But I don't know if she is saying no, we cannot let them kill me, or no, we cannot leave. I feel like someone has tied a rope around my chest and is pulling it tighter, tighter. The sweat on my neck and palms feels cold even though I know the room is warm.

"Where will we go?" asks Chui, the exhaustion plain in his voice. I'm surprised that he's so sure that we will all move to ensure my safety, and I feel bad for what I thought earlier. He's trying to protect me even when he's so tired. We've been traveling for days, sleeping on roads and under trees and bushes. I'm tired, too. Tiredness has sifted into all my joints, making them feel like they are filled with hot sand. For those few minutes before Auntie saw me, it felt like we had found a good place to stay. But, as usual, I've messed everything up, and now we have to move on again.

"Will we go home?" Chui asks.

Home, I think, remembering.

It's early evening, the sun just sinking behind the hills, and we are all sitting together outside, waiting to eat dinner. Enzi is leaning against the wall, talking with Mother as she cooks. They're both smiling. I'm too young yet to think about going to the little village school, and Chui and Asu chat away about their day and what they learned. I sit quietly and let the others' talk swirl around me like smoke, watching as Mother pounds the ugali *around and around in the battered pot, spreading it up the sides to cook, and then pushing it into a ball so it doesn't burn. A last ray of sun slices through the air around us and it looks like all the dust of the world has turned into gold. When this happens, Asu scoops me up into a hug and kisses my head before settling me in her lap and finishing her conversation with Chui. I know then that the long-shadowed light of the setting sun has reminded her of me, her golden brother. I sit there, safe in her lap, and watch the gold dust settle over us all.*

"What would we go home to?" Mother's voice snaps me into reality. She's right, of course. "Home" is our little village outside of Arusha. But we didn't have enough money to stay there in the first place, and now there's nothing to go home to. No house, no farm, no father.

"How much money do you have?" asks Auntie.

Mother tells her. It's a pitiful amount. Auntie crunches her forehead into her head scarf again and plants her hand on her hip. Her other hand swishes the tea around and around in her cup.

"You won't get two streets over with so little. And with three children? How did you even stay alive on your way here?" It's not a question that she expects to get an answer for, and none of us gives one. Auntie gets up and begins to pace. "I don't have any money to give you," she says, answering a question we haven't asked. "We saved for two years to pay for Adin to go to university so that he can become a manager at the VicFish factory. If you had arrived a week ago, I could have given you that money. But it's already paid; he has already started classes. We only have enough for the food we need to eat now."

"What will we do?" Mother asks in a whisper. She is rocking slowly where she sits. "What do we do?"

I am beginning to think that we will have an entire conversation made up of questions that don't get answered, but, surprisingly, Auntie answers this one.

"You should go to Dar es Salaam."

My family's faces are almost funny in their disbelief. Chui's mouth has dropped open, and he looks like a fish. I close my own mouth.

She must be joking. Dar es Salaam is hundreds of kilometers away from here, halfway across the country, on the ocean. It's twice as far as the journey we just took, days and days of travel. There's no way we can go there. We don't know anyone there. Who would we stay with? How would we live?

Auntie continues on, as if it wasn't like talking about going to the moon.

"Nowhere in the Lake District is safe, and you cannot farm without a man to help you. Yes, Dar es Salaam is the only place for you to go. It's an enormous city, filled with people of every kind. You can get jobs there in cleaning or something. There have been no albino killings there. They even have albino ministers of parliament. One is a lady albino MP, at that."

"Killings," Mothers whispers, as if she didn't hear anything else Auntie said.

"Hmph," says Auntie. She clatters over to the stove to boil more water for tea. The others must have been able to finish their cups. Mine sits, cold and still, at my feet. I can see small hairs and dust have settled on it, pinching the surface like water bugs' feet. I want to vomit. Auntie bustles into the room again with the tea.

"So," she says, "you must leave as soon as possible, but you can't leave until you have more money than you do now." She runs her eyes over us again. "You'll need train fare and enough to get started in the city. At least two hundred and fifty or three hundred thousand shillings." She pauses, considering.

"More would be better."

It's a number so high that it's lodged in the cracks between the stars. Mother starts to cry again. "We will never be that rich," she sobs.

"Well," says Auntie, "you'll have to try to get that rich as fast as you can. You must work hard at whatever jobs I can find you until you have the money you need." Then she turns and levels a finger straight at me.

"All except you," she says. "You will hide."

7.

I CROUCH BEHIND the tall sacks of corn in the pantry, listening to the voices in the next room rise and fall. The dry kernels push out against the side of the bag like babies waiting to be born. Auntie and the older cousins have arranged the sacks so that it looks as if they're thrown in a pile in the corner, but really there's a narrow space underneath. I can crawl in near the wall and pull a light sack of millet over the opening and then I'm hidden from view.

The first time I went into this space I was afraid.

"What if he dies in there?" asked Kito, Auntie's youngest son.

"He won't," replied Chui, with a confidence I only wished I shared. It was cramped under the sacks; I had to lie on my belly with my arms curled under my head.

"What if he can't breathe?" asked Kito.

"He can breathe," said Chui. "You can breathe, can't you, Habo?"

"I can breathe, and I can hear you, too, Chui," I muttered through tight teeth. "There's no need to shout."

"How was I supposed to know that? I can't see you."

"Well, that's the point, isn't it?" snapped Asu from the doorway. She had initially refused to be a part of the construction of my corn cave, as the younger cousins were calling it, but all the talk of me suffocating had brought her into the room after all. Through a tiny crack I saw Asu surveying my hiding spot, standing with her arms crossed so tightly that her *khanga* pinched in at the elbows.

It was hot, and I could feel the moisture from my breath beading on my forearms. Mwanza is warmer than Arusha is, because it's not in the mountains. Even though Auntie and her family bundle up in the evenings, my family and I don't need to. Of course this means that during the day, it's uncomfortably humid and warm for the dry season. I began to wonder whether maybe Kito was right after all about suffocating.

"Can I come out now?" I asked.

"You should try to stay in there longer." Auntie's voice came from somewhere beyond what I could see. "You can stay in the back room when it's just us, but whenever anyone comes by, you'll have to be in there. If they visit for a while, you need to be able to stay there without making any noise."

That's easy for you to say, I thought, but it turned out that Auntie had been right. People dropped by all the time and, every time they did, I had to hide.

The first day it felt like I was diving in and out, dragging my little millet sack behind me, all day long. I've gotten used to it over the past three weeks, but I also asked my cousins to help me rearrange the corn bags so there was a bigger space in the middle with more vents to breathe through. They were happy enough to help, even talking to me a little, but they still had trouble looking me in the face when they did it.

Now when I'm in my corn cave I still have to be lying down, but I can stretch out a bit and I don't have to be frozen in the same position for twenty or forty minutes while some stupid neighbor-lady tells Auntie all about the latest goings-on in fish town.

Today the rumble of voices in the background belongs to Mother, Auntie, and the local schoolteacher. Every now and again I hear the younger tones of Chui or one of the cousins. I'm still having trouble keeping the cousins straight in my head, because I mostly have to memorize who's who just by listening. I don't get out much when everyone's home, because visitors are so much more likely. Most of my time out is during the day when they're at work and school. Even if I'm out with the family, when everyone's home they all talk at the same time, and figuring out names is really hard.

When I ask Mother or Asu or Chui, they give me useless advice, like, "Pili's the tall handsome one" or "oh, Kondo is easy to tell apart, he has a mustache."

"And just what does a mustache sound like?" I asked Chui once, losing my patience. "And how does handsome sound, hmm?" Chui told me not to be so cranky—I had asked him, after all, and if I wasn't interested in what he had to tell me, I could just figure it out on my own. I've tried to keep my temper since then.

The only cousin I can tell apart from the others right away is little Kito. It helps that he has the highest voice and still sometimes uses baby words, but it's more than that, too. Out of all the children, Kito is the most fascinated by my secret cave. Because of this he got over his shyness around me more quickly than anyone else. When the people in the house aren't paying attention to him, he often sneaks away and whispers to me. I'm a little worried this will draw attention to my hiding place, but it's so nice to have someone to talk to when I'm buried under the sacks that I haven't said anything to him about it.

Kito can't reach his opposite ear yet, so he doesn't go to school. Which means that, instead of being invited into the main room to talk with the schoolteacher, he's sitting on top of my hiding place, telling me what's going on.

"They're talking about school," he hisses through the crack, as if this was a major announcement.

"I figured they would, since he's the schoolteacher, Kito," I whisper back.

"Oh," says Kito. He's silent for a while, thinking that through. Then, "They're talking about Chui going to school."

I sigh. Sometimes a five-year-old's grasp of what's news is a little hard to take. Especially when it's so hot. I feel like I'm roasting in an oven, and the smell of the dry, hot corn all around makes me hungry and nauseated at the same time. I hear the schoolteacher ask Mother how many school-age children she has, and I strain to hear her answer.

"Kito!" I whisper-shout. "Kito, what are they saying now?"

Kito listens and then says, "Your mother said that Asu's too old for school and Chui's the only other child she has here. She says her other sons stayed in Arusha."

I wonder what it would be like if Mother's statement were true and I had stayed with Enzi to finish out the coffee harvest season. For a small part of a second I imagine how nice it would be, just the two of us, living together and working and making money. But then I sigh and remind myself of the truth: Looking the way that I do, I would never be allowed to work in the village, and Enzi never really liked spending time with me, anyway. The silly dream unravels.

I realize that Kito has been talking for a while without noticing that I'm not listening to him anymore.

"What did you say, Kito? I missed that."

"The schoolteacher's leaving now, Habo. Your brother's going to start school tomorrow. Is school fun, Habo?"

I think about my old school in our little village. Every day during the midday break I would go sit under the wild mango tree at the edge of the school yard. I would close my eyes and focus on the feeling of the wind as it hissed through the grass and swept over me, and I watched the other boys playing. They ran and shouted around the sun-baked playing field. They held races. They kicked a tattered football around between two sets of goalposts. I would watch and watch, but could never join in. I hated watching.

When I was young enough not to know any better, I went home and complained to Asu, but what could she do about the boys in the yard?

"You're like a lion," she told me, "golden all over. Does a lion run around playing with the little black antelopes? No. He sits on the hill and watches them. Nothing that's golden is common, Habo. You must stay uncommonly still." And that was that. In the six years I went to that village school, I spent my days watching the antelopes play without me.

It's lucky that I'm still in my corn cave so Kito can't see the anger on my face. I keep my voice happy.

"*Ndiyo*, Kito. School is fun. You'll like it when you're old enough to go."

"Do you wish you could go to school with Chui?"

"No, Kito. I can't go outside. I'm happy to stay here where it's safe." Again, I'm glad Kito can't see my face as I lie.

"Okay, he's gone," says Kito. "You can come out now." I hear the *shush* of Kito's backside against the sackcloth as he slides to the floor and tugs away my millet door.

"Thank you," I say, and pull myself slowly into the world of the real people.

Up until the schoolteacher's visit, Chui had been doing odd jobs in the neighborhood: picking up trash, running errands, shining shoes with a piece of old shirt. Everyone has been doing what they can to make money so we're not so much of a burden on Auntie. Four more mouths is a lot to feed. Especially when one mouth spends all day hiding instead of helping. But

Tanzanian law states that all children over the age of seven have to go to school, and now the schoolteacher has found us out and Chui will have to go. I wonder if Chui will have trouble catching up. It doesn't seem like so much time has passed, but it's mid-August now and he's missed over three weeks of school. Now it will be just Asu and Mother who work to pay for our keep. Now it will take that much longer to save up the money we need to travel to Dar es Salaam.

Auntie has a job at the new Victoria Fish processing factory. She managed to get a job for Mother at VicFish, too, since her husband's uncle is the floor manager's stepfather, but she wasn't able to extend her influence enough to get Asu a job. Mother and Auntie take a *dala-dala* out to the fish factory every morning at five, before it is fully light.

Since she couldn't get a factory job with them, Asu had to find something else to do. It took two weeks of walking around the rich neighborhoods, knocking on every door, for Asu to find something. Being a farm girl with a different accent and hard hands made it impossible for her to get work as a housemaid or nanny, which she was hoping for, but she finally found work as a laundry girl for a few rich families. Now, every morning, Asu gets all cleaned up and takes a purple *dala-dala* over to the fancy neighborhoods of Isamilo and Nyakahoja to work.

The first day Chui goes to school, the house is eerily silent. The two oldest cousins, Asu, Mother, and Auntie are all working out of the house. The two younger cousins and my brother are all at school. It's just me and Kito in the house until lunchtime, when the half-day schools let out. Auntie told me to watch Kito the best I can, but to hide when anyone comes. There's an old woman down the street who sometimes comes by to give him food and make sure he's all right, and sometimes a neighbor or two or a child skipping school will come in and play. I always have half my attention on him and half on the door. Even though there aren't that many people who come to visit, it still feels like I spend most of my time hiding under the sacks.

Albino, I whisper to myself as I lie there, rolling the word around on my tongue, tasting it. Just like the long clothing Asu always forced me into as a child, the weight of the label is uncomfortable, but it fits and I have to wear it. *Albino.* After a few weeks of practice, I decide I like it. At least, I like it better than *zeruzeru.* That name meant "nothing." At least being an albino is something.

Today, though, when I dive into the corn cave at the sound of the door opening, I'm surprised to hear Asu's voice.

"I'm home!" she calls.

"Asu!" cries Kito.

"*Habari gani,* sweet one," I hear her say. Then, "Habo, it's okay. I'm by myself. You can come out."

I wriggle my way out gratefully.

"Why are you home so early?" I ask. Asu is standing inside the door, a huge bundle of laundry tied in a sheet beside her.

Beads of sweat dot acrossher nose.

"The washing machine in the Njoolay house is broken." She grins. "And the repairman cannot come until tomorrow, no matter how much Mrs. Njoolay screamed at him on the phone. So that means that today"—she waves to the pile beside her with a flourish—"I'm going to be washing the laundry here."

I grin. Having Asu home for the day is a rare treat.

"We'll help, won't we, Kito?"

We head out to the back patio, where the fire pit is. Kito helps Asu lay the fire, and she hangs the big laundry kettle over it.

"You stay there," says Asu, filling the kettle a bucket at a time from the tap in the side of the house. I try not to bristle at the fact that the tone she's using is the same one I use when I'm talking to Kito.

"But I want to help you."

Asu shakes her head. "No. It's too dangerous."

I peek around the door and calculate angles.

"If I crouch down behind the woodpile, against the wall, no one will be able to see me from the road," I argue.

Asu chews on her lower lip, thinking about it.

"And I'll still be in the shade, so you don't even have to worry about me getting burnt," I add.

For a few moments, Asu just stands there, considereing. I inch out and settle myself behind the woodpile, not waiting for her permission, pleased to see that I was right about being invisible and shaded.

"See?" I say. I know Mother and Auntie would kill me themselves if they knew I was out in the yard in the middle of the day, but I want to get out of the kitchen, and the chance to finally be helpful outweighs my unease. Anyway, I want to show Asu that I can look out for myself.

From my hidden corner, I reach out and start feeding dry corncobs into the fire. I smile widely up at her. She sighs.

"Oh, all right," she says, and goes to get another bucket of water.

I don't say anything more but inside I'm crowing in triumph.

✳

When steam rises off the top of the pot in great billows, Asu throws the soap flakes and sheets into the pot and starts to beat them around in the water with Auntie's laundry pole. I'm in all my usual long clothes, and Asu is standing right over the laundry pot. Both of us are sweating a lot. Mwanza is not only hot but sticky too, even in the dry season. Kito doesn't seem to notice the heat. Right now he's chasing bugs around the edges of the fire. When he catches them, he brings them over to Asu or me. We tell him what a clever little boy he is.

"Asu, tell me about your day," I say.

"What do you want to know?"

"Everything," I grumble. "I'm stuck in a pile of grain sacks for half the day, and I've never seen Mwanza except the night we came in the pitch-black. Tell me everything. Then I'll be able to think of that when you're gone."

Asu looks off in the distance for a moment.

"Well, today is a Tuesday, so I work for the Njoolay family. But let me tell you about the Msembo house, because they're more interesting." She winks at me and continues. "When I'm going to work at the Msembo house, I take the purple *dala-dala* from the corner of the fish market and ride down Makongoro Road. We turn onto Uhuru Street and cross the city, heading away from the wharves. People get on and off. I can smell the food from the street vendors." She puts a hand on her belly, dramatically. "I always want to eat, but I don't want to get my clothes dirty before work, so I don't. In the center of town I switch to the yellow and blue *dala-dala*. This gets me to Isamilo, and from there I can walk to the Msembos' house."

Asu pauses to heft a steaming sheet out of the kettle with the paddle and put it into the rinsing bucket. She beats it around in the cold water there until all the soap is gone from the cloth, then lifts it out again. She takes one end and I take the other and we twist the sheet between us, making sure it doesn't ever touch the dirt, until most of the water is gone out of it. Water drips off Asu's elbows as she lifts the sheet over the line. Then she's at the soapy pot, beginning the process again with the next sheet.

"Once I get to the front of the Msembos' house," she continues, "I'm still not inside. It's a very grand house. There is a huge garden around it on all sides, so green it hurts your eyes to look at it. And around the garden, there's a great, tall wall with broken glass and barbed wire along the top. To get into the house I have to go up to the gate and talk to the man on guard. He stands there all day with his big gun on his shoulder and opens and closes the gate for people."

"Is it scary to talk to the guard with the big gun?" Kito asks.

Asu flashes him a quick smile. "I bet he's almost as bored as Habo in the grain sacks," she says, "standing there all day long in his little hut, not able to go anywhere or talk to anyone. No, he's not so scary."

Again she moves the sheet through the washing and rinsing process. My sleeves are wet now from helping her wring the laundry dry, and I shove them up past my elbows so they don't annoy me as much. My white arms gleam wetly against the white sheets as I twist.

"Once you're in the house, what's that like?" I ask, to get her talking again.

"The house is huge. It's probably bigger than all the houses on our street put together. Mrs. Msembo likes it clean, and there are seven girls who work there every day to make sure everything gleams. Even though I'm only supposed to be doing laundry, I help the other girls in the house when I can, because otherwise it would just be too much to do. Mrs. Msembo checks the work, you know."

"How does she check it?" asks Kito, letting his latest bug crawl up his wrist.

"She'll come up and hold her hand over a table or counter." Asu purses her lips together, puts one hand on her hip, and holds the other out in front of her, palm up, miming Mrs. Msembo's actions. "And if she can't see the reflection of her hand clearly enough to see the rims of her fingernails, you have to clean it again."

As we slowly work our way through the pile of laundry, Asu tells us all about the Msembos: Governor Msembo, who has eyes like a lizard and is up for reelection in a month's time, and the two children, who are spoiled and throw tantrums and break things when they don't get what they want. She tells us about the room full of hunting trophies from Mr. Msembo's *safaris,* the room full of fine china and crystal that Mrs. Msembo uses to host great dinner parties, and the cabinet full of magic talismans that she discovered one day when she was dusting.

"I wonder if any of Alasiri's elephant ended up in that cabinet," I say when she tells us all the things she found there: animal feet and teeth, powders rolled in snakeskin, bundles of twigs tied together with strips of hide.

"Your elephant, too, remember? You and Chui were hunters that day," Asu reminds me.

I make a face at her.

"Me, I would never feel right with that much luck medicine in my house," Asu continues. "You can bet I closed up the cabinet quickly and went on with my dusting!"

As the sun creeps across the sky and the rest of the family begins to return home, Asu tells us about the gleaming modern kitchen with its two large refrigerators to keep things cold all the time and the large electric ovens and stoves where the girl who cooks prepares meals for the family. She tells us about the pet dog that yaps and bites, but that Mrs. Msembo treats like a third child, insisting it have its own plate of food at mealtimes.

"And they have meat at least once every day, sometimes twice! Can you imagine?"

I can't.

Asu tells us then about the other girls she works with: Halima, the shy cleaning-girl, and Aisha, who complains so loudly you can hear her from three rooms away, but her cooking is so good that Mrs. Msembo will never fire her. She tells us about the gardeners and the guards who come in and share lunch with the house girls, and how they all chat about their families and plans for the future when they're rich. Asu talks and talks, and although my hands are wrinkled and sore from wringing wet sheets, I'm happy because my mind is finally full of images of a world beyond the kitchen of Auntie's house.

❈

The next morning, after everyone has left for the day, I'm sunk into a daydream where I'm walking with Asu through every bizarre and beautiful room of the Msembo house when Kito comes up and demands my attention.

"I'm bored, Habo," he says. "Make me something." He's holding a piece of firewood and a knife.

I smile. This has become a familiar game for us since we're left in the house alone together all the time. At first I was so bored hiding in the corn cave that I whittled pieces of wood into chips to use as fire starters, nothing more. But one day I saw Kito looking out the window at a boy playing with a top and decided I would make him a toy. I made a very bad top: It was not at all balanced and kept falling over to one side, but you would have thought I'd given Kito the world. His eyes lit up and he rolled that lopsided top across the floor for hours.

That's when I started whittling in earnest. I tried to make him a truck and, when that failed, I turned it into a boat. I made two more boats so he could have a fishing fleet. He put corncobs in the boats, pretending they were fishermen, and brought me millions of imaginary fish. I carved him a little dog to accompany the fishermen. Again, it wasn't any good, but again, he loved it. So I kept carving.

Now, nearly a month after we started this game, Kito has a little village of houses, and donkeys and dogs and cats, and a dozen little wooden fish for his corncobs to catch in nets we made out of spare string. On my fifth try, I even managed to make him a truck.

"That piece won't do, Kito," I say, taking the wood out of his hands. I hold it sideways for him. "See, there's a big hard knot here, and bugs have made trails through the rest of it. It'll crack the minute I put a knife to it."

Kito frowns. I heave myself onto my feet and take his hand. "Come on, let's go pick out a better one."

I take Kito outside the house and over to the woodpile. I put the termite-ridden piece on top. "Look for one with no bugs," I tell him, and we hunt around for a better piece of wood. Soon, I've found one. It's straight, with no bug holes or knots, and it's not so dry it's splintering.

"Here, this one's good," I say. I turn to Kito to ask him what he wants me to make for him today, and find myself looking into a familiar shining smile.

"Hello again," says Alasiri softly.

8

8.

NO, HE CAN'T *be here.* I watched him return to the wilderness. He can't be here, leaning against the railing of the side yard, looking at me with a smile that is like coins in someone else's hand, all shine and no warmth.

Yet here he is.

At the sound of Alasiri's greeting, Kito whirls around from where he was digging in the woodpile. His eyes go wide as he sees the tall man talking to me, seeing me. No doubt his mind, like mine, is replaying Auntie's many warnings about not being seen, about the importance of hiding. Of what could happen to me if I'm found.

Auntie's voice shrieks in my head, reminding me that it's the middle of the day and I've come outside without checking first to make sure the road was empty. That I simply walked out, as if I didn't have a care in the world, playing with bits of wood for everyone to see. Alasiri or no, I have to get inside. It's not safe for me to be out like this in Mwanza.

Kito must have come to the same conclusion, because he runs up to me and starts to push me toward the house. His little brown hands pushing against my belly are almost comical, but the fright in his voice is not.

"Habo, go!" he whispers loudly. "Go! Hide!"

I retreat a few steps until the tall woodpile and the side of the house shield me from view of the road. In the doorway I stop and look at Alasiri. He's still leaning on the fence, and now he's laughing.

"Why must you go hide, Dhahabo?" he asks. "Have you no hospitality to offer an old friend?" His use of my full name, *gold*, makes my skin crawl.

"What do you want?" I ask. It's not polite, I know, but I deeply feel the danger of talking to him like this. Every second we stand out here talking is one more chance for someone to walk by and learn my secret. Kito is tugging at my shirt, trying to pull me into the house. But I don't want to go inside until I've made Alasiri go away. The last thing I want is him following me.

"What do I want?" His voice is soft, and I have to lean forward to catch his words. He pauses for a moment, looking down at his feet. Then he looks up at me. "What I want, Golden Boy, is to know where your mother is."

"What do you want with Mother?" I ask. His eyes never leave mine. The small hairs between my shoulder blades are standing up.

"I told you. I want to know where she is." Alasiri hasn't moved from the gate, but somehow the fact that he's talking so softly makes it seem like he's getting closer and closer.

"She's at work," I say without thinking. "So go away. She won't be home until later. If you want to talk to Mother, you'll have to come then."

I wait for him to leave. I imagine him pushing off from the fence, dusting his hands on his pants, and walking away. I will the image to come true. But it doesn't. Instead, Alasiri examines his long fingers.

"Ahh, she's at work," he continues in that same soft, smooth voice. "She won't be here until later. *Ndiyo*, I see."

"So you should go," I repeat. Alasiri seems not to have heard me. He continues.

"No doubt she's at work at the factory where your aunt got her a job. Your auntie is at work, too, isn't she? I watched your pretty sister arrive at Governor Msembo's house this morning. So she, too, is at work. Your brother is at school. And your cousins are not in the house or that little one would have gone to fetch them by now, am I right?" He flicks his eyes to Kito, who ducks behind me. I can feel him shaking where his hands are fisted into the material of my shirt. I don't like that Alasiri knows so much about my family, and I don't answer him.

"So it seems, Golden One, that you and I are alone with only this little boy for company. Am I right again?" His eyes start to sparkle, and I feel sickness curl through my stomach. A distant part of my brain identifies the feeling as fear. Because I've seen that look in Alasiri's eyes before. It's the look he had during the last stretch of our ride to the elephant, when he was close enough that he could see the kill.

For a moment, neither of us moves. Then, slowly, Alasiri pushes open the gate and walks into the yard. Finally following Kito's advice, I race away into the house, slamming and locking the door behind me, and run frantically toward my corn cave.

Kito is pasted to my side, crying openly in terror. I stand in the middle of the kitchen floor, frozen for a moment, wondering whether I should bring Kito into my hiding place with me. I can hear Alasiri rattling the doorknob.

I have only seconds to decide. If I leave him outside, Alasiri could make Kito tell him where I am. If I take him in with me, I don't know if we'll both fit. A foot sticking out would give us away. Also, if Alasiri found me, he would find both of us and could hurt Kito. No, although it terrifies me to be alone with the poacher, I decide I have to get Kito out of here. I will not be the reason he gets hurt.

Whirling, I grab Kito by the arm, hard, and push him away from me. He cries out in alarm.

"Kito!" I say to him in a harsh whisper. "Kito, stop crying! You have to go run and find help."

"No!" he practically shouts at me. "No, don't make me! I'm scared!"

"Shut up!" I shake him roughly. "You have to go, Kito. That man is not a nice man." I can hear a rasping sound as Alasiri pushes a blade through the doorjamb to trip the lock. "Run down the road until you get to the fish market. There will be many people there. Tell them a man broke into your house and scared you. Try to find a man to come with you, or the police, before you come back into the house. Now, go!"

I shove him in the direction of the front room, just as I hear the *snick* of the latch giving in. I dive toward the wall and burrow into my cave, pulling the little sack of millet in behind me. My one consolation, as I hear the poacher enter the kitchen, is the scuffling sound of Kito's little feet as he runs out, slamming the front door behind him.

With a curse, Alasiri sprints across the house. He's beyond what I can see from the vents in my hiding place, and I hold my breath so I can hear what he's doing.

I hear the squeak of his shoes against the floor when he pulls up in front of the door, the protesting of the door on its hinges when he yanks it open to look after Kito. There's a brief beat of silence when all I hear is my heart pounding loudly in my ears. Then there's a soft *thunk* as the door closes gently, and the snap of the bolt being thrown. *He's locking us in,* I think, and my breaths—in-out in-out—are too fast, and I realize I'm making a wheezing noise. *Quiet, Habo!* I scold myself. *Stop it!* I close my eyes and try to return my muffled gasps to their normal rhythm.

"So, Golden Boy, you're still in here. Somewhere." My eyes snap open. Alasiri's footsteps in the other room are slow and measured, like his words. Without realizing I'm doing it, I start holding my breath again.

"Your little cousin was running as fast as his stubby little legs could go. So you know, we really don't have much time for this," Alasiri's disembodied voice continues smoothly. "You should just come out from wherever you're hiding, instead of making me come find you." I hear a crash. He must have turned over the table in the front room.

"You should have known there was only one way for this to end, your little hiding game, your ridiculous little life. You didn't possibly think that you could stay hidden, did you? You couldn't possibly have thought that you'd be safe here, in Mwanza of all places?" His voice is honey poured over hot stones. The sound of a knife slicing through Auntie's mattress is like a scream of pain on a dark night. I pull my knees up against my chest as I lie there and try to think myself into invisibility.

"You and your mother and your pretty sister all should have known." His voice is closer, clearer. This is a problem with Auntie's house. Although her family is much better off than we ever were, and her house is bigger and better-built than ours was, it's still a small house. Once he finished with the front room and the two small bedrooms, there's only the kitchen and the yard left for him to search. The light behind my clenched eyelids flashes, and I know his shadow has passed over one of my peepholes. I gather my courage and look out.

Alasiri is standing in the middle of the kitchen with his head up, arms held loosely at his sides. He is scanning the room leisurely, taking in possible places I could be hiding. In his right hand is a long hunting knife, the same one that he used to cut up the elephant.

It's that detail that finally gets my brain working again. He has a knife. A hunting knife. This is no game of hide-and-seek.

This man means to kill me. He means to kill me, cut me up into pieces, take the pieces that interest him, and leave the rest of me lying on the floor to bloat in the heat, just like the elephant carcass in the bush.

Anger bubbles up in me like boiling water. I'm furious that this man should come into Auntie's house to try to kill me so that he can sell bits of me to that horrible *waganga* with the crazy eyes. I'm not a game animal. I'm not a thing. Black spots dance in front of my eyes, and without thinking, I shove myself out of my corn cave, stand up, and hurl one of the sacks at his head. Alasiri is facing away from me, kicking open the cupboards as I come out, but at the sound of my movement, he whirls around. The sack I threw hits him in the chest and he slashes at it with the knife, reflexively. Grain sprays everywhere and, in the confusion, I manage to climb over the rest of the pile and grab one of the bigger stools. I hold it out between me and Alasiri.

"Fine! I'm out, you stupid monster!" I have no idea what I'm saying. My anger is a haze at the edges of my vision, and I shout with all the breath in my lungs. "What are you going to do now? Kill me? Are you going to kill me? Well, I won't let you!"

For a brief second, Alasiri looks surprised. Then his smile is back, stretching across his face like an open sore.

"Well, well," he says, "so you do have some spine after all. I thought I was going to have to kill you where you hid, like a boy hunting frogs."

"I'm not a frog! Get out of here!"

Alasiri starts walking slowly toward me, swinging the knife loosely in his hand.

"*Sawa*, not a frog. Now you're a snake, squirming away and bearing fangs at me. But I'm still bigger than you are, little snake, bigger and stronger. Eventually, I'll win."

My anger is fading and my fear returning.

"Get out!" I say again, but with less force this time. Alasiri moves closer and sideways, and I see he's trying to corner me. I step quickly to the left and away from him, so that I'm lined up with the doorway to the front room. Somehow, I have to get out of this house and into the street. Surely he wouldn't threaten me with a knife in the street. *Would he?*

As if he can read my thoughts, Alasiri says, "Why are you running, Golden Boy? Do you think you'd be safer out there? Do you think that anyone in the street would stop me from killing you?" He pauses and takes an appraising look at me. "Do you even know what you're worth?"

If I just keep backing away, I can reach the door before him. Surely I can unlatch it and get out before he could lunge at me with the knife. Surely he's lying. Surely.

"Don't think I'm lying," he says, again reading my thoughts. "Your hands and hair alone are worth more than a year's salary. Your skin is enough to buy a car. Your legs—ah, your legs." He looks down and I realize that my legs have stopped moving. I force myself away from him with a lurch. He laughs and continues his slow prowl toward me. "Your legs are worth a great deal more than all the rest of you put together. Because it's your legs, Habo, that will win Mr. Msembo this next election. Your legs will get me a position in the government, and a nice house. No more tourists for me." He smiles, and I feel a little bit like I'm going to faint. I'm remembering how Asu told me about the cabinet of luck medicine she found while cleaning the Msembos' house. I have a sudden, terrible image of Asu cleaning around a cabinet that contains bits of my dead body, never knowing it. I feel vomit climbing up my throat and I force it down.

"You're lying," I manage, weakly.

"No," Alasiri says simply, taking another slow step forward. Then, "Did you know it was your sister who helped me get this job?"

I stare at him with my mouth open.

Alasiri smiles. "Oh yes," he says. "Let me tell you a story while we dance across the room. It's a story about a silly older sister who works in a fine house." He takes another step toward me and I step away to match him, out of habit. My brain is no longer working.

"One day, this silly sister tells the other maids about her little albino brother. Isn't that sweet?" Again, we take matching steps. "And who should overhear but the mistress of the house? Now, it just so happens that this particular mistress of the house has been looking for news of an albino. She has heard of a wonderful magic made from albino legs that can guarantee an election victory for her husband and so, when she hears this silly sister talking in the kitchen, she contacts her favorite *waganga* and promises him any price for this medicine. Are you following along, Dhahabo?" I jerk the stool up to my chest from where it's been slipping when he says my name. Alasiri just smiles and keeps talking in that low, sing-song storyteller voice.

"The *waganga* agrees and calls up his favorite hunter. He's pleased when he learns that the hunter already knows this boy. And so it's agreed. For a very great deal of money, in American dollars, the hunter will bring the boy to the *waganga*, and the Msembos will have all the luck they need." Alasiri's eyes muse over me once again.

"Your family named you well when they called you Dhahabo, for you might as well be made of gold. Pure gold," he says quietly, as if to himself. His eyes lock onto mine.

With a start I realize that he's much closer than he was before. I've let my nerves get the better of me and have frozen in place again. As he talked, he has closed the distance between us, and now he's only just a little farther than arm's length away. Instantly, I snap the stool out a little, shaking it at him, and take a few quick steps backward. My shoulders crash into the wall. No, not the wall. I can feel the latch handle bruising my ribs. I have managed to back up into the door.

9.

ONCE, WHEN I WAS only five, I tried to get away with taking off my clothes in the middle of the day. I peeled off the long-sleeved layers Asu and Mother had put me in before they left to work in the maize fields and I ran down to the river. I flapped my arms up and down as I ran and let the breeze I made by running cool me. I got to the river and let my white, white toes sink into the dark mud of the riverbank. I smoothed the dirt up my ankles and wondered what I'd look like if my skin was the good color of the river mud instead of the color of cow bones. But my strange face peered up at me from the surface of the water until I dove in to make it scatter away.

All that afternoon I played in the sunny pools rather than the shaded ones. It felt wonderful. The water sparkled every time I splashed it into the air, and the sun fell over my bare shoulders like a warm blanket.

But that night, I was miserable. It was as if my skin had

pulled in all the heat of the day and wouldn't let it go. I was bright red and had a terrible headache, and my skin was tight all over, like I was being pinched by the hot hands of an angry god.

At first both Mother and Asu gave me a terrible scolding because I had disobeyed them, but when Asu saw that I was in pain, she softened.

"You mustn't ever do this again, Habo," she said. "The sun is jealous of you. If you go out, he'll burn you again. Stay inside where it's dark." And Asu had held me and sung to me while she rubbed my skin with aloe and goat butter. Mother stood off to the side and told her if she missed a spot. Asu rubbed and sang, rubbed and sang, until I fell asleep. The heat from the burns dried the tears off my face, and in the morning there was nothing left but dry tracks down to my ears that crinkled when I moved.

As I stand here, facing Alasiri, that morning comes to me with such clarity that for a moment I am blinded by the sparkle of the river. There have been many times that my differences caused me pain. But I never thought that they would be the reason for my death. Now, with Alasiri staring down at me with a mad sheen in his eyes and a hunting knife in his hand, I know I'm going to die.

No! You're not going to die! I yell at myself. *Think! Think of a way out of this!*

But in order to reach behind me and unlatch the door, I'll have to let go of one side of the stool. If the stool slips, will I give him the chance he needs to stab me?

Noticing that I've finally hit something and can't retreat anymore, Alasiri moves. His grip on the knife tightens. His left arm darts out and grabs a leg of the stool. He yanks it forward, slashing over the top with the knife. I have only a second to make my choice, but I know that if I don't get out that door, I'm dead. So instead of letting go of the stool or pulling away from the blow as he expects me to, I shove forward, pushing the stool into his chest, blocking my face with my free arm. The move throws him off balance and he staggers.

I'm not ready for the burning agony that rips from my wrist to my elbow, but fear gives me the power to reel away from him, unlock the latch, and wrench the door open. Alasiri shoves clear of the stool and it clatters against the far wall, but I'm already out the door, pulling it closed after me. Then I turn and run with all my strength, ignoring the sun burning my skin and the blood dripping down my arm, downhill into Mwanza, toward people and away from the madman with the knife.

✳

I spend the day darting through the crazy rock formations on the hillsides around Mwanza. I run for hours from one hiding place to another, making sure the people who see me go in are not the people who see me leave so that, even if Alasiri is trying to track me, no one can point him in a straight line.

At first I'm worried everyone who sees me will try to kill me, but most people just stare. This is probably because I'm all the wrong colors, but it might just be because I'm running. And bleeding. And crying. I don't spend long enough in any one place to find out. But I do force myself to slow down and stop crying.

I spend the first half of the day working my way farther and farther away from Auntie's house, and the second half working my way back, because I don't know where else to go. I make it as far as the edge of the fish market just down the street from Auntie's house by midafternoon.

By now I'm starting to burn and need a place to hide. As soon as there's a commotion in the market to cover my movements, I sneak under one of the boats that has been pulled up on shore and turned upside down. Here, in the shade of the boat and the relative safety of the market, surrounded by people who aren't looking for me, I wait for night to fall and try to figure out what to do.

I'm hungry and sweating, my legs are trembling from the effort of running after all the weeks I've spent with no exercise, and the pain along my arm is constant. In my first hiding spot, a lean-to full of goats pushed up against a pile of boulders, I ripped off one sleeve of my shirt and tied it over the cut, which was still bleeding everywhere. I've been afraid to look at it since.

I flop over and stare up at the curving wood above me, waiting for my heaving chest to settle into its usual rhythm, and try to think. *Can I go to the police?* It's a tempting thought, but I throw it away. Auntie said that the police did nothing when Charlie was killed. Who knows whether they'd be on my side or not. My stomach twists. Right now I feel like I can't trust anyone in this whole wretched district.

Another thought follows that one the way a stray cat slinks in between the fence rails, knowing it will be unwelcome. If even going to the police won't protect me, then I can't stay at Auntie's house any longer. For a while I just lie there and let the knowledge that I have to leave settle into my heart like a roof collapsing. Then I force myself to crawl out of the rubble and keep thinking.

This isn't just about you, I remind myself. *Kito nearly got killed today, too. If you stay there, you're a danger to the whole family.* This, after all, is the reason Auntie didn't want us in the first place. I look at my blood-soaked sleeve and wish we had listened to her then, poor as we were, and just turned right around and left. I brush the wetness off my face angrily. *It's not as if I liked it there anyway. Stupid corn cave.*

If I'm not going to Auntie's, where am I going to go? Enzi is in Arusha. For a moment I imagine I could go there and live with him. But this is an old dream, already worn shabby by reality. There was barely enough work for the normal boys in our old village, unless it was helping on a farm, which I can't do, and I'm tired of hiding in a house while everyone else works to feed me. *When does the coffee season end, anyway?* I try to remember, but can't. Enzi had said he would finish working the harvest and then follow us to Mwanza. I'm pretty sure they harvest coffee all the way through the dry season, but I can just imagine, with my luck, showing up at our little village looking for Enzi after he's already left. Alone, without a job, I would starve.

I stare up at the hull of the boat arching over me, despairing. Then, from a deep memory, come Auntie's words, urging Mother to take me away: *"You should go to Dar es Salaam. There have been no albino killings there."*

If they let albinos be ministers of parliament, then surely they would let an albino boy do other, smaller jobs. If I can get to Dar es Salaam, maybe I could make a life for myself. I try not to let the word *alone* echo too loudly as I think this.

Of course, the city is thousands of kilometers away. And I have no money.

Overwhelmed by everything, I curl into a tight ball in the point of the boat and fall asleep.

❋

I wake to the sound of one of the few rainstorms of the dry season drumming on the wood over my head. I'm achy and famished. It's full dark, and I can't put off my decision any longer. I heave myself into a crouch and look out from under the boat. No one is on the beach that I can see. The market is deserted other than the ugly angular forms of the marabou storks, guarding the hills of dried fish. I briefly consider eating some of those fish, but under the glassy eyes of the storks, I can't quite make myself do it.

The noise of the rain on the high tin-and-plastic roof of the pavilion covers any noise I make as I drag myself out from under the warm wood and let the rain soak me. Crouching in the shallow water of the lake, I soak the ripped-sleeve bandage until the dried blood in it dissolves and I can peel it off. When I do, I'm surprised to see that the cut, though long and ugly and painful, is not deep at all. The knife must have only glanced along my arm. I rinse my forearm in the water and press lightly against the fragile scab that has already formed over the cut. As long as I'm careful not to open it up again, I think it'll be fine.

My shirt, however, is another story. Smelling like a rusty pipe, covered with dull brown bloodstains, and with one sleeve ripped off to make my makeshift bandage, it's not a shirt I can wear again. Not only will it not protect me from the sun, but I can't really hope to sneak out of Mwanza looking like a butcher's apprentice. I'll have to go to Auntie's house and get the rest of my clothes.

And while I'm at it, I'll get some food, too.

My bare white arm glows faintly in the darkness as I sneak through the fish pavilion, the hairs between my shoulders standing straight up. Fifty-pound sacks of dried fish are piled in neat columns four times the height of a man, some nearly as high as the roof. Usually this place is crowded with people shouting to be heard over their own noise. But when the rain shower ends as abruptly as it started, the rows between the stacks are filled with nothing but blackness and an eerie silence, broken irregularly by the harsh croak of the marabou storks. I slip between the columns, the dried corpses of thousands of tiny fish sifting under my feet.

Once out the other side of the pavilion, I duck from one

boulder formation to another, hiding in the deep shadows of night as I work my way up the hill toward Auntie's house and trying not to splash my feet in the puddles left by the short storm. When I get close, I crouch in the thin bushes across the path and observe the house.

All the lights are on and I can see shapes moving about inside. My first impulse is to run straight into the warmly lit rooms. I imagine throwing myself into waiting arms and letting them squeeze the terror of the day out of me like juice from a lime. It's a tempting vision. What I wouldn't give to be warm and dry and feel safe and surrounded by family again. But no, I won't go searching for hugs and reassurances. I now know the feeling of safety is a lie. You can't win an argument with a hunting knife. If I went in, they might try to convince me otherwise, and I can't let them do that.

Instead, I watch for the glow of a lit cigarette, listen for an unusual rustle in the bushes. Anything that would indicate the presence of my hunter. I don't see anything, but even so I stay hidden, motionless for an hour, two hours, watching, waiting, and arguing with myself.

I need money, food, and fresh clothes from the house. I have to go inside. But I won't go in until everyone else is asleep. I will no longer be a coward, hiding behind women who take care of me. I will be a man and not put them in danger.

Besides, between the blood and the mess and Kito's story, they probably think I'm already dead. It would be cruel to come back to life only to leave again. If they think I'm dead then they won't follow me, won't miss me, won't be worried for me. I curl my head into my arms and wait for them to fall asleep.

Who knows? says a poisonous little voice in my head. *Perhaps they're relieved.*

Night in the city is filled with its own noises. The wind through the trees is like the sound of distant rain, and dogs bark at one another constantly. The sounds of car and truck engines echo off the sides of the buildings when they pass. Music, upbeat and happy, swells and fades as people drive by on the main road down the hill, leaving the silence behind them a little lonelier. It's hours after midnight by the time I creep across the road and around to the rear of the darkened house. The kitchen door with its destroyed lock swings open at my touch, and I sneak like a thief into the place I've been calling home for over three weeks. Just across the threshold I pause and listen. I hear even breathing from many mouths. This is good; I've waited long enough. Silently, I creep across the kitchen.

The moon coming through the window throws the kitchen into harsh lines of black and white. I try to block out the images of what happened here this morning, but it's difficult. I find that I'm standing still, shivering, reliving it scene by scene. I shake myself. Freezing like a terrified rabbit isn't a good way to escape; it's a good way to get caught. I force myself to move again.

After living in the house for weeks, I know all the places that Auntie hides the money that everyone brings in. There's the jar with the screw-top under the sink that holds small money: coins and little bills for shopping at the market and paying vendors who come by the house. I reach under and pick it up. Then there's the bigger money, brought in by Asu and the older cousins, that's behind a loose wallboard in the main room. This is more difficult to get to because my family is sleeping on mats spread all around the room between it and me, but I need it as well.

I slip in on soft feet and move through the sleeping forms. I hope they're all too exhausted from the stress of the day and cleaning up the broken furniture to wake up. Guilt coils in my stomach when I see that Asu has a deep furrow between her eyebrows and is tossing her head as if she's having nightmares. I tiptoe past her and make it to the far wall.

The next trick is prying the board up without making any noise. I grab the plank in both hands and begin levering it away slowly, oh so slowly. My injured arm screams at me, but the cut doesn't reopen so I don't listen to it. I twitch my muscles a centimeter at a time and wait for over a minute to let the wood relax into the new angle before moving it again. Sweat is pouring down the sides of my face and my muscles are burning by the time I have the board lifted high enough to reach a hand in and grasp the roll of shillings.

Slowly now, I tell myself. *Don't just let it snap down like an idiot would. Lower it slowly, the same way you got it up.* My fingers are slick with sweat, but I manage to return the board to its place without a single squeak.

For a moment I just crouch there, trembling, clutching the money in my hands. I can't believe I'm stealing from my family. No good boy would ever do such a thing.

You're not a good boy, the voice in my head reminds me. *You're nothing but a dirty* zeruzeru. *And if you don't get out of Mwanza as quick as you can with those shillings, you'll be a dead* zeruzeru. I get to my feet.

I was originally planning to take the biggest money from under Auntie's mattress as well—the money from her and Mother's factory paychecks—but my experience with the loose board makes me decide it's not worth it. Instead of attempting a third robbery, I creep back through the main room. I'll get some food and take all my sun clothes from their bundle in the corn cave. Then I'll get out of here.

A part of me wants to kick something "accidentally" so that everyone will wake up and see how brave I'm being and talk me out of leaving. But the moonlight shows me bright lines on Chui's face, like old snail tracks, and I don't know what to think about the fact that Chui cried for me, so I go on to the kitchen, as quiet as a ghost.

The corn has been restacked against the wall, although a few stray kernels in the corners of the kitchen show that the mess is not completely cleaned up yet. I pull at the sack on the end and, sure enough, they have even taken the trouble to re-create my corn cave. I don't know whether to feel touched that they hoped I'd come back or angry that they thought I'd crawl into a hiding place that didn't work the first time.

I get down on my hands and knees and scoot into the cave to grab my clothes roll. I'm coming out, my head and shoulders still inside, when a hand touches my side.

I jump up in alarm, banging my shoulders and neck against the roof of the corn sack cave. I shove myself out, my heart hammering, and whirl around to see who's found me.

"Habo?"

I brace for an attack, my eyes darting in the darkness. Then I notice a small form huddled against the side of the nearest sack, shaking.

"Kito, you frightened me!" I whisper, hoping he'll take my cue and keep his voice down.

"Is it really you? You're not dead? Really not dead?" My prompting didn't do any good: His voice is a high squeak, getting louder by the second. I hear a rustling from the other room.

The little boy is terrified, and I don't want to make him scream, but I need to get him to be quiet. I reach out to him.

"Shh, Kito. It's me. I'm okay." He tentatively takes my hand. I pull him into a hug. I tell myself it's just so that I can whisper in his ear and muffle his mouth against my chest, but it also feels good to hold someone.

"Shh," I say again. "I got away, Kito, it's okay."

Kito starts to sob, and now I do use my shoulder to muffle his noise. Quickly, I scoop him up in my arms and carry him out onto the patio.

"Kito, Kito, shh. I'm not hurt." *Much.* My arm still twinges with every move. Kito is blubbering.

"I thought you were dead! I ran and ran, and I found some neighbors, but only women, and you said 'bring a man,' and so I ran all the way to the police station." He gasps for breath.

"But the police wouldn't believe me and I had to tell my story over and over, and then they called Mother from the factory and we all went home and everything was everywhere and there was blood! And you were gone! Gone! And—"

I cut him off. "Enough, Kito!" The boy is starting to wheeze from the effort of telling his story, and he's getting louder, too. "You did a good job. Do you hear me, Kito? You did the right thing. All the right things. *Asante*."

Kito sniffles and burrows his head against my shoulder. I look out over his hair and scan: the street for danger, the houses for lights, the sky for signs of dawn. My ears strain for a sound that tells me I've been caught. After two minutes that feel like forty, I gently push him off. I link my fingers through his and hold our brown and white fingers up to his face.

"Look," I say, "we're a zebra."

He breaks into a tear-streaked smile.

"Kito," I continue, squeezing his fingers in mine, "I have to go." His eyes widen in panic, but I can't let him get worked up about this. These final hours before dawn are the only thing between me and a guarantee of being caught. I have to go now. If I don't leave before the rest of the family wakes up, I'll never make it. Seeing Kito is hard enough. I'd never manage to go if Asu was asking me to stay, or Mother.

"Kito, I have to. The bad man will keep coming if I'm here. The only way to get him to leave you all alone is if I go away. Then the bad man won't come anymore." I smile when I say these things. I don't want the boy having any more nightmares than he already will.

"Will the bad man chase you?" he asks.

A thorn of fear pierces my throat. For a moment I can't say anything. Then I swallow hard and keep talking. The fear scrapes all the way down, making my voice raw when I answer him.

"Of course not," I say. "He'll hunt elephants again."

Kito heaves a sigh of relief. Then his brow wrinkles up. "But where will you go? And when will you come home?"

I take a breath. "Kito, I have to go far away. I'm going to try to make it all the way to Dar es Salaam. I'll be safe there, and the bad man won't ever be able to find me. But that means I have to stay away."

Kito starts to cry again.

Think like a five-year-old! I scold myself. *Going away is as bad as dying to him.*

"I'll call you on the phone!" The rash promise is out of my mouth before I can stop it. *Punguani!* my inner voice raves. *Idiot!* But Kito's face has relaxed again, and I don't dare take it back. "I'll call all the time," I lie. "I'll call the phone in the store down the street, and when they answer it I'll say, 'Hello, my name is Habo. I'm calling from Dar es Salaam. I need to speak to Kito, please.' And the shopkeeper will run all the way up the big hill, panting, wondering who is so important to be getting a phone call from the biggest city in all of Tanzania. And they'll be so surprised to see it's you! And you'll walk down to the shop and talk to me on the phone, and everyone will be so jealous of Kito, the boy who gets phone calls."

"I'd like that," he says.

"I know. But if I'm going to call you from the city, I have to get there first, don't I? So I'm going to get some food and then I'll be on my way. But remember," I say, putting a finger on his pudgy little lips, "we can't make any noise at all."

"Okay," he says.

"And in the morning you shouldn't tell anyone you saw me, either," I say, hoping against my better judgment that Kito will be able to keep my secret, at least until I'm too far away for them to catch up to me. "That way, when I call, it'll be a fun surprise for everyone."

Half an hour later I'm again tiptoeing through the bushes on the far side of the street. But this time I have a pack of belongings and food balanced on my head, a fresh shirt, and money.

I'm on my way.

10.

ONCE PAST the house, I fade into the darkness, debating what I should do next. My first thought is to
get away from people and find somewhere to hide, so instead
of heading down into town I head up, into the wilder hillsides. The night air is cool and humid on my face, and at first
while I climb I can hear the sounds of night in the city—far-
away dance music and laughter, honking horns—but at the
top there is no one to laugh, no music playing.

You're alone, I tell myself. *You can relax a bit.*

But just as I think these things, my foot lands on something that squishes a little and twists my ankle under me.
There is a screech in the blackness and I feel claws ripping
at my ankles. I stumble and fall. A light, furry shape bounds
over me, hissing and spitting. My heart gallops in my ears and
I lie in the weeds for a minute, fighting down the waves of
dread that make the edges of everything sharper.

It was just a cat, I tell myself. *You just stepped on a sleeping cat, that's all, nothing to lose your mind over.* I pull myself into a crouch and look around for somewhere to hide. Surely all that racket will bring people running, and I don't want to be here when they arrive. I huddle under a bush and wait. And wait.

No one comes.

A terrible thought occurs to me: If it had been Alasiri I had bumped into and I was the one screaming, no one would have heard me, either. Though I feel more comfortable hiding far away from people, it's too easy to be killed here. I break into a sweat, even though the August night air is brisk, and turn around and head for the center of town.

I creep along the side roads until I get to Makongoro, the main road that leads from the airport to the center of town. I remember Asu telling me how she would take the purple *dala-dala* this way to work. I hurry along in the shadows and try not to think about Asu. Getting angry about what Alasiri said would just slow me down now.

As the night creeps closer and closer toward dawn, it becomes more and more difficult for me to move around unnoticed, but since my goal has changed from hiding to trying to be around people, I no longer see this as a bad thing. Slowly, light fills the sky. I walk through the streets of the city, checking over my shoulder again and again to make sure Alasiri hasn't suddenly appeared behind me.

By now I'm near the center of town, but most people just stare for a bit and then go back to whatever they were doing, like yesterday, and I start to feel a little better.

See? I tell the frightened animal in my mind. *Not everyone here is trying to kill you. You're going to be all right.*

Have you forgotten Auntie's warnings? the voice whines. *Have you forgotten that yesterday you were chased with a knife?*

I'm hoping against hope to run into a bus or train station without having to ask where to find it. I'm walking quickly, not really paying attention to where I'm going, arguing with the voice, when a pack of young street boys, most not much bigger than Kito, start to follow me. I notice this when they start to clap their hands, calling out "Deal! Deal!"

I wonder whether they're saying this to get money. *Do they think I'm a white person?* I turn around to face them, to explain in Kiswahili that I'm Tanzanian, too, and I don't have any money to give them, when they start to chant.

"There goes a *zeruzeru*," chants the first. The others keep up a steady chant of "Deal! Deal!" in the background. His friend joins in.

"If we kill him we'd be rich!"

"Deal! Deal!"

"What's he worth? What's he worth?"

"Oh, you know he's a deal!" the second boy finishes triumphantly, and the whole ratty pack of them start to circle me, laughing.

I run.

I don't run because I'm afraid of being killed by a bunch of unarmed five- and six-year-olds. I don't run because it is a smart way to go faster to somewhere I need to be. I run because Auntie's comment comes back to me—*Even the children know about it*—and I finally understand what she meant.

Albinos are killed so often in Mwanza that the children chant about it in the streets.

I dodge around central Mwanza at a blind run. The children's jeers have faded behind me, but still I run until my lungs burn and my legs ache.

Finally, unable to run anymore, I duck behind an office building and crawl into the filthy shade between a row of large metal bins and the peeling concrete wall of the building. It smells terrible, but this stench in my nose is better than the sound of those children in my ears. I lean my head against the rusting metal and force myself to breathe normally again.

How am I going to get out of here? The very air in this city rubs against me like a rough cloth against a sunburn, making me feel raw all over. I have to get away.

Walking feels too slow. If a group of five-year-olds can chase me, I would be caught by a group of men. I bang my forehead gently against the bin a few times to clear it. The metal is cold and slightly slick from the waste oil that has dribbled over the top.

Maybe I could just go live in the bush like a wild man. The stupidity of that thought actually makes me laugh, a small, hollow sound. I'm not a nomad like the Maasai. My family were farmers. I'm used to living in a house, near a village, and having food close by. I could never survive on my own.

Stop banging your head and think! I sit back and wipe the sheen of oil and the flakes of rust off my forehead before they can fall into my eyes.

So. Fine. I must live in a village or a town or a city. But

if I'm going to live somewhere with people, it will be far, far away from Mwanza. I refuse to live in this province. I refuse to die in this province.

I pull out the money I took from my family and count it. I have just under thirty thousand shillings. That seems like a lot of money. I squeeze my eyes shut and try to remember how much Auntie said Mother would need to save for the train. It was a really big number, but that was for four people. Now it's just me. I hold the money in front of me, brushing my face over the edges of the bills like they're a fan. *This should be enough to buy just one train ticket, shouldn't it?* I don't know how far it will take me, but at least it will get me away from here.

A bus might be cheaper, but I don't know if there is a bus all the way to Dar es Salaam, and I remember Auntie complaining that, because most of the going and coming in Mwanza happens by boat, the bus station is eleven kilometers outside of town, beyond the military barracks. It's a long way to walk if I'm not even sure it'll work. Plus, buses make a lot of stops. Riding a train would make it more difficult for Alasiri to catch up to me. I hope.

Also, if I'm honest with myself, I have to admit that I've always wanted to ride a train. I've been on a bus, but I've never been on a train. It might be fun.

Standing, I pick up my bundle of clothes and reknot the pack tightly. I push my hat down low over my eyebrows so that it's harder to see the color of my face and hair and balance the pack on top of my head. I fist my hands up into my sleeves, take a deep breath, and step out from behind the bin.

As I march down the street, I can feel the curious glances. No one says anything to me or tries to stop me, but I find myself hurrying nonetheless. I remind myself not to walk stiffly. *You're just a normal Mwanza boy*, I remind myself, *out running his morning errands. You are not a* zeruzeru. *You are not afraid. You are not in a hurry.* I repeat that over and over, hoping it changes how I seem to those around me, willing them to ignore me.

I need to ask someone where to go, but who? I look at the people around me as I walk, looking for someone to trust with my life. That man in the expensive suit? No, Alasiri told me it was the governor himself who wants my legs. I don't trust anyone rich enough to buy me.

That shopkeeper over there? The lady selling roasted ears of corn? No, she will stay in one place all day. If Alasiri looks for me, she would be too easy to ask. Not a shopkeeper then.

A child? I shudder as I remember the street boys. No, not a child. They'd talk about seeing me all day long. I need someone too busy to take much notice of me who won't stay in this area for long. I stand for a moment on the street corner, frustrated, glaring into the murky early-morning light and breathing in the gray dust and the diesel exhaust of the cars and *dala-dalas* passing me by, trying not to think about how good that woman's roasted corn smells and the fact that I haven't had any breakfast.

Finally, I see a young woman running to catch a *dala-dala* that she just misses. It pulls away from the corner, and she calls after it in frustration. She's perfect. She is late and annoyed and will not stay here long, but must wait for the next *dala-dala* so she has a few minutes to spare.

I walk up to her.

"*Sabahani,*" I say. "Excuse me, could you please tell me where to find the train station?" I'm hoping she's too busy to really pay much attention to me, and she is. As she answers she keeps scanning the street beyond me, checking for the next *dala-dala*.

"It's not far," she says. "You go past Nyamagana Stadium. At the roundabout there you can walk off Kenyatta Road onto Station Road. Then you can't miss it."

"*Asante sana, Bibi,*" I say, relieved. I remember seeing Kenyatta Road as I ran in circles earlier. I'm fairly sure I can find my way there.

"*Bibi?*" she asks, laughing, turning to me. "I'm too young yet for a boy your age to be calling me *bibi!*" She has a pretty laugh, but it fades as she actually looks at me for the first time. She sees my hunched shoulders, my tightly tied pack, my face. Her smile disappears entirely, as if it had never been.

"Ahh," she says softly. "The train station." Her eyes are sad. "*Ndiyo,* you should go. This is not a good city for you. Go to the train station, polite boy, go and be safe."

We hold each other's gaze for an awkward moment, and then I look down, embarrassed, and turn away.

"*Asante,*" I say again, because there is nothing else I can think of to say.

11.

I MAKE IT without incident across the various roads and roundabouts until I can smell hot engine oil and see the tracks stretching away to freedom. I crouch across the way and watch the station. The lack of sleep has made my sight even weaker than it usually is, and I can feel my stupid albino eyes jiggling back and forth, making it hard to see clearly.

The train station is a small building, with people going in and out through the dark arches of the doors like ants exploring a piece of fruit on the road. I hesitate. The minute I walk up to the ticket window, people will see me and know what train I'm going on. If there's a long time between when I buy the ticket and when the train leaves, it would be that much easier for Alasiri to find me.

For a few minutes I argue with myself, doing nothing. Finally, I tell myself that a strange albino boy staring at the train station from across the street is just as noteworthy as a strange albino boy buying a ticket, and I push myself to my feet. Slapping the dust off my pants, I resettle my bundle on my head and walk up to the ticket window. Although the window faces the street, it's too dark for me to see if there's anyone inside. I lace my fingers through the iron bars in front of the window and lean forward. The smell of metal worn shiny by many hands greets me.

"Hello," I call into the darkness. "Please, could you tell me how I buy a ticket?"

"What?" a deep voice asks from beyond the bars.

"I'd like to buy a ticket, please," I say. My hands are sweating, and I wipe them on the sides of my shirt.

"Yes?" asks the voice. "A ticket to where?"

I pause. For some reason this question makes it all come crashing down onto me. I'm leaving. I'm really leaving my family. I'm going someplace completely unknown, and I'm going to pay stolen money to this man to make it so.

"How much to Dar es Salaam?" I manage, although my voice is a little higher and tighter than it was a moment ago.

"Eighteen thousand, nine hundred shillings." My head reels. Not only at the amount, but at the fact that I'm currently carrying enough inside my shirt that I can even have a conversation about such a number. I'm sweating into a small fortune. The man is still talking. ". . . and it will take you forty hours to get there."

The voice in my head gasps. *That long? Two whole days??* I try to remain calm. I want to ask the man whether there is anywhere else I could go and be safe, but that's not a question

I can say out loud. *Two days on the train!* my inner voice groans.

The man is getting impatient. "Well? Do you want it or not?"

"*Ndiyo*," I say, and dig in my shirt for the folded bills. "Yes, please." The bills are plastered against the skin of my chest, but I peel off a few and hand them over. I can only hope that they're the right amount. As tired as I am, I can't see well enough to tell the numbers on the bills anymore. I figure he'll tell me if I underpaid. Since he says nothing, I figure I've at least paid him enough, maybe overpaid. A hand pushes a ticket at me out of the darkness.

"Do I get any change?" I ask with all the calm I can muster.

He hands me a few small bills. I sigh. The change may or may not be accurate, but I have no way of knowing.

"*Asante*," I say. "How long until my train leaves, please, and where do I catch it?"

A small, awkward pause follows my question.

"Boy," says the voice, "there is only one train. There is only one track. You have twenty minutes to figure it out." A finger jabs out of the darkness in front of me to point over my shoulder at the farthest arch. I assume that's the entrance to the tracks.

I turn away from the window, clutching my ticket.

"Oh, and boy?" he adds. I turn around and look in the direction of the dark window. "If you miss this train, the next one isn't until Sunday. The train only runs twice a week."

"*Asante*," I say again, blessing whatever luck brought me here on a Thursday, and I walk through the arch farthest to

the left into the shadowy, crowded passageway of the Mwanza train station.

Instantly, smells and sounds take over sights for me.
(Sweat. Lye soap. Fry oil. Dust. Hot machinery.) My eyes become nearly useless in the low light, and all I sense are waves
of heat when somebody pushes past me. (Swishing clothing. The slap of sandals against worn heels. A woman talking loudly on a mobile phone. The bleating of a goat beyond
the tracks.) I get jostled, and my bag slips off my head. I cry
out and turn around, bending down to find it. (Feet. Dirt.
Dog urine.) People move around me and I feel like I'm in the
middle of a herd of cows that has been spooked. I'm afraid
of getting crushed, but I'm even more afraid of losing all my
belongings, so I stay on the floor and feel around until I find
them. Just as I close my hands around my pack, two leather
sandals full of dusty toes stop an inch from my face.

"You! There on the floor! What is wrong with you, huh?"
Large hands grab my shoulders and pull me up to face a hulk-
ing, sweaty man in a khaki uniform. (Voice like gravel under
tires. Cheap cologne. Armpit. Garlic with dinner last night.)
The light from the platform beyond him makes it impossible for me to see his features, but I don't think he's anyone I
know. I clutch my bundle to my chest.

"I'm sorry, *Bwana*. I dropped my bag."

"Well? Did you have to crawl all over the floor like an animal to pick it up?"

I flush, humiliated. His voice is not quiet, and I'm sure
there are people staring at us now. I'm leaving easy tracks for

my hunter to follow.

"I'm sorry, *Bwana*," I say again. "I don't see well."

"Hmph." His grip loosens, and I step away from him. I shuffle toward the light, jerking to a stop whenever someone's shadow passes in front of me to avoid bumping into them.

I come out of the station and stand against a chain-link fence that separates the courtyard of the station from the tracks. I squint around. People waiting for the train are clustered around a small shop painted red with *Coca-Cola* written all over it. Other than a thin stretch of packed earth, there isn't a platform. The long metal rods of the train tracks are set into the dirt about ten feet to the left of where I'm standing. There aren't any people on the far side of the tracks, so I assume that where I'm standing is the right place to catch my train. I'm glad for that, but still, until the train comes, I need to get out of sight.

I walk through the gate in the chain-link fence and look around, scanning for places to hide that would still give me a good view. There's a small shed off to my right, away from the tracks, and I decide to walk over and check it out. Behind it a small triangle of ground is sandwiched between a large blue plastic rain barrel, the wooden north wall of the shed, and a pile of old bags of concrete, fused to rock by the humidity. It's like a concrete version of my corn cave. It's perfect.

The only trick will be getting into it without being seen. I loiter for a bit over near the fence, my fingers laced through the chain-link, my head tipped forward so that my hat covers my face, waiting for everyone to lose interest in me. Three minutes creep by, then five. Finally, I get the chance I've been waiting for.

On the far side of the Coca-Cola stand, a boy playing with his brothers runs into an old lady carrying little bags of rice to sell at the market. Some of the food goes flying and lands in the dirt. The woman is furious and grabs the boy by the scruff of his neck. When everyone turns to watch the shouting and scuffling, I slip into my hidden corner without anyone seeing me.

Once I'm wedged in, I set my pack beside me and arrange myself in a sitting position that keeps all my skin covered. I inch my pants down off my hips and roll my toes into the cuffs; I make sure my hat flap overlaps my shirt collar; I tip my head forward until the tip of my nose disappears under the shade of the brim; I put my hands under my knees. *Yes, perfect.* I'm safe from the sun and from prying eyes, and I'm so used to hiding in the corn cave that I could stay here comfortably for hours if I need to. There's even a crack between the wall and the side of the rain barrel that lets me see out.

I'm just settling into these happy thoughts when I catch sight of a familiar figure stepping out of the station arch. Even though I'm well-hidden and he's nowhere near me yet, when Alasiri walks onto the dirt platform, my heart stops.

I have to remind myself to start breathing again as I watch him walk up to the Coca-Cola stand and start talking to an elderly couple sitting there in the shade. I'm much too far away to hear what he's saying, but I can imagine well enough. When he holds a hand out in front of his chest to indicate height, I know he's asking about me. In an instant I'm back in the corn cave, feeling the walls close in around me. My breath comes in gasps and I'm overwhelmed with the desire to run.

I splay my fingers against the rough wood of the shed beside me and force myself to breathe only on counts of ten. My lungs tighten, telling me I'm not getting enough air, but I ignore them and keep counting. *Think!* I tell myself sternly. *This is no time to panic! You have to think.*

Run! Run! Run! chitters the small voice of fear.

I keep breathing. So, Alasiri is still following me. He's here and I'm here. The only question is whether he'll find me. *Well,* I think, *now I'll see whether* this *hiding place works.* The calmness of the thought surprises me, but I suppose the body only has so much space in it for terror and then it just doesn't hold any more. I must have used all mine up.

I press my face to my peephole again. The old man is pointing at the station, waving his hand. Alasiri straightens, says something over his shoulder to the old people on the bench, and walks back the way he came. He pauses for a moment at the gate in the fence that leads into the station, hands on hips, looking carefully through the crowd. I hold my breath again, willing him to go away. The space that I'm in looks too small to hide a person; the way the concrete bags are stacked makes it look like they fill the whole space. I hope that this illusion will be good enough to make Alasiri leave entirely. For a minute I think he might come over and look behind the shed, but instead he turns away and is swallowed by the dark arch of the station.

As Alasiri disappears into the shadows, I discover I have the ability to breathe normally again. I also notice I was gripping the planking of the shed so hard that I've split a fingernail on the rough wood. I put the finger in my mouth and suck on it as I think about what I should do now. The wild voice in my head is still gibbering out crazy ideas, like hiding in the bush or running away on foot, but I decide to ignore it until it starts talking sense. Because really, the fact that Alasiri is still chasing me doesn't change my plans at all. It just makes it even clearer that I have to get out of Mwanza as quickly as possible. *And that*, I remind the whimpering voice in my head, *is still going to happen fastest by riding a train.*

Once I've come to my decision, I settle into my earlier position, squatting in the shade, eye pressed to barrel crack, to wait. I imagine the voice huffing off into a corner of my mind and sulking at my maturity. It makes me smile.

The next half hour passes slowly, not helped by the fact that my stomach is grumbling about a missed dinner and breakfast. But there's no way I'm going to wander out and buy something from the food stand, and I refuse to unwrap the food I brought with me until I'm on the train. From time to time I squint up and try to gauge the passage of time by the progress of sun, but eventually I give up and just wait.

Finally, I hear a soft, rhythmic chugging and I see the people on the platform begin to stand and stretch. Children scamper and point and I know that a train is on the way. Now I'm nervous again. I don't want to stay hiding so long that I miss my train, but I also don't want to jump out too early.

I can only imagine how awful it would be to stand around, waiting for the train to arrive and open its doors as everyone on the platform stared at me. I would never know, until it was too late, if one of them was rich enough to have a mobile phone, and unpleasant enough to know Alasiri. My palms begin to sweat.

I pull myself into a crouch and knot my knuckles into my bundle. I have no feeling in my arm or my hip, and my skin is pitted with little dents from the time spent pressed against the rotting wall of the shed. I swear I hear my hips creak when I move. I stretch as much as I can in the small space, getting ready to dash for the train.

The scarred engine pulls slowly into the station in the middle of a cloud of foul-smelling smoke and a painful shrieking of brakes. The large doors on the side are shoved open and people start getting off, some stepping down carefully and reaching up for their luggage or babies, and some throwing their bags out ahead and leaping after them. People from the platform crowd in among the passengers getting off, pushing their way onto the train.

I'm so enthralled, watching all this, that I almost forget I need to get on that train, too. Almost, but not quite. When the platform is nearly clear, I put my bundle on top of the bags of cement and heave myself over. Then I pick up my pack and jog toward the train. But I'm already too late: I see a man in uniform start to swing the heavy train door shut.

"Wait!" I call, terrified at the thought of being left behind and having to wait in hiding until Sunday. "Please! Wait!"

The man sees me and holds the door open a little, with a noise of annoyance. The train gives a shudder and starts to inch back the way it came, out of Mwanza. I jog faster.

I'm nearly there, on the packed earth leading to the train, when a movement ahead of me pulls my attention away from the door. There, leaning in the shade against the corner of the station, is a man.

Alasiri.

I stop without meaning to. Yes, it's him. He's pushing himself off the building, a slightly stunned look on his face, as if he didn't really expect me to be here, either.

I realize I'm trapped. Alasiri is standing at the station gate. The train is pulling out of the station in his direction. To catch the train, I'll have to go toward the man who is trying to kill me. My brain shuts down for an instant.

Screeching softly, the train speeds up. The door I need to get into, the last one open on the train, moves away from me, closer to Alasiri.

I have no choice: I have to make it to that door before it leaves the station. I break into a run.

For a moment, Alasiri seems content to let me run toward him. Then he sees that my running might get me to the door before I get to him. With a curse, he breaks into a run, too. He has a man's strength to power his stride. I have the pure fuel of fear driving my short legs. It's a race to the door. I cross the expanse of packed earth so quickly, I can feel the impact of my feet on the ground all the way up into my shoulders.

Each step takes me closer to the open door.

Each step takes me closer to Alasiri.

The train is really picking up speed, and I run alongside it, trying to reach the door with the conductor as if my life depends on it. Which it does. My toes are now stumbling along the ragged rocky edges of the tracks themselves, and the train is getting almost too fast to catch.

My vision blurs with my terror. The sound of Alasiri's breath growing louder mingles with my own panicked gasps in my ears. He's so close now, I can see the little hairs on his face telling me he didn't shave this morning. There's a gleam of triumph in his eyes as he reaches for me.

I sprint forward, lungs screaming from the effort, and launch myself sideways toward the open door of the train. I feel the brush of fingers, a grabbing hand that has just missed me. My body slams onto the dirty metal floor of the train, my legs dangling out the door. I drag myself in the rest of the way, then whirl around. It feels like the air is ripping my lungs as I gasp in and out, and I've scraped my palms and knees, but it's worth it. Because there, behind the last train carriage and shrinking in the distance, is the lone figure of Alasiri, cursing in frustration. He hasn't caught me. I collapse onto the grimy floor and laugh with relief.

"Show me your ticket, boy, or I'll throw you off again," booms a voice from above me. "I won't have kids riding the train for fun without paying."

"I'm not riding without paying!" I wheeze. "Look, here's my ticket." I pull it out of my pocket and give it to the train conductor who held the door for me.

"That's a ticket, all right, but it's third class! How dare you jump into the first class door as if you belong here?"

"I didn't know." He's still holding my ticket between two fingers, as if it was slimy. I want it back. "Give me my ticket and show me where the third class car is, *Bwana,* and I'll go there." I hold out my hand.

The man gives an unpleasant little laugh, shoves my ticket at me, and turns away.

"Wretched boys," I hear him mutter. Then, louder, "Follow me!"

Carefully pushing my precious ticket deep into my pocket, I hug my bundle to my chest and follow the man down the corridor.

12.

"NO! I CAN'T DO IT!"

I'm frozen in the door between train cars, my knuckles in a death grip on the thin metal bars on one side, my other hand clutching my bundle to my chest. My eyes are glued to the space in front of me that the train orderly expects me to jump across. Panic crawls up my throat like a hairy spider.

"No!" I say again, starting to back away.

"*Punguani!* Go on!" he bellows in my ear. I wince. But even his bellowing can't stop the slow inch of the panic spider.

After I had gotten on my feet again, the orderly led me from the passenger-entry door to the end of the carriage. Now, directly in front of me is the next train car, with an open door at the rear of it just like the one I'm standing in. The cars sway with each imperfection in the track and bump in the landscape, and they each sway just a little differently, making the door I need to go into jolt unpredictably. All that's between my car and the other car is a rusted connection and one single chain. And below that—nothing. Nothing but the rocks and red dust of Tanzania, blurring past. The chain tenses and slackens, tenses and slackens, pulling the cars closer together and then letting them drift farther apart. With my bad eyes, I can barely judge the distance between the two doors, but only a blind man couldn't see that a misstep would end horribly.

I imagine myself being pulled under the train and sliced in half, or having the two cars jolt together and crush my legs. I swallow down a mouthful of bile. No, I've just spent two days fighting to keep my legs. I want to keep them a little longer. I turn to the man.

"I don't think I can . . ." I start, but his dark brows crunch down over his eyes and he gives me a rough shove, sending me flying. I land hard against the other door, hands scrabbling for the rails. I find them and pull myself in to safety. My bundle lands on the floor with a thump as I plaster myself to the train wall, shaking.

The big man comes in behind me a split second later, taking the gap in one long stride. My eyes must be worse than I thought. It must not be such a big gap after all. Again I wish I wasn't an albino, with all its problems. But I have no time to curse my useless eyes, because the man grabs the collar of my shirt with one hand and scoops my bundle off the floor in the other and, instead of being allowed to walk as I was in the last car, I am dragged through the second class carriage like a misbehaving child. I don't want to cause any more of a scene than we're already causing, so I go with him quietly.

I have to jump over two more car interchanges before the

orderly finally lets go of me with a shove. He dumps my stuff on the floor in front of me. I quickly bend down and pick it up, pulling it up close against my chest again.

"This is the third class cabin," he says, loudly enough for everyone nearby to hear him. "Stay here or I will put you off the train at the next station. No more of your tricks, *zeruzeru!*"

With that, he spins on his heel and walks away from me. He reaches the intersection between cars and jumps over lightly. With the benefit of many years of experience and no reluctant boy in tow, he is almost graceful. I wish him a horrible death falling under the train.

Anger helps no one, chides Asu's voice in my head. But a voice that sounds like Chui is laughing. I turn and look for a place to sit.

The third class car does not have private rooms off of a hallway like the first class car did. Nor does it have spacious rows of padded individual seats, like second class. Instead, the seats in the third class cabin look almost like bus stop benches, with long slats of wood nailed together to make the seats and the upright backs. The benches are arranged in rows all the way down both sides, with only a narrow aisle in between.

After my sudden arrival and the orderly's outburst, everyone in the car has turned and is staring at me. For an awkward moment they all consider me. I shuffle quickly down the aisle, looking for an open seat at one end or the other. Having spent a lifetime at the edges of things, I don't even consider taking one of the open seats in the middle of the car.

I find what I'm looking for on the third bench from the end on the right-hand side. This is an added benefit, because I'm facing forward. The swaying motion of the train hasn't bothered me except when I was being forced to jump, but I'm glad that I don't have to spend the next two days facing backward. I mumble my apologies to the men and women there and perch on the bench. I sit and tuck my head down, clutching my bag to my chest with both arms, every muscle tight, waiting for everyone to go back to whatever they were doing again and stop staring at me.

Eventually they do. I hear the murmur of conversations restart, the rustle of snacks being unwrapped, the creaking of the wooden slats when fat people adjust their positions. I wait a little longer, then raise my head. There are two men sitting on the bench with me and a younger man and an old couple on the bench facing me. They look at me with open interest. The older man speaks first.

"What are you, boy?"

I hesitate. What should I say? I'm a *zeruzeru* being hunted like an animal? I'm a child running away from his family? I'm nobody, son of no one? No, better a half-truth. I don't want to appear too vulnerable.

"I am an albino," I say. Saying the word out loud to a stranger for the first time is like drinking coffee with no milk: bitter, but you're not surprised because that's what coffee is. I shift slightly in my seat. "I'm on my way to stay with my grandparents in Dar es Salaam. I'm going to help out in the shop there."

The man grunts, accepting my story. He turns to his wife and they talk about me in quiet voices. The young man with them keeps staring at me, though. I turn my head away from him, pretending to look out the window.

I don't know whether the other two men sitting beside me understood what I said, because it's clear that they're from another tribe. Their faces have bold features and are accentuated by patterned scars on their cheeks and foreheads. Their skin is so black it's almost purple, and they stare unblinkingly out at the moving landscape. They seem rather fierce, and I'm sure that's why my seat was left empty. People will rarely sit with those from another group if they have a choice. But to me, the men are comforting. In their own way, they're as out of place as I am. And perhaps sitting next to such large, frightening-looking men will make anyone trying to kidnap me think twice. I slowly let my fists unclench and my shoulders drop below my ears.

I'll relax a little, I tell myself, *just enough to get comfortable, but I won't let my guard down.*

But those brave words can't compete with the effect of relative peace, quiet, and the gentle rocking of the train. The last time I had a good night's sleep was two nights ago, and I've been doing nothing but running and hiding since then. I have stolen, lied, and left my family and all that is familiar to me. I've been terrified, enraged, and just plain miserable. My head drops against the hard slats of the seat and, against my will, I am soon deeply asleep.

The train lurches as it passes over a junction in the tracks, who knows how much later, and I awake with a start. At first I'm completely disoriented, thinking I'm at home and the warm form beside me is someone in my family. But a quick glance upward shows me a tattoo-accented jawline and a dark, intelligent eye above it, watching me. I jerk away.

I can't believe it! After all that telling myself to be careful, I fell asleep. Worse than that, I've been sleeping against the shoulder of the stranger beside me. I feel my face redden with embarrassment.

"Forgive me, *Bwana*," I stammer. "I didn't mean to fall asleep on you."

The man laughs and shakes his head slightly. He says a few words in a language I don't understand, but their message is clear: *It's okay.*

I smile back, then look around.

I was right: Riding a train *is* a lot of fun. It's amazing how fast we're going. As soon as you see what something is, *whoosh!*, it's whisked away again, gone! The landscape outside flashes past in a way that reminds me how we sped along the Serengeti road in Alasiri's Jeep. But that thought is linked to many others I don't want to think about. I glance quickly up and down the train, making sure that no faces have left or arrived and that none of them is Alasiri. Then I make myself think about something else.

Over the next hours, I busy myself eating some of the food I packed and looking out the train windows. I'm mesmerized by the land outside, my land. I see the low scrub stretch far away into the distance where the purple thumbprints of mountains smudge the edge of the sky. Sometimes we pass little villages, nothing more than a cluster of small square houses, drying corncobs on their wavy tin rooftops. I imagine my family living in these villages, what our life would have been like there.

They remind me of our village in the Loilenok Hills. These villages are so tiny, so far away from everything. I understand now how small my world used to be. And yet, I miss it. I miss knowing the routine: knowing I would go to school, knowing it would be awful, knowing I would come home and eat, knowing I would herd the goats, knowing I would have dinner with my family and sleep, knowing that I would do it all again in the morning. Now I'm on my own and I have no idea what will happen or what I'm going to do.

The train does not stop at any of these villages.

The speed of the train and the changing landscape keep me amused for a long time. But the fun hours are followed by hours that crawl. Men and women talk or sleep or look out the window. They eat the food they packed and take trips to the end of the car to use the bathroom. I wish I had someone to talk to; Asu or Mother or Kito—even Chui, I suppose. Fighting with him would at least be *something*. I know I should really be saving my food, but I take out some more *ugali* and nibble at it out of sheer boredom.

Finally we begin to pass houses clustered closer together and then more modern buildings. I sit up eagerly and turn to the young man across from me.

"Excuse me," I ask, "where are we?"

The man laughs, loudly, in my face. He elbows the old man beside him, who had fallen asleep.

"*Bwana*," he says. "This white boy wants to know where we are. Should I tell him we're in Dar es Salaam already?" He laughs like this is some great joke. I scowl at him. Even I can tell two days haven't passed. I just wanted to know what town we're in. I turn away from his rudeness. The old man doesn't join him in laughing at me, which is slightly comforting. Instead, he leans toward the window and looks at the approaching station.

"Oh no, boy," he says softly to me. "No, this is not Dar es Salaam. We have not yet gone even a third of the way. This is Shinyanga station. Ten hours more and we will come to Tabora. Then there is only the little station at Manyoni between us and Dodoma . . . and that is only halfway to Dar es Salaam." He gives me a tired smile. "It's hard to be patient when you are young."

I smile at him for his kindness in explaining this to me, but inside I'm screaming. We've only gone a third of the way? I don't know if I can take it.

Of course, I know I have to. Because even though every time we pull into a station my heart hammers in my chest as I scan the people waiting to get on, looking for Alasiri, every station we leave behind makes me feel just a little bit safer. I'm getting farther and farther away from him and, from what I can tell, he doesn't seem to be following me. I still find myself starting to panic whenever I fall asleep or whenever my healing arm aches, reminding me of yesterday, but I can talk myself into calmness more and more easily the farther we get from Mwanza.

At Shinyanga I stand and reach a few hundred shillings out the window to one of the boys selling sweets and buy myself a chocolate bar and a Coca-Cola. I've had chocolate twice before in my life, but I've never had a Coke. The chocolate memories come from the early days at home, when Mother still smiled easily. My father had left us, but the farm was still doing well. For two years in a row that I remember, Mother bought a bar of chocolate for us to share on the holidays. Each small bar had four squares. Mother gave one square each to Asu, Enzi, Chui, and me. At Chui's insistence, we each broke off a corner and shared it with Mother.

I let the chocolate dissolve on my tongue and think about how I'd describe it to Kito. I choke on the bubbles in the Coke and laugh when they tickle my nose and imagine I'm watching him do the same. But these thoughts make me sad. And, after eating a whole bar of chocolate and a whole tin of Coke, I have a bellyache to fall asleep to.

When night comes, everyone pillows their heads on what they brought with them and falls asleep where they sit. I hear people mumbling about how second class seats recline and first class passengers have little beds all to themselves. I try not to feel too miserable when I hear this. I sleep sitting up, like the rest of third class, waking every time we hit a juncture or pass a streetlamp.

Once during the night I wake up not because of movement,

but because we're not moving. At first I think it's just another station, but there are no lights outside my window and, as the time stretches on and we're still not moving, I begin to think it might be something else.

Alasiri! I think. *Alasiri has caught up to me and has found a way to stop the train.* My heart starts to hammer in my chest.

I look around and see that a few other people are awake around me, including the old man I spoke to earlier.

"*Bwana,*" I whisper at him so as not to wake his wife. He looks up at me. "Why have we stopped?"

The old man gives a dry laugh.

"They say there is something wrong with the engine." His voice is thin and reedy, like his body. "We will be here until the mechanic can fix it."

Something wrong with the engine. Visions flash through my head. Alasiri, unhooking key parts of the train and then laughing madly as the train engineers try to fix it. Alasiri, using the distraction of the engine to slowly prowl up and down the train, staring into the faces of the sleeping passengers, looking for me. I swivel in my seat and look up and down the compartment I'm in. Other than a few other passengers woken up by our unscheduled stop, no one else is moving around. I swallow against the dryness in my mouth.

"How long will it take to fix the engine?" I ask.

"Who knows, boy? Who knows."

We lapse into silence again and the old man dozes back off, but I hunch in my seat, straining to hear the sound of a compartment door opening, frantically trying to think what

I'll do if I hear it. Would the people around me protect me or hand me over? Should I hide in the train or run outside? It's black as a cave outside and have no idea where I am, whether we're in the middle of a wilderness or near a city or town. The windows reflect my face back to me, pale and tense.

It takes hours for them to fix the engine, but I do not go back to sleep.

By the time the train finally lurces forward again, the first streaks of pink are coloring the sky outside the window and my eyes are grainy and heavy-lidded with exhaustion.

The next day seems even longer than the first, and the train ride doesn't feel like an adventure anymore. I'm uncomfortable and tired. I have no more exciting snacks. I hear the people around me complain that our delay last night is making the train run especially late this trip. It doesn't look like we will get to Dar es Salaam until tomorrow morning.

I sigh and prepare myself for another uncomfortable night.

It's only after my second sunrise breakfast on the train that my spirits begin to improve. Partly, this is because I got to eat again and I always enjoy eating, and partly it's because people start to double-check their bags and talk loudly about what their plans are once they get off the train. All of this is medicine for my bad mood because it makes me realize that I'm finally getting close to the end of my journey.

But as I listen to everyone talk about their plans in the city, I realize with a jolt that I have none. Should I try to get a job? Should I beg? Should I even stay in Dar es Salaam, or should I just keep running out into the surrounding countryside?

I have a headache from frowning while I think, but I still haven't come up with any good answers when the train begins to slow down, moving cautiously through concrete homes and warehouses.

The sun is completely up by the time we're pulling into the station. I see people, animals, and cars clogging the city streets. Children and stray dogs run alongside us for no reason other than the joy of the chase. Dar es Salaam is bigger than Mwanza, which is frightening, but it's also better than Mwanza, because here, Auntie said, they have not killed any albinos.

With a final lurch, the train pulls into the station, the doors open, and I'm out.

※

My feet land on the slanted concrete of the Dar es Salaam station platform, and for a moment I stand there stunned, looking around, squinting in the early morning light, letting the people from the train stream around me like a herd of goats going around a tree. It's much bigger than the other stations we've passed, complete with a high wrought iron fence to keep people from the street off the platform and an enormous corrugated tin roof to keep the sun off the people waiting for the train. It has all the size of the Kirumba fish market without the salty-sack smell.

Now what? the voice in my head asks me.

I have no good response. When I was running from Alasiri,

I had no thought beyond getting out of Mwanza. When I was hiding in the city, I had no thought beyond getting on the train. When I was on the train, I had no thought other than getting to Dar es Salaam. Now I'm here, and I seem to have no thoughts at all.

Instead of sulking and sleeping and eating chocolate, you should have worked harder at figuring out what to do when you got here! I yell at myself. But yelling now does me no good. I'm stuck here, with not much money left, no place to go, no one I know to take me in, and a lingering worry that Auntie may be wrong and the people here will also want me dead.

This reminder makes me look quickly around at the people in the station. Is anyone taking too much of an interest in me? Not the people from the train who are streaming by. The ticket collectors? No; though their smart uniforms and guns make me nervous, they're glaring at everybody equally. The candy boys? Yes, they're staring and whispering, but kids have done that everywhere. The people leaning against the yellow wall with the timetable board, waiting for the next train? Maybe. Some of them are staring at me. Although I suppose by standing here, gawking, I'm making myself more obvious. Quickly, I start to walk along with the general flow heading into the station. This doesn't improve my mood, because the Dar es Salaam station's hallway is even darker than the Mwanza station's, and the minute I step from the open-sided platform into the long, dim exit corridor, I'm blind again.

There are few things quite so terrifying as the combination of being surrounded by strangers, not knowing where to go, and not being able to see. For a second I stay perfectly still. Then someone runs into me from behind and I have to move forward. I have no idea how to get out and I'm afraid to call attention to myself by asking for help, so I start to just put one foot in front of the other and hope my feet are taking me somewhere I want to go.

After bumping into more than a few people, bruising my shins on a low wooden railing, and stumbling over a piece of concrete flooring set higher than the others, I finally find myself out in the sunshine again. The light hurts my eyes, and the heat of the morning, held off before by the station roof, settles onto my shoulders like cinder blocks. The air here in Dar es Salaam is much hotter than in Arusha or even Mwanza, and thick with the shimmering fumes of cars. On instinct, I continue my stumbling walk forward, crossing the street and finding a sheltered doorway to stand in before I take a look around me. I shade my eyes and squint into my first view of the city.

Dar es Salaam is choking on cars and people. Taxis honk their horns, buses pull in and out of spaces that seem much too small for them, and people yell at one another to be heard above the traffic. The buildings soar: glass, bright paint, and advertisements that block out tall sections of sky. The streets smell like people cooking food that is not like the food I ate at home and echo with the sound of people speaking many languages. It is complete chaos, but it's a welcome sight. I imagine Alasiri stepping off the train, looking around for me, and not having any idea where, in all this noise and bustle,

I might have gone. *Of course,* I remind myself dourly, *this is also a good place for you to disappear against your will.* My smile fades. Yes, it would be all too easy to kidnap me, right off this exact street corner, without anyone really noticing or being the wiser when I vanished.

So. Here I am. Now what do I do? The little voice in my head, so ready to chip in uselessly at all other times, is completely silent.

I suppose I could look for a guesthouse, but that would cost money, and I don't want to go throwing my money away until I find a way to make more. I could find a tree to sleep under, like we did in the Serengeti, but all the trees I see here are surrounded by concrete sidewalks. I wouldn't feel safe sleeping out in the open here in the middle of the city, but perhaps if I go outside it, just a little ways?

Without further thought, I hoist my belongings onto my head, pick a direction at random, and start walking up the busy street.

13.

AFTER JUST ONE block I stop in the shade of a hospital. I pull my floppy hat out of my bag and put on an extra long-sleeved shirt, even though I don't want to. I'm hot and sticky already and it makes me stand out since everyone here seems to be in short sleeves. But I know that with the layers on I'll be able to walk through the morning without getting burnt.

If this is what the dry season is like here, I think to myself as I sweat, *I'd hate to see how hot the wet season is.*

At noon, when the sun is at its most dangerous, I huddle on a shadowed stoop, eating the last of the dried fruit I took from Auntie's house. Funny how it looked like so much food when Kito and I were packing it, and now, just eight small meals later, it's gone.

The next time I want to eat I'll have to pay for it with money or work, which is a scary thought. I have a sudden bleak vision: No one will pay an albino to work; my stolen money dwindles away; I spend the rest of my life begging on the streets of Dar es Salaam, hungry, dirty, homeless, alone. In a way, these thoughts are almost worse than thinking of being murdered. At least if you're murdered, it's over. A street urchin can live miserably for a long time.

These thoughts aren't doing me any good. They're is only making me depressed when I have to keep my wits about me. *You never know*, I remind myself. *People here may not have any problem giving you a job. Remember, they have albino MPs!* My inner urchin is not completely convinced by this little pep talk, but I pull myself onto my feet, turn my face up a new road at random, and start walking again.

Every time I start to come to a place that looks less than friendly, or I catch someone looking at me too intently, I change direction. I tell myself that it's impossible to be lost if you never knew where you were going to begin with and that it's good for me to confuse my tracks in case anyone tries to follow me, but these excuses give me very little comfort. I walk on, trying to fight the feeling that I'm wasting my time going in circles.

I'm hoping the crowds, traffic, and buildings will begin to thin out, but as the evening cools, I find that Dar es Salaam just goes on and on, no matter what direction I walk. I no longer have any sense of how far I've gone, but I see no end to the city. *No country tree for me tonight.* I'll have to start looking around for somewhere to sleep.

No dinner, either, my stomach reminds me. My stomach hurts, but I still don't really want to go up to someone to buy food. Although I've been walking all day, I can't stop looking over my shoulder, checking for Alasiri. I still feels too close to the train station to spend time in a shop, being noticed.

I push my fists into my belly to make it quit grumbling and start looking around for places to hide. It's dusk now, a good time of day because the sun is low and can't hurt me or show me clearly to strangers, and I'm wandering up the large, open expanse of a wide avenue called Bagamoyo Road. Though the houses are getting less fancy, even the poorest of them are made of cinder blocks and have zinc roofs instead of mud.

When I see a grassy square dotted with rounded pieces of rock, I think I've found the perfect place to spend the night: There's a tall hedge between it and the road, and it will be quiet and peaceful. The gate has a sign on it. I lean in close and sound out the letters one at a time: *Orthodox Cemetery*. I'd rather not sleep surrounded by other people's dead, but I still prefer it to sleeping out in the open and maybe ending up dead myself.

I swallow my doubts and head in, looking forward to a good rest. But it's not to be. I'm just settling myself in the corner of the wall, feeling safe and out of the way, when a couple walks in through the gate. They see me and yell, "Get out of here! Have you no respect for the dead?"

I run.

After I've run a block or two, I slow to a walk and look for somewhere else. Nowhere is as good as the cemetery, but I have no choice but to keep walking, looking. Finally, when it's almost too dark to see and the people on the road are getting scarier, I hear a rhythmic rushing sound.

There, off to the side of the road, is a wide sandy expanse with a vast stretch of dark water behind it, like Lake Victoria. It's off the road and there's some cover. It will do.

I clamber down onto the beach and look until I find a large palm tree that has blown over in a storm. I scoop the sand out from under it with my hands until there is a dent the length of my body. Then I crawl in and, tucked out of sight under the trunk, I fall asleep.

❋

The next morning I wake up to find that damp sand has slithered its way into all my clothes, my hair, and my eyes. But I've made it through my first night in the big city safely, and that alone is reason to be glad. I look over the water, tinted red by the rising sun, and wonder at it. It's like Lake Victoria— stretching away so that you can't see any land on the other side—but this water is different. It moves up and down the beach in long, rolling waves, frothing white. I lick my lips and, tasting salt, realize I must be looking at the ocean.

For a few minutes I just sit there, taking it in. And then my stomach reminds me that, although the sea is pretty to look at, it's not something that I can either eat or drink. I get up, dust the sand off as well as I can, and climb up onto the sidewalk.

By late morning I'm sick of the neverending city. By midafternoon I have gone beyond hungry to a place I've never been before, where my body moves mechanically and my mind has switched off. Without thinking, I walk through the hottest part of the day. When the pain of my developing sunburn snaps me out of my trance, I find shade and chew on some wild plants by the side of the road. They make me a little queasy, but after the sun has slackened I have the energy to keep going.

Each time I've reached for my money to buy food in some store, fear has pushed me past it. But by my second evening with no food, I'm ready to do something drastic. I turn down a house-lined street at random and decide to find myself some food any way I can.

I walk down the side street I've chosen. It has a mixture of houses. Some are small and others are larger with wrought iron grills over the windows. They are all leaking the wonderful smells and sounds of dinners being prepared. I stand, fists shoved into pockets, and look up and down the street, considering what to do. I *might* be able to walk up to any house and ask for traditional hospitality. Then again, I'm in a major city, which means I'm more likely to be turned away as a beggar. Worse, any of these homes could belong to a *waganga* or some other poacher of people. In that case, I might be fed, but it would likely be my last meal. My stomach whines as I shift from foot to foot in indecision.

No, I decide, it's better not to take the risk of approaching someone's front door. Perhaps there's somewhere I can sneak in, take some food, and leave some money in its place. That way I won't be a beggar or a thief.

I look around at the houses with new eyes. Which one will suit my needs? Not the one I'm standing in front of right now; there are about twelve children inside, hopping around as their mother prepares their meal. For a moment I feel a twinge of loss, but I fight it off and keep walking. Having been a child waiting his turn to eat, I know that enough eyes will be on that pot to make it impossible for me to get near it. I push away memories of my family sitting around the fire pit, sharing dinner, and move on. The next yard has a dog, and then two more houses have either too many people or are dark. I'm beginning to think that my idea wasn't such a good one after all, and then I find it. The perfect house.

Refusing to let a rash move get me into trouble, I hide under a tree facing the house and examine it closely. It's a house out of place on this street of open yards: a walled compound. I climb the lower branches of the tree to get a better look inside. As long as there's no one too scary there, the high cinder block wall could actually help me: No one from the road will see what I'm doing.

I squint between the branches of the tree. The moving shadows of the leaves in the breeze make it hard to see well, but since they also make *me* hard to see, I'm not complaining. The house is set forward, with a large open space behind it cluttered with objects, surrounded by a beaten dirt yard. I can't tell what the shadowy objects are from this distance, but they're not moving, so none of them are dogs or children, that much is clear. The house is a little bigger than some of the others I've passed, so I won't be taking food from a poor person. Just beyond the house I see a small cooking fire, tended by a lone old man. The breeze suddenly changes directions, and the smells of a perfect dinner wash over me: cornmeal, peppers, meat. I sniff appreciatively. Even better, the old man is inattentive. With the light of the fire shining on his face, I can see from here that he's just staring off into nothing while he waits for his dinner.

A distracted old man with a gift for cooking. Perfect. If I can sneak up on him, I can take some food and be gone before he even notices I'm there. He's so absentminded, I bet he won't even notice the missing food. I bet he'll think the money he finds was just money he dropped one day. I laugh silently to myself as I picture his baffled face. And if I don't manage to sneak up on him, I can just throw the money at him, grab the food, and take off. I'm no athlete, but I still think I can outrun a skinny old man. I smile. Yes, this is perfect. *Silence, stomach,* I command. *I'm off to get you your dinner!*

My stomach, obligingly, doesn't grumble even a little as I slink across the road in the deepening dusk. A quick look tells me that I haven't been seen by any of the neighbors. Then it's up a second tree and over the wall into the yard. My feet land with the tiniest of puffs in the dirt.

I'm surprised by how easy it is for me to cross the yard. For an old man living alone, he has the patio swept so neatly that the dust lies in an unbroken sheet in all directions. Not so much as a twig to crack underfoot as I sneak over to the wall of the house and crouch down in its shadow.

Wrapped again in a double darkness of night and shadow,

I feel invincible. I slide one foot in front of the other along the wall, making no more noise than a snake on sand. Bending forward slightly, I peer around the corner of the house. The old man is sitting between me and the fire with his back to me. I plaster myself to the side of the house and wait for him to do something. My breathing is as soft as moth wings. I wait.

After all the days spent running, it makes me feel powerful to be on the other side of the hunt, waiting for a sign to pounce. I'm hungry, though, and every minute of waiting is almost painful. My mouth is watering at the smells, and I have to push my fists into my belly again to keep it from grumbling and giving me away. If only the old man would *move*! In the entire time I've been watching him, he has sat in the same position, staring off into nothing. I wonder if he's in some sort of a trance. This thought makes me reconsider my plan. If he's a *waganga* in a trance, he could be really dangerous. I shuffle back a few steps and look in through the window where the moon is shining on his possessions. I see nothing in there that looks at all like medicine or magic. I breathe a sigh of relief and creep to the corner and peek around again. So he's only a batty old man, lost in thought. I'll simply have to wait him out.

Just when I'm beginning to think that I'm going to die of hunger, or old age, or both, before I get any dinner, the old man finally moves. He pushes himself slowly off the ground, dusts off his hands, and turns and walks into his house. For a moment I hesitate, confused by his actions. Why would he

leave his dinner out in the yard without eating it? Then I realize he must have forgotten a spoon or a bowl or something
and gone to get it.

I couldn't have created a more perfect opportunity. Reaching into my shirt, I pull out enough shilling notes to cover a
homemade meal and ball them in my fist. I'll drop them on
his stool by the fire, and then I'll grab his pot and leave it,
empty, by his door tomorrow. A slow smile creeps across my
face at my own daring, and I slink forward, ready to place the
bills on the stool. I reach toward the pot, eager to eat.

And that's when a long, hard stick crashes over my shoulders. I fall down from the force of the blow, crying out in pain.

Whack! The stick whistles through the air and I pull my
arms up over my head to protect it. *Whack! Whack!*

"Stop!" I shout.

"Stop?" barks a strong voice. "Stop? Why should I stop
beating a thief?"

Whack!

"I'm not a thief!"

"Huh. A thief and a liar!" *Whack! Whack!*

"No, really, I was going to pay for the dinner! Look! Look at
the money in my hand!"

There's a pause in the beating. I peek up through the tangle
of my arms and see the old man looming above me, his hands
holding the stick high over his shoulder, his head tilted slightly to the side.

"What are you talking about?" The muscles in his arms relax a little, and he rests the stick against his shoulder.

I'm so grateful to see him lower the stick, even a little, that I start to blubber.

"I was hungry, and I didn't know where to go. I don't know the city and I don't know where to get food, so I decided to take some from someone . . ." I see his hands tighten on the stick and I rush on. "But not to steal it! I was going to leave money on your stool, enough money to pay for the meal. Really, I would have, it's right here in my hand. See? I was going to leave that and take the food because I was hungry and didn't know where else to go, and your food smelled so good from the road and . . ." I realize I'm rambling and beginning to repeat myself, so I just trail off. I extend my hand toward him, shaking a little. "You can have the money anyway if you like, *Bwana*. Just please don't beat me anymore. I wasn't trying to steal, I promise."

Nothing happens for a moment as I hold my hand up in the air, clutching the fistful of shilling notes, and he stands above me, still as a statue. I'm afraid he's going to start hitting me again. I push the money out against his leg.

"Take it," I say, cringing.

The moment I touch his leg, one of his hands darts down from his shoulder and grabs mine. I gasp. I definitely picked the wrong old man to rob. This one has the strength of an ox. His large, calloused fingers close over mine like a trap, tight and hard. Then his eyebrows shoot up in surprise.

"What's this?" he asks.

"The money, *Bwana*. The money I was going to leave for the dinner. See, I wasn't lying."

The old man makes a funny noise in his throat. It might be a growl. It might be a laugh. I shove the shilling notes into his hand and pull my arm over my head again in case he decides to keep beating me. Instead, he raises the shilling notes to his face and sniffs them. I watch him, baffled. Then he lowers the stick to his side, one hand still leaning on it, but no longer outwardly threatening.

"So, you really were going to pay for the food?"

Now that my initial terror is over, I can feel every burning welt left by his stick on my sun-tender skin. My arms and back scream with pain, and my forearm with the knife cut from Alasiri has started to bleed again. I begin to feel annoyed at this man. This man who hits so hard with a stick and then is too stupid to see the money I'm holding right in his face.

"Yes!" I snap, a little more curtly than is probably wise. "I said I was. You have the money, you can see for yourself!"

"Hmm," says the man. I can tell from the way he's holding his shoulders that he still doesn't believe me. "No, that still doesn't make sense. If you're so willing to pay for food, boy, why didn't you buy food from a street vendor? Why steal an old man's dinner in the dark? No, that is the work of a thief."

This really makes me lose my temper, and before I know what I'm doing, I'm scrambling to my feet and yelling at him.

"I. Am. Not. A. Thief!" How dare he insult me, even after I've given him the money? "How am I supposed to buy something, *Bwana*?" I snap. "I have no idea what the people in this city think about people like me. I couldn't just go up to a street vendor."

"What do you mean, boy, people like you?"

I stare at him dumbly. I know it's dark, but we're right beside the fire, and even I can see the slight glow coming off my white skin. Then I understand. This old man is mocking me. He's standing there, holding my money in one hand and a stick to beat me with in the other, and he's playing word games with me. I begin to hate him.

"If you can't see for yourself what I mean, then I'm hardly going to tell you!"

The old man cocks his head slightly at me, hearing my hostility.

"Well then, I guess I won't ever know," he says. Slowly, he stretches out his arm and offers my money to me. I hesitate for a moment, then take it. It may be a trap, but I need that money. He lets me take it, then drops his arm to his side. I clutch the money tightly against my chest and start backing up.

"What do you mean?" I ask when I'm out of range.

"I mean, boy, that I will never know. You have just said you will not tell me, and I cannot see for myself what you mean." His sudden smile surprises me. It's as if he's about to tell a great joke and is anticipating the ending. "I am blind."

I stare at him with my mouth hanging open like a fish. Of all the things I expected, this was not one of htem. Not from a man that could hit so hard and so accurately. Not from the man who, just a moment ago, had me curled on the ground, begging him to take my money. My brain cannot process what he just said.

The old man's laugh fills the silence like the October rains: a quick burst, then gone. He shuffles to his stool, using the stick to find it, and then sits down.

"So, boy-full-of-secrets-who-is-not-a-thief, would you like to join me for some dinner?"

I can't help it. I laugh. And although it stretches my bruised shoulders painfully, it feels so good, I do it again. The old man's smile catches the firelight.

"*Ndiyo*," I say, hiccuping. "Thank you, I think I would."

14.

I LOWER MYSELF gingerly onto the dirt beside the old man's stool. He serves out a portion of his dinner for himself, and then scoops some into another bowl for me. It's killing me to wait until he's done eating, with the bowl sitting in my lap, filling my nose with dreams of goat, chilies, and corn, its warmth seeping into my thighs. I try not to drool. And then I laugh, realizing I could drool all I want: The old man is blind!

"What's so funny, boy?"

I collect myself quickly. "Nothing, *Bwana*. It's just that my evening isn't turning out at all like I expected it to."

The old man smiles. "No, I'm sure it's not! It's not every day that a young boy like you gets beaten so soundly by an old man like me." And now he's laughing, too, and even though it's at my expense, I join in. Then he says, "So, you're a polite boy; I can hear that you're waiting to eat until I'm done."

"*Ndiyo, Bwana*," I say, surprised.

"Hmph. Excellent. Well, while you wait, you should do something with that mouth of yours. If you won't fill it with food, fill it with words." He waves his left hand in my general direction. "Keep your secrets if you want, but tell me something else."

"What else, *Bwana*?"

"Smart boy like you should be able to come up with something. Tell me about yourself."

I am momentarily baffled. I'll keep my secret, but without saying I'm an albino, I don't know what to tell him about myself. It has always been the first thing everyone saw about me, the most obvious way I thought about myself. To tell my story without talking about the way I look is strangely difficult. The old man gives a little grunt to remind me he's waiting. I shake my head and begin talking.

"Well, my name is Dhahabo, but everyone calls me Habo for short." I pause.

"Gold," the old man grunts. "Unusual name."

I don't explain why I have it.

"My name is Kweli," he says. "Everyone calls me Kweli for short."

I can't help but laugh again. Somehow this makes it easier to go on.

"My family and I used to live in a small village outside of Arusha, but my father left when I was young." I feel like I'm telling only half the story and the pieces fit together oddly, forming a picture I barely recognize. "When our farm failed in the drought, we had to go to Mwanza, where my mother's sister lives with her family."

"That's a long way. How did you get there?"

This part is easy. Our trip across the Serengeti doesn't have much to do with me, and so I tell him all about Enzi staying behind to finish the coffee picking, running out of money for the bus, and walking across the game lands until we met Alasiri. I choke a little on his name, remembering too late that some people believe saying a person's name can call them to you from far away. I don't know if I believe that, but it doesn't hurt to be cautious. I curse myself for being so stupid. Kweli notices my stutter.

"You didn't like this man?"

"No, I didn't. I don't. He came and found us later and tried to hurt me." Again, half the story. I rush on before the holes in my story seem too big.

"So I left my family and took the train from Mwanza to Dar es Salaam. I arrived yesterday and I've been walking around the city since then, and tonight I tried to take food from the wrong old man."

Kweli's laugh barks out again at that.

"And what, boy, did you plan to do here in the largest city in Tanzania, other than steal dinners from helpless old men?"

My mouth is open, but no words rush out. The weight of a thousand unplanned days crushes my lungs. My voice, when it comes out, is high and fragile, like a small child's.

"I . . . I didn't have a plan."

"What?" Kweli's head snaps up. "You paid good money to travel halfway across the country with no plan?"

"Yes."

"Do you have any family here?"

"No."

"Any friends?"

"No."

"Any skills other than dinner thieving?"

"No." My voice is barely a whisper. "And I'm not even very good at that."

Kweli chews in silence for a moment while I study the fire. Then: "Does your family know where you are?"

This is a dangerous question. I barely know this man. To tell him that I'm all alone in the world and no one knows where I am seems unwise. It would highlight just how vulnerable I am. I lie.

"*Ndiyo*, they do."

Kweli gives another *hmph*, this one in a tone that tells me he doesn't quite believe me, but he doesn't challenge me. For being blind, this old man sees far too much.

"Eat," he says when he finishes his bowl, and I do.

The food is as delicious as it smelled, but I don't appreciate it nearly as much as I should. My brain is still too busy thinking about the problem Kweli has set in front of me to be able to completely enjoy the stew. I chew in silence, and for a while there is nothing but the soft hiss and pop of the wood in the fire and the bellowing of tree frogs in the bushes.

I'm nearly finished when I hear a sigh. I look up in surprise. I've been so sunk in my own thoughts that I had almost forgotten the statue of a man sitting next to me in the darkness.

"I can't believe I'm doing this," I hear him mutter. Then, loudly, to me, "Boy, what kinds of work can you do?"

I think quickly. "I can fetch and carry things. I can take care of animals and vegetable gardens . . ." I trail off, hopeful. "Why, *Bwana*? What do you need done? If I haven't done it before, I'm sure I could learn. Quickly."

"Maybe you can. Maybe you can't. We'll see." There is a tree frog–filled pause, and then, "It is possible that I have a few days of work you can help me with. You can stay here and I will feed you in return for your work. That will give you a few days to figure out what you're going to do and give you a chance to contact your family again."

I can't believe my luck.

"Thank you, *Bwana*! Thank you very much! That will be a great help to me. I'll work hard, *Bwana*, you'll see!"

I realize I'm babbling and shut my mouth, but I can't suppress the enormous grin that splits my face. Somewhere to stay! Food! And a little more time to figure out what to do with myself now that I'm on my own. As to what he said about calling my family . . . emotions tangle inside me and I don't know how to sort them out.

There's no need to rush into that, I tell myself. *Best to leave things the way they are until you know exactly what you're doing and have something definite to tell them.* I'll wait a few more days and call them then. That's all I need, I'm sure of it. A few more days to figure out whether Dar es Salaam is a safe place for me to stay or whether I need to keep running.

When I wake up the next morning on a blanket just inside Kweli's front door, I'm still smiling. The sun is a bright band on the dirt a few inches from my face, but I can tell from the silence of the house that the old man isn't awake yet. I suppose sunrise would make no difference to a blind man, but to me it feels like a holiday to still be lying in my blankets when the sun is already up.

I stand and stretch slowly, letting my bruised muscles un-cramp. Even though the packed-dirt floor was hard, I slept better here than I have in days. Every time I woke up in the middle of the night, frightened, confused about where I was, braced to run, I remembered the high wall around me and the fact that there's no trace of my path through the largest city in Tanzania, and I would smile and go back to sleep.

Today is the first day I will be doing work for Kweli. How I'm going to do enough work to earn my keep without burn-ing my skin is something I'm not sure about. But, for the first time in a long time, getting burnt is not my main concern. If I have to get burnt to keep my end of the bargain, so be it. *No matter what,* I tell myself, *you have to stay strong and get the work done here. This is too much good luck to pass up just because you're afraid of a little sunburn.*

Perhaps, responds a voice in my head, sounding remark-ably like Asu, *but there's still no call to be silly about it. Go put your hat on!*

I smile, remembering the thousands of times Asu snapped those words at me when I was little, and go put on my hat, my long pants, and a double layer of shirts just like yesterday. I peel the makeshift bandage off that I tied over my arm after dinner last night. The cut has scabbed over again, so I leave the bandage off. After poking at the cut, though, I'm no longer smiling. Asu is the one who got me into this mess, by telling her friends about me. It's how Alasiri found out where I was. *He would probably have found me anyway*, I remind myself. But the betrayal still stings like limejuice on a wound. I don't like thinking bad thoughts about Asu, but I can't make myself think good thoughts about her just now, either. So I think about something else. It's daylight. I can look around at Kweli's house and belongings. I slip out the front door to explore.

The house itself and the front yard are fairly normal, but when I walk around the house to the backyard where we ate dinner last night, I catch my breath in surprise. The things that were just shadows in the moonlight now have hard edges and color. There are tools of all shapes and logs of all sizes leaning up against the wall. In the far corner of the yard, a blue plastic tarp is stretched as a roof between four tall poles. Under it is a large log, almost a tree trunk, partly peeled, with a hatchet embedded into the middle. There are wood chips all over the ground. But what really makes me gasp is what I see in a lean-to attached to the house. There, protected from the weather on three sides, is a collection of carvings more amazing than any I could ever have imagined.

They are all made from a dark wood, polished so smooth they glow. People and animals twist and knot about one another. They stretch for the sky, screaming, or bend double and curl around, laughing, weeping, grinning. They are beautiful.

They are horrible.

I find that I've crossed the yard without realizing my feet have moved. I'm up close, staring at the tortured leer of a mask. I feel slightly dizzy, surrounded by the writhing forms. I take a step backward and run into a man.

I shout in surprise, turning around and punching at his chest while trying to get away, my eyes still filled with the screaming masks and my body reacting on instinct to feeling trapped. Hands close over my flailing wrists like manacles, and my hands are wrestled down to my sides.

"What's wrong with you, boy?"

I look up, startled, and see that it's Kweli who has me, not Alasiri. I sob with relief, and then shame.

"I'm sorry, *Bwana*, so sorry. I was frightened. I thought you were someone else."

His face softens. "Well, that's some greeting you gave me. If I let you go now, will you try to strike me again?"

"No, *Bwana*."

He drops my hands. I rub my wrists. I'm going to have bruises there, too, now. This old man is a rock.

"So, what were you doing out here? I woke up and went to find you and you were gone."

I wince, realizing what that would have looked like, how he must have thought I'd abandoned our agreement and run off in the night, maybe even taking some of his things with me.

"I'm sorry," I say again. It feels like I'm saying that a lot to this man. "I was just taking a look around and I got distracted by these carvings."

"Ha!" Kweli barks. "And? What do you think of 'these carvings'?"

I pause, not sure what to say. Clearly the old man collects them for a reason, so he must like them, but I can't help but feel uncomfortable around them.

"I . . . don't know," I say, but Kweli is shaking his head, telling me that answer isn't good enough. I try again; decide to be honest. "They're very good. I used to do little carvings for my cousin, and these are much better than those were. But . . . I don't know if I like them. They're too . . . They show too much feeling." I curse my clay tongue, not knowing how to say what I feel. "They seem aggressive or something." Still not right. I give up. "I don't know," I say again.

This time, though, Kweli is nodding. "*Ndiyo*, you're right."

I look up in surprise. I had expected him to defend the statues, tell me that they were wonderful. Though I suppose, being blind, maybe he doesn't know? *Why would a blind man collect statues anyway?*

"I am?"

"*Ndiyo*, they're aggressive. They are Makonde sculptures, the sculptures of my people. They show us how we really are: the raw emotion of humanity. Good. Evil. Love. Hate. Everything. They aren't supposed to be pretty little carvings. You have good eyes."

I *don't* have good eyes. I have stupid, worthless albino eyes, and I want to ask him how he can know that I have good eyes when he's blind and can't see the wretched statues anyway, but I keep my mouth shut.

Kweli continues, "And now you know what I do, hmm?"

I'm not entirely sure, really, because Kweli doesn't seem to be rich enough to collect art for fun, but I take a guess anyway, since he's waiting for my answer.

"You . . . collect carvings? You . . . sell them?"

The old man laughs, making me feel even more stupid than I already do. Why would a blind man collect art?

"No, silly boy! I make them."

I know that my mouth is hanging open and I'm glad he can't see me.

"But . . . you're . . . I mean . . ." I stammer off into silence, not sure how to finish without sounding insulting.

"You mean, how can I be a sculptor when I'm blind?"

I nod, and then mentally kick myself because, of course, he can't see me.

"*Ndiyo, Bwana,* that's what I was thinking."

I sound like an idiot.

"Many people have the same question," Kweli answers, stepping forward into the lean-to. He reaches out and runs his fingers along the twisting, almost life-size body of one of his sculpture-people. He is quiet for so long that I think he might be finished speaking to me. I wonder if I should maybe slip away and let him have some time alone, but then he continues, almost as if he's talking to himself.

"The answer has two parts. One part is that I was not always blind. My father was a Makonde sculptor as well, and he taught me as a child how to shape the *mpingo* blackwood and make it tell my story. I had been carving for six or seven years before I went blind." He pauses again. I'm fascinated, willing him to go on.

"I was angry for a long time after that." His voice is soft. "And yet, I suppose I was lucky. I could have been a painter and lost everything, but no, I was a sculptor. Once I got past my anger, I learned that I could still shape the blackwood. The difference was, I could no longer make it tell my story; I had to listen to the wood and shape it slowly into the story it already held. I feel the sculpture now, in my hands, even though I cannot see it with my eyes." He turns to me with a sad smile. "Some say my sculptures are even better now than when I was younger. But I don't know if that's true. All I know is that I'm grateful I didn't have to lose my art when I lost my sight. I don't think I could have survived losing both."

I'm stunned by his story, hearing the softness in his voice, watching his fingers slowly trace the outline of a man screaming in rage at the sky. Then he lets his hand drop and I realize that, on the statue he has been touching, the man has no eyes.

"So!" says Kweli, with such force that I jump. "That's my story, and that is enough of that. Now, let's get to work. I have a lot to do today."

❋

I learn quickly that working for Kweli isn't going to be easy. He tends to shout when he wants something and he expects you to run to get him what he needs.

He needs water from the well.

He needs the hatchet from the bench.

Not that hatchet, *punguani*, the little one.

Once, I left the broom on the ground between chores and Kweli tripped over it walking to the house. He screamed at me like I'd killed his cattle. It makes sense, with his being blind, that everything has to stay in its place, but I had my hands up in front of my face in case he started in on me with his fists—he was that angry. Luckily he didn't hit me; I just learned some new vocabulary.

As we sit by the fire that evening, sharing another pot of stew in the dusk, I think about what a day it's been. My clothes are stiff with sweat and dust, cracking when I move. My leg muscles ache from all the fetching, and I have blisters in the crooks of my thumbs from sweeping up all the wood chips Kweli produced as he hacked at the log under the tarp. But for all that, I feel content as I chew on the spiced green banana in my bowl. Kweli worked me like a regular boy. This is maybe the first day in my entire life that I've worked just as hard as anyone else, and the feeling is almost as warm in my belly as the stew. Today, I was normal. And with my extra precautions, my arm is still healing and I didn't even get burnt.

Kweli's voice snaps me out of my thoughts.

"So, boy, what did you learn today?"

"*Bwana?*"

"You saw me work. What did you learn?"

"Umm," I stall. *I didn't know there was going to be a test!* I quickly think over what I saw him do. "You used the hatchet to break big chunks off the log . . . You started at the top and then worked your way down—"

"No, no." Kweli is waving his hand at me. "That's what I *did*. That's not what you *learned*. Think about it and then let me know." With that he gets up and walks inside the house.

What's that supposed to mean? *I learned that I can do a full day's work, just like a normal person*, I want to shout after him, but I don't. Kweli is the one person who, because he can't see at all, doesn't see me as odd. I'm not about to mess that up just because I'm frustrated by his stupid question. Still, I'd better come up with some answer.

I think over the day again, this time not just on the things that I did, but on everything that was going on: how I would jump at the sounds of people passing by on the road before I remembered the wall, the dogfight up the street near noon, the heat of the sun, the clear taste of the water from the tap in Kweli's wall, the sight of Kweli working.

It was amazing to watch, really, and I spent a lot of the day spying on him even when I was doing other things like sweeping the courtyard, getting water, and tidying up. He started off the day running his hands over the log, brushing his fingers over the dents and cuts already made, memorizing everything. Then, with a force and precision that was terrifying, he picked up the hatchet and began to chop at it. He would find a spot with his left hand and then raise his right arm high above his head and slam the hatchet down next to his left, again and again. I had visions of him missing, even once, and chopping off his hand, but his aim never wavered, and the rhythmic biting and ripping sounds of the hatchet became a backdrop for my day to the point that I only noticed when it changed tempo or he took a break.

I wondered why he wouldn't take a smaller risk and only tap the wood with the hatchet, so one time when Kweli was in the outhouse, I snuck over and tested my theory on a piece of scrap wood. I soon found out why Kweli has muscles like he does: Blackwood is as hard as iron. I tapped at it with the hatchet, and the metal blade just slid off, nearly costing *me* a finger. There wasn't even a scratch on it. It was only when I raised the hatchet high over my head, with two hands, and brought it slamming down that the scrap wood split in half, the pieces flying in opposite directions. I don't know how he can control the cut when he's putting that much force behind it, but I decided I'd tested my luck enough and quickly returned the hatchet to where he'd left it. I only just managed to pick up my two halves and toss them on the scrap heap before Kweli came back. He didn't say anything to me then, but there was a secretive little smile on his face, and I wonder if he somehow knew what I did.

He spent most of the day working at the log, chopping great hunks off the wood with long, fluid sweeps of the blade. By late afternoon, the wood no longer looked like a log, but more like a crocodile—all twisting jagged edges and flat bits covered in choppy scales. It still didn't look like a statue, really, but it was definitely different. At that point, Kweli had paused. He had set the hatchet aside, stretched out his shoulders, and taken a long drink of water. Well, really, he had told *me* to put the hatchet away, sweep up his mess so he had space to stretch, and get him a drink of water. Then he ran his hands over the wood one more time, memorizing it again in its new form. Then it was *Boy! Get me a carving blade!* and he was at it again, this time with a smaller, much sharper piece of metal. And he spent the rest of the day with that, chip, chip, chipping away at the scales of the crocodile.

I look up from the fire. I'm still not entirely sure what I'll say, but now at least I've thought about it. I rub my bowl with ashes. The ash brushes away the last crumbs of *ugali* and cleans away the grease of the sauce. It also turns my fingers black. I look like some funny animal, with white fingers that turn black at the tips. I sigh and head inside. Nesting the bowl inside the others stacked on the table, I turn to the lump in the darkness that is Kweli. I can tell from the lack of snoring that he's still awake. I take a deep breath.

"I learned that it takes a long time to make a statue. I learned that blackwood is very hard, harder than any wood I've worked with before. I learned that you have to have the area neat and that you memorize your work with your fingers. I learned that different blades work the wood differently. And I learned that you don't make something perfect all in one go. You start with rough shapes and then make them smoother and smoother."

In the silence, I hear Kweli turn over to face the wall.

"*Bwana?*"

"What, boy?"

"That's what I learned."

"I heard you."

"Oh."

"Now go to sleep."

I turn away, dejected for some reason I can't quite name. Then I hear the rough voice come out of the darkness again.

"Tomorrow you'll learn more."

I smile.

15.

THE NEXT MORNING we're sitting together in the backyard, eating breakfast, when Kweli hands me a piece of wood and a carving knife.

"Carve me a dog," he says, and heaves himself to his feet and is gone.

I watch his retreating form for a moment, then look down at the wood and the knife that he thrust at me. I grip them awkwardly, like a man holds a newborn. From his workstation under the tarp, I hear the *tch-tch-tch* of Kweli starting into the crocodile again with the little hatchet.

"Boy!" he barks from across the yard. "Go get the whetstone and sharpen this blade for me! It's too dull!"

I jump to my feet and leave the wood and the knife on my stool. It seems I'll still have to do chores today. In a way, I'm glad. It gives me a chance to think about how I'm going to carve my dog.

I've made dogs before, for Kito, but five-year-olds are easy to please. You can put a block in front of them and say, *Look, it's a house,* and they'll smile and nod and play with it for the rest of the day. I know Kweli won't be so easy to convince, even though he's blind.

As I move through the chores of the day, I think about all the dogs I've seen—the way they run, the way they growl and fight, the way they flop in the sun and sleep like they're dead. Should I make my dog standing up? Should he sit? Should he sleep? Will Kweli ever stop giving me chores so I can go work on him?

The answer to that last question seems to be no, and the day drags its dusty body across us, crushing me with the weight of a hundred tiny tasks. It's not until late afternoon, the hottest part of the day, when Kweli decides to take a nap in the shade of the tree, that I get a chance to work on my dog.

I pick up the knife and the piece of wood from my stool where it has sat abandoned all day and sit just inside the doorway. There I'm covered by the shadow of the house but I can still feel the breeze from the yard. I turn the piece of wood over in my hands. It's more square than circular, though it's more like a rectangle than anything else. It's not blackwood, but some pale, soft wood that I can dent with my thumbnail if I press hard. I guess Kweli doesn't think I have the skill to make a *mpingo* dog. He's right, of course.

I close my eyes and rub my fingers over the wood, trying to sense the dog inside like Kweli does. But that only makes me feel foolish, so I open them again quickly and pick up the knife.

Well, here goes, I think, and push the knife against the wood with no clear plan.

Immediately the knife bites out an irregular chunk, breaking off one corner in the process. I curse myself silently so as not to wake the old chore-finder under the tree.

Punguani! Slow down! You're ruining it and you've barely even started.

I take a deep breath, put the knife down, and look at my mutilated little piece of wood again. Well, the loss of that corner will make it nearly impossible to make a standing dog, unless he's laughably short. So it'll be a sitting dog. This time, I lay the knife very gently on the block and inch the blade toward me.

I'm rewarded by a thin curl of wood falling into my lap. I grin. I can't help it. I have no dog yet, just a block of wood with one chunk and one slice gone out of it, but even if I stop now I have something to tell Kweli I learned.

I hardly notice the time passing as I sit on the stoop and carve. I'm only mildly aware that I've had to shift my legs twice to keep them out of the moving sun and that the sounds of the small hatchet are again filling the middle distance. I don't even look up. My knuckles ache from gripping the knife so tightly, and every now and again sweat drips off of my nose onto the blade and I have to flick it away. I hunch my shoulders and bite my lower lip, and slowly, slowly, a curved back and two pointy ears are freed from the block. A round chest follows, and a blocky muzzle and feet. My dog.

I stare at him with a fondness that a part of me realizes

is ridiculous. I flex my cramped fingers, and I'm just bending over to work on the details when Kweli hollers across the yard that it's time to come for dinner. I push my dog into my pocket and go over to the tap in the wall to fill a bucket with the water that we'll use to cook the cornmeal into *ugali*.

When I join him by the fire, Kweli says abruptly, "There's a woman named Eshe who lives a few streets away."

"*Bwana?*" I ask, confused.

"She has a mobile phone," Kweli goes on, "and she lets people use it for a fee. When you decide you want to let your family know where you are, you can take your money to Eshe, and she will help you make a call. Just walk to the right for three blocks when you go out my door, then left for a block, and ask anyone on the street which one is Eshe's house. Everyone knows her."

So he didn't believe me about my family knowing where I am. Still, that information is good to know. Even though I don't plan on going anywhere near Eshe, I feel safer knowing that Kweli wants me to tell my family where I am.

"*Asante, Bwana,*" I mumble, stirring the ingredients together. "I'll keep that in mind."

Once the meal's ready, I plough through my *ugali*, shoving handfuls of the cornmeal porridge into my mouth so quickly I burn my tongue, waiting for the question. Finally, it comes:

"So, boy. What have you learned?"

"I learned that you gave me a soft wood, so I have to keep the knife at an angle. I learned that if you break something a little, you can still work with it, but you have to change your plan, and"—I pause for dramatic effect—"I learned how to carve a sitting dog."

"Ha! Very well then, let's have this dog of yours." He holds out his hand.

"Well . . . it's not entirely finished yet, but here's what I have so far." I try to keep the pride out of my voice as I put the dog into his hand.

"Hmmm," he says, and runs his fingers over it. Suddenly, in his hands, I see every ragged edge, every skipped detail. I see how blocky the head and feet are, how out of proportion the head is to the chest. I see that I could have made the fur wavy with cuts; that, had I curved the tail the other way, it would've been more realistic. A vision of the beautiful, smooth, complex statues Kweli creates flashes through my mind. I realize, as I watch him, that I haven't created anything special after all. My dog is just a badly cut piece of wood. I bury my face in my hands and brace myself for the criticism that is sure to come.

I wait.

And wait.

Finally, I look up. My dog is sitting on the ground, and Kweli has gone into the house. I clench my fists. My dog was too poorly done for him to even waste words criticizing it. I stand up and, with a savage kick, send the dog flying into the far corner of the courtyard. *Stupid dog! Stay there!* I shout at it in my mind.

I rub a piece of charcoal around my bowl without paying any attention to whether it's getting clean or not, and then stomp into the house. I slam my bowl on the counter and barrel across the house toward my sleeping mat—and smash right into Kweli.

The impact nearly sends both of us to the floor.

"Goodness, boy! Watch where you're going!"

"You watch where . . ." I start, and then trail off, flushing with shame at my rudeness. I keep forgetting that he's blind. "Sorry, *Bwana*," I end, lamely.

"Well, all right, but be a little more careful in the future. You nearly knocked me over."

I mumble something incoherent, wishing he would leave me alone.

"I came in here to get this," he says, and pushes something at me. I take it. Some distant part of my brain registers that it's wood.

"Tomorrow," says Kweli, "make a cat."

❋

The next morning, at breakfast, I'm savoring the feeling of safety that a full belly and a tall wall give me, thinking about how I'm goinb to carve my cat, when Kweli ruins everything by saying, "I need to go into Mwenge today. Why don't you come with me and I can show you around? Then, on the way back, we can stop in at Eshe's house and you can make your phone call."

I feel like I've swallowed a mouthful of river water, I'm so suddenly cold. *No!* I don't trust the city; don't know if people here will hunt me or hurt me. By now Alasiri could have caught the Sunday train and be looking for me here. The last thing I want to do is to take that kind of a chance. Also, if I go into town with Kweli, someone will be sure to say something to him about my unusual looks, and that will be the end of my staying here.

"Um . . ." I start, but then don't know where to go from there. The silence stretches as I race to think of something to say. Kweli tips his head to one side, like a bird.

"Then again," he says after a beat, "I suppose if you want to get a head start on your cat, you could stay here. Today I'm just setting up and running a few errands; Friday will be the day I need to work in my shop. I could head in alone today and then, on Friday, you could come in with me and help out."

"Oh, yes!" I say right away, without thinking it through. "That's a good idea, *Bwana*."

"Very well," says Kweli, and he gets up to gather his things. I shuffle around awkwardly, not sure what to do with myself. Kweli pauses in the doorway. "And Habo?"

"Yes?"

"While I'm gone, please think about when you'll be willing to talk to your family."

I mumble something incoherent. Kweli gets his long stick from where it's leaning on the wall and opens the gate. Before I close it behind him, I can see why. He rests the top of the pole on his shoulder and has the bottom part pushing along the ground ahead of him. He keeps one hand on the stick as he walks and sways it from side to side, showing that the path ahead of him is clear. The stick leaves a curved line in the dust like a snake track as he walks away from home and into town unassisted. I feel a pang of guilt for not going with him, but I close the gate firmly.

Once Kweli's gone, I try to focus on starting my cat, but I find that I can't get the problem of Friday out of my head, or the question of my family. *There's no point in calling them until you know for sure what you're doing,* I remind myself, but the words feel hollow.

I end up putting the cat-wood to one side and hunting around the far corner of the compound until I find my dog again. I sit just outside the front door, aimlessly carving swirls into my dog's fur, trying to think of how I'll manage to convince Kweli that I should stay behind on Friday too.

Why, *why* did I agree to help him?

I'm jolted out of my reverie by a sound: the scraping of a key in the gate.

That was fast. Did he forget something?

It's only as I see the gate crack open that a chilling thought occurs to me: *What if it's not Kweli?* It feels like I'm watching the door swing open in slow motion as that thought sinks in, and then I drop my dog and my knife and race into the house. Questions pelt the inside of my skull like hail.

Who is it?

Where can I hide?

How do they have a key?

Where are they less likely to look?

I scramble inside and crouch down on my sleeping mat just

to the right of the doorway, listening to the metal door in the outside wall creak open and closed on its rusty hinges.

Stupid, stupid, stupid! This is a terrible hiding place: I have no cover and no ability to hide anyplace else, because by now the person will have walked into the compound and be able to see into the house through the open door I'm crouching behind. I can't run across their line of sight and, unless the person coming in is as blind as Kweli, they're going to see me if they come in the house.

"Great-Uncle!" I hear a voice call out. "Great-Uncle, are you there?"

I cower farther into the shadows of the corner. Great. Kweli has a family. I suppose this shouldn't surprise me, but it does. I've pictured Kweli in my mind as if he was one of his own statues: tall and proud and standing alone, unconnected to anything around him.

The voice is young and high: a girl or a very young boy. On some level I'm deeply grateful that the voice is not older, not male, and therefore could not possibly be Alasiri come to hunt me out of my hiding place again, but I'm not comforted very much. This person, whoever they are, may not be a danger to me in the same way that Alasiri is, but they're related to Kweli, and if they see me they'll tell him what I really am.

I hear a soft clatter from the courtyard. A voice mumbles, "This doesn't look like Great-Uncle's work."

My dog! My knife!

I start to sweat. Through my own stupidity, I am again hiding from someone who is holding a knife. The voice changes.

Less welcoming now; wary.

"Hello? Is anyone there?"

No, I think desperately. *No one's here. Go away.*

"Great-Uncle?" I hear again. Definitely a girl. I shift my weight onto my heels to ease the burning in my calves. The mat underneath me makes a soft shushing noise as it moves under my feet.

There is a pause where we both listen with all our attention, and then: "If anyone's here, I want you to know that I have a knife." There is a quaver in her voice now. I think she's getting scared, too. She goes on: "And if you don't come out, I'm going to call the police and have them search the house. Then you'll be sorry."

I consider. That would be a bad thing. The police would definitely make me sorry. They would tell Kweli what I was for sure in their report. This person—Kweli's great-niece, whoever she is—maybe I could reason with her, bargain with her. I haven't been here very long, but already I don't want to leave. But if this girl gets too scared and goes to the police, then I'll have to grab my things and run away before they can get here. I'll have to disappear. Without saying good-bye to Kweli. Without coming back.

I'm so wrapped up in weighing my options, that I stop paying very good attention to what's going on around me. I'm startled out of my thoughts by a gasp. My head snaps up, and there, framed against the bright square of the doorway, is the figure of a girl.

A girl with a knife.

16.

WITH THE LIGHT behind her, I can't make out her features with any clarity other than to see, from the way the folds of her *khanga* fall over her hips, that she is indeed a girl. In her right fist, she's carrying my knife. In her other hand is a blocky shape that might be my dog.

Great. I've given her two weapons. I'm disgusted with myself. But, though she looks to be about my age, she's a little bit shorter than me. If I had to, I could wrestle the knife away from her. I might get cut up a little in the process, but I'd win in the long run.

"Who are you?" she asks, holding the knife out in front of her a little. "What are you doing here? Where's my great-uncle?"

Though not as terrified as I was a moment ago, I still feel shaky and empty. I can't quite pull my mind together to answer her questions with anything except simple truths.

"My name is Habo," I say, standing up slowly. She keeps

the point of the knife level with my chest, but she doesn't move any closer. Of course, she doesn't move farther away, either. "I'm here helping Kweli around the house. We met a few days ago, and he invited me to stay on with him until I make other plans." I decide to leave out the fact that I was trying to take his dinner at the time and he beat me handily with a stick. "He's in town right now, at the market, setting up and running errands."

I wait for more questions and hold my palms out toward her to show her that I'm not dangerous.

"You look strange. Why do you look like that? Are you an albino?"

I sigh. I hate meeting people for the first time.

"If I tell you, will you put the knife down?" It's uncomfortable to talk to someone when you've never seen their face, but they've seen yours.

She considers this, her head cocked to the side. The gesture looks just like her uncle, or great-uncle, or whatever Kweli is to her.

"No," she says finally. "I don't know who, or what, you are, and even if you looked normal, you would still be someone I don't know, who I'm alone with, inside high walls. So no, I'm not going to put the knife down." She pauses, forehead creased, considering. "But if you want to come out into the front yard, we can sit down facing each other. And if you promise not to come any closer while we talk, I promise not to use it against you."

I consider her offer. I wish I could see her face as she says these things so I could see her intentions. Is she someone like Chui, enjoying holding power over me? Someone like Alasiri, lying to me and waiting for the right moment to pounce? Someone like Asu, feeling terrible that, to keep herself safe, she has to threaten me? Whatever her motivations, I decide this is probably the best offer I'm going to get.

"*Sawa*," I say. "Let's go."

The girl moves one careful step at a time so that she doesn't have to look away from me to keep from tripping. I follow, pace for pace, a reverse dance to freedom. Finally, we're out. For a moment I blink in the brightness, getting my weak eyes used to daylight again. Then I look at her. She isn't like Chui or Alasiri or Asu. In her face I see a calculation, but no evil intent. In her crinkled brow I see intelligence. In the jut of her chin, stubbornness.

And she's pretty.

In fact, if only she wasn't scowling—which pushes a deep line between her eyebrows—she would be very pretty. Her cheeks and forehead are round, her hair is pulled off her face in little braids, her eyes are big and widely set. And suspicious.

"Well?" she demands.

I take a deep breath to start answering her question and realize that I don't remember what it was. *Punguani!* I thought it was hard to talk to an invisible girl, but I'm finding it even harder to talk to a pretty one.

"What did you want to know?" I hedge for time.

"Why do you look like that?"

Oh, right, that was her question. Of course.

"Oh . . . um . . . well, yes," I stammer. "I'm an albino."

"Really? I thought so!" The girl squints at me, taking me in. "I've heard about that," she informs me. "You're all the wrong color, right?"

"*Ndiyo.*"

She stares at my face, interested. I look back at her, trying to seem honest and friendly. She's definitely my age. I wonder where she lives.

"Why are you the wrong color?"

"I don't know. I was just born this way."

She continues to study me for a minute. I'm pleased to notice that the longer our conversation goes on, the lower the knifepoint has dropped. She now holds it loosely by her side.

"Really?" she says. "You don't know?"

I shrug.

"My brothers are black, and my sister, too." I see the question in her eyes before she has a chance to say it. "And both of my parents are black. And I've seen white people before. I don't look like them, either."

"You're right, you don't."

"Well, that's all. I'm the only one out of my family, the only one out of my village like this."

She considers this a moment. Her fingers are now hardly gripping the hilt of the knife at all. I begin to hope I can get her to put it down entirely.

"But it's not just me, you know," I go on. "I've heard that there are plenty of albino people. In the Lake District, they kill them. That's why I'm here. I had to run away because a man there tried to kill me. With a knife." She jerks her hand tight around it again, but I think this time the look in her eyes might be guilt. Her gaze flicks back and forth between the knife and me. She switches it to her other hand and wipes her palm on her *khanga*. I press my advantage. "Are you sure you wouldn't be willing to put down that knife now? I promise not to hurt you. Why would I hurt someone who's related to Kweli when he's letting me live here and he's the only person I know in the whole city?"

She tips her head to the side, chewing on her bottom lip. Finally she says, "I'll put it in my pocket." Then she glares at me again. "That way you won't be nervous, but if you try to come at me, I can still get it."

"That's fair." *You're friendly and trustworthy*, I remind myself. I smile at her.

She carefully slips the knife into the loop of fabric in her *khanga* that serves as a pouch and then holds out her open palm to me as proof of her good faith.

"What about my dog?" I point at her other hand.

"Oh. This is your dog?"

"*Ndiyo*. Kweli asked me to show him that I could carve a dog. I worked on it all day yesterday, and I'd rather you not take it."

She turns the dog over in her hands, considering it.

"I knew it wasn't one of Great-Uncle's," she finally says. "I mean, you can tell it's a dog, but it just doesn't look like his carvings."

That makes me mad. I know it looks nothing like Kweli's

beautiful statues, but I worked for hours on that! Who is she anyway to talk about my carving? Just because she's related to a master carver doesn't make her one.

"Since it's mine, not his, I'd like it back."

"I didn't mean that in a bad way," she says. "No need to get huffy. Here, catch."

I'm not being huffy! I think, but I'm too busy trying to catch the statue to snap at her.

I'm terrible at catching things. It was one of the reasons the other boys never let me play with them, even after they all got over their fear that I was a ghost. I've always been useless at games that require you to judge the distance and speed of something and get in the right place for it. Which is pretty much every sport ever created. Even the boys who were willing to be a little nice to me wouldn't risk losing every day by having me on their team. So I went and sat under my wild mango tree and let them win without me.

As usual, my bad eyesight takes over. I fumble with the dog for a split second, thinking I might have, for once, judged distances correctly, but I lose control and it lands in a small puff of dust by my feet. I bend down to pick it up, furious for no good reason. It's not like this girl was testing me out to join her sports team. After today I'll probably never see her again. Then I remember: She's related to Kweli. The odds are I *will* see her again. It's almost *guaranteed* that she'll come see Kweli again.

I need to make sure she doesn't tell anyone about me. *But how?* I realize I have to keep this girl around for a while, get

her to trust me, get her to like me. Get her to keep my secret. How do normal people make friends? I squint at her,
considering.

"Why are you looking at me like that?"

I start. "Oh, um . . . I was just . . . thinking."

"Thinking? Looks like it was a strain. Maybe you should
stop."

I scowl at her, ready to say something ugly, but I see the
sparkle in her eyes just in time and realize that she's joking.
I quickly swallow my anger. I should joke, too. Maybe I can
make her like me that way. I hold up my dog.

"I think almost as well as I carve," I say and, to my great
relief, she laughs. Then she looks around.

"So, you said Great-Uncle is at the market?"

"Ndiyo."

"Well, I don't feel like walking all the way into Mwenge to
find him. So instead, maybe you can show me how good you
are at making tea."

I smile and wave her inside like we're already friends and
it's my house, instead of her having a knife in her pocket and
me being a squatter.

"Just you wait," I say. "I'm even better at making tea than
I am at thinking."

"I can't wait," she says. "And oh, by the way." I look up in
time to see the twinkle is back in her eyes. "I'm Davu."

We walk through the house and head out into the back
yard together, but as I rekindle the breakfast fire and pour
the water into the pot to make tea, a silence begins to stretch

and I'm not sure what to do about it. Davu is tracing patterns in the dust with the toe of her sandal. It's pink leather and looks expensive.

"So . . ."

"Yes?" she says, looking up from her feet.

I have no idea where I was going with that. I force myself to make conversation. Something, *anything*, is better than this stretching silence. I pick up the wooden spoon and start to stir the tea leaves around, just to have something to do.

"So you're Kweli's great-niece."

"*Ndiyo* . . ." Davu looks at me like maybe I'm a little slow.

"Uh, how old are you?" I ask.

"I'll be thirteen next month."

I was right. We're nearly the same age.

"How old are you?" Davu asks back, spreading her fingers in her lap and studying her fingernails. They're painted the same pink as her sandals. The ones on her right hand are chipped.

"Thirteen," I say, happy to be older.

The silence starts to stretch again. Thankfully, Davu says something.

"How long have you been living with Great-Uncle Kweli?"

"Three?" I think for a second. "No, today is my fourth day here, if you count the night I arrived."

"That would explain why I didn't see you when I came by last week," she muses.

"Oh? Do you live nearby?"

"Just a few streets over." She stops playing with her fingers and looks up at me with sudden interest. "Where are you from?"

This stumps me for a minute, but then I think of a way to pull the pieces together.

"I grew up in a little village outside of Arusha, but recently my family moved to Mwanza. I took the train from Mwanza to get to Dar es Salaam."

"You said someone tried to kill you Mwanza. Why would they do that? And why did you have to leave Arusha?" Davu leans forward.

I don't correct her when she says we lived in Arusha. I also don't tell her that we had to leave because we didn't have the money to stay on our farm. Anyone wearing those sandals wouldn't understand that sort of thing. I skip ahead to her other questions.

"We went to Mwanza to be with my auntie." I take a deep breath. This is hard to tell, but if I want her help keeping my skin color from Kweli, she has to know why it's important. "I left Mwanza because a man tried to kill me in order to sell my body to a *waganga* to make luck medicine."

"I've heard that they do that up in Mwanza, but I guess I never really thought about it." Davu looks down, frowning. "How did you get away?" she asks.

"Well, I was hiding in my auntie's house, but this poacher found me anyway. He came after me with a hunting knife about this long"—I hold my hands up to show the length of the blade—"but he only managed to cut me once when I pushed into him to get out the door. See?" I roll up my sleeve and show her the long, puckered scab on my forearm. She looks at it with round eyes, then back up at me. I like that all this makes me sound brave, but I still feel kind of queasy when I think about it. I take a deep breath and go on. "I ran out the door and spent the day running and hiding. When it was night and I was sure he was gone, I went back to the house, got train fare from my family and came here to Dar es Salaam because my auntie said there haven't been any albino killings here."

"That's so awful." Davu shudders and the little beads at the ends of her braids click together. Then her face turns quizzical "Why didn't your family come with you?"

"We only had enough money for one ticket, and I had to get away." It's not entirely a lie. I rub the palms of my hands against the sides of my pants. Talking about this has made me break into a cold sweat. I want to change the topic.

"You must miss them,". she says. Her dark eyes are wide and sad. "I can't imagine traveling all alone to a place I'd never been before."

I shrug, not wanting to talk about my family either. I finish my story. "Well, once I was here, I found Kweli. He's paying me in food to stay and help him around the house while I figure out what to do next."

"Hmm." Davu chews on the edge of her thumb, chipping the pink paint even further. There's a faraway look in her eyes. "I guess that's okay then. I mean, it's good for you that you found somwere to stay. And it's good for Great-Uncle not to be alone all the time. He won't let us help him very much, and Mother's always worried about him." She focuses on me again, her gaze sharp. "How long are you going to stay here helping him?"

"Um . . ." Again I run up against the wall of not having a plan. "I don't know. I'm happy to stay here for as long as he'll keep me. I like helping him." I gesture toward the wall. "Also, no one can see me in here. I feel safer that way."

This comment is getting into dangerous territory, because it's pretty close to my telling her that I'm lying to her great-uncle about what I am. I know I should push further and ask her to keep my secret, but when I try, I can't. I sit there with my mouth open a little, waiting for the words that will clearly explain what I need from her, but they never arrive.

"You really need the wall to feel safe?" Davu asks, circling back around to our earlier topic. "I don't think that people here kill albinos the way they do in Mwanza."

"You *think*," I say. "I'm not about to trust my life just to a thought!"

Davu shrugs in agreement. "I guess I can understand that," she says. "But really, I don't think I've ever heard of that here. People killing people because they're in a gang, yes. Or because they have a fued, or were doing something illegal. But I've never heard of anyone being killed here just because of the way they look."

This is comforting, but it doesn't change my mind about wanting to keep the way I look a secret. I try to move the conversation into safer territory.

"Anyway, I like learning carving. Kweli is letting me carve, you know."

"*Ndiyo*," she says, smiling again. "Remember? I saw your dog."

We both laugh.

"Me," says Davu, "I can't stand carving. Kweli keeps trying to teach me, but I don't have the patience for it." She wiggles her fingers in front of her. "You spend all this time on a silly piece of wood, and then something goes wrong and the whole thing is ruined. No thank you."

"It's not always impossible to fix," I say. "I messed up a bit with my dog and I was able to make it work out." I see Davu's look. "Not perfectly," I add defensively, "but better than a complete failure."

"Hmm," says Davu, but I don't hear any judgement in her tone. I pull the pot off the fire and pour the tea. For a while we sip in silence. Then Davu says,

"You know, I'm not sure why Great Uncle is still willing to carve wood at all."

"What do you mean?" I ask.

"Well, because of how he went blind. You know." She gestures vaguely.

"No, I don't." This is interesting. "He's never told me how he went blind, just that he wasn't always blind."

Davu looks at me sideways, as if measuring my worthiness for the story. Then, apparently coming to a decision, she leans forward.

"Well, one day, when Great-Uncle was about our age, he and his friend Kebwe were out herding the goats together and they needed switches. Great-Uncle picked one up from the side of the path, but *Kebwe* reached out to an animal fence to grab a switch."

She pauses, her eyebrows arched high to tell me this should mean something to me. I think over what she's said and figure out what it must be.

"Was it a *manyara* fence?"

Davu nods solemnly.

I know the *manyara* bush—every country child does. The sticks are lashed together for fencing to keep out wild animals. Though the sticks don't have spines and aren't particularly strong, no animal will cross them because of how poisonous the sap is. I had been warned away from the green wood of the *manyara* fences when they were fresh many times as a child. *Your eyes are bad enough*, Mother had said. *You don't need to hurt them further.* Because the sap, the poisonous sap, blinds.

I gasp. "Did they know the sticks were *manyara*?"

"Kebwe knew what he was taking, but he didn't think that it would be a problem since they were just herding goats. But then . . ." Davu drops her voice almost to a whisper. "Then the two boys started to play swords."

She pauses again. I have to admit, Davu is a good storyteller. Her pauses and mysterious voice make me want to hear more.

"Go on!"

"So the two boys played. Great-Uncle's stick was dry and worked better as a sword. Kebwe's was still green. To make up for this, Kebwe struck harder, trying to win." Davu waves her hands in front of her face, showing the frenzy of the fight. "Then Kebwe's stick snapped in two," she freezes, miming the action of a stick snapping, "and the sap sprayed all over Great-Uncle's face."

I'm holding my breath.

"And then he rubbed his eyes." Her voice is no longer completely caught up in the story. Now she's looking around at the simple house, the meticulously tidy yard of a blind man, and her voice is sad.

"Oh no," I say. Even though I know how the story must end, I still want it to end differently. I hate Kebwe, hate him without even knowing him. "That's awful."

"*Ndiyo*, it is," says Davu. Then she looks up at me and I don't know how to read her expression. "But do you know the funny thing about all this?"

"No. What?" I feel like she's trying to have two conversations with me, one with her words and one with her eyes. But I don't know what she's saying.

"Kweli still keeps in touch with Kebwe. He's never once blamed Kebwe for making him go blind. He says it was an accident and no one should be condemned because of an accident." She pauses, considering me solemnly. "You said you'd stay as long as Great-Uncle let you. I think, as long as you're nice, he'll let you stay as long as you want to."

I don't know what to say. I pull my gaze away from Davu and look down. After a moment the playfulness is back in Davu's voice.

"Me, I would have beaten Kebwe up," she says.

I have to laugh at that. "I bet, even blind, Kweli *could* have beaten him up. He's really good with that stick of his." And this launches us into another story about Kweli and sticks, but in this one, Kweli wins.

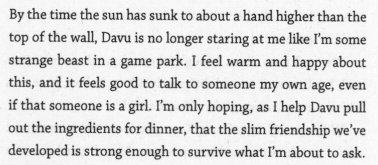

By the time the sun has sunk to about a hand higher than the top of the wall, Davu is no longer staring at me like I'm some strange beast in a game park. I feel warm and happy about this, and it feels good to talk to someone my own age, even if that someone is a girl. I'm only hoping, as I help Davu pull out the ingredients for dinner, that the slim friendship we've developed is strong enough to survive what I'm about to ask.

"Davu . . ."

"Yes?"

I pause. I should have been rehearsing how to say this all afternoon, but instead I got distracted having fun. Now I can't put this off any longer. Just like when I stepped off the train into Dar es Salaam, I feel lost, anxious, overwhelmed. I'm kicking myself for not having thought about how to deal with this when I had the time. Nothing for it—I'll just have to make it up as I go.

"Kweli should be home soon."

Davu looks up at the sky. "*Ndiyo*," she says. "So? You're not going to tell me now that you really were an intruder all this time, are you?" Her voice is serious, but behind it her eyes are laughing at me. I take a deep breath.

"No . . . No, it's something else."

She tips her head to the side. "What?"

"Well"—*here goes*—"because Kweli's blind he doesn't know I'm an albino . . . and, well, I was kind of hoping that you wouldn't tell him."

For a moment Davu only looks at me, her face stony with disbelief. Her silence scares me. Before I know it, I'm racing on, filling the silence with too many words.

"You can't tell him, you just can't! I'm safe here. And Kweli may even be thinking about teaching me how to carve, but even if he never does, he's letting me stay here and he treats me like a normal person. But if he knew I was an albino, he'd throw me out for sure, and I don't know anyone else in the whole city, and I'd have to live on the streets. So please don't tell him. Davu?"

She's still looking at me, stunned.

"You mean you never told him?" she asks.

"No, and neither can you. Y-you don't even have to lie to him if you don't want to!" I'm starting to stammer. "Just don't go out of your way to tell him. It won't even come up in the conversation if you don't put it there. I swear, Kweli thinks I'm normal."

"I don't think you know him as well as you think you do," she finally says. "He probably *does* know you're different. And anyway, even if I did tell him, he wouldn't treat you any differently."

This stupidity makes me mad, and before I can stop myself,

I'm shouting at her.

"Oh, really? He would treat me just the same? Like you did when you saw me and asked *what* I was?" She looks away from my eyes when I say that, but I'm like a cart rolling down a steep hill with nothing to slow me down. "Like the kids in my village who never let me play with them? Like Alasiri and the *waganga* who decided I was a *thing* they needed to cut into pieces?" My face is hot, and I'm having trouble breathing. I hate myself, hate everyone. "My own mother has barely touched me in my entire life, and you think that this old man, this *stranger who I barely know*, is going to just say, 'oh, that's not a problem at all, please, come right this way, Mr. Albino, and share my house and my work'? *You're* the one who doesn't know what she's talking about!"

I turn away from her and stomp out into the courtyard. I stand there, taking big shuddering breaths until I feel calm enough to go in again and keep talking. But I don't get the chance to, because just then, I hear the protesting hinges of the front gate.

Kweli is home.

17.

"**HABO?** Are you there? Come help me with this!" In comes Kweli, his walking stick in one hand and a black plastic bag in the other.

I can feel the danger of Davu looming behind me, but I move automatically to help him.

"*Sawa!*" I say. "How was your day at the market?"

"About the usual," he says, holding out the bag and turning toward the sound of my voice. "A few tourists shopping and gossip floating around like car exhaust." He hands me the bag. "Here, look inside. I got something to go with dinner tonight."

He sounds excited, and I peel apart the edges of the bag. There's a fish wrapped in newspaper at the bottom.

"Very nice, *Bwana*," I say. "Very fresh."

"I thought we'd have a coconut fish stew tonight with our *ugali* instead of just vegetables. They sold one of my statues at the shop today. Even after I took out the money to pay the bills, there was still some left over, so I decided we should have a feast."

"One fish is not much of a feast, Great-Uncle," says Davu by my elbow. She has snuck up on both of us. "It's lucky that you have me here to help you cook it."

"Davu! Is that you? What are you doing here?" A smile breaks out on Kweli's face and he reaches forward. Davu leans her cheek into his palm and lets his fingers play across her face. "It's wonderful to see you again! Is Chatha here, too?"

"No," says Davu, leaning away and taking the fish from my unprotesting fingers. "Mother stayed home. She had some extra work to do, but today was a day off of school, so she said I should come over and see how you were getting on."

"Well, isn't that nice. My own niece sending someone else to do her dirty work!"

Davu laughs lightly when he says this, but I thought his tone was a little bitter.

"I assume you've met Habo?" Kweli says.

I look at Davu and our eyes catch. *Please, please, please,* I beg with my eyes. She glances away. No promises.

"Yes, I have. We spent most of the day here together. We cleaned up a bit. Really, Great-Uncle, you should keep the place more tidy!"

This, of course, is another joke, since not so much as a blade of grass dares to grow sideways in all of Kweli's compound. He laughs.

"Well then, that's settled! Come inside, you two, and let's eat! With three of us to share it, the fish will really be a feast!"

Davu takes Kweli's hand and walks in with him, chatting

about people they both know but who I have never heard of. I want to run away, but I realize I have to do the opposite. If I hang back too far then it'll be easy for the conversation to go in directions I don't want it to. Maybe if I'm there I can steer the talk away from myself. I hurry to catch up.

Davu and I help Kweli prepare the stew, and I force myself to take part in their easy banter. I'm tense, and more than once my laugh is too loud, too grating, and there's an awkward pause afterward. But, miraculously, we get through the preparation, cooking, and eating of the fish without the color of my skin coming up once.

As we scrub out the dishes with ash afterward, Kweli finally says, "Well, Davu, it was wonderful to see you, but you should probably be getting home. Is it dark out yet?"

Davu and I look out the open door.

"*Ndiyo*, Great-Uncle."

"Hmm. Then Habo should go with you for safety."

"I . . . uh . . ." I interrupt, then realize I have nowhere to go with that sentence. *Come on! What would a normal boy complain about? Think!* I try again. "I don't know the way. And it's dark. What if I get lost?" My voice breaks at the end, and I hate myself for it. Kweli cocks his head toward me.

"It's not so far. Do you really think you won't be able to find your way through the city?"

"I don't know," I mumble.

"Well, you're not used to cities, so I suppose I can understand that." Kweli heaves himself to his feet from where he'd been sitting. "Come on, I'll go with you. That way you won't get lost, and maybe next time Davu comes to visit you'll remember the way by yourself."

Trapped! He's taken away my only rational reason for wanting to stay here. I can feel my terror mounting. Davu must have seen it, too, because she breaks into the conversation.

"Really, Great-Uncle, it's all right. I can find the way alone. I've done it plenty of times before. You and Habo should stay here and get some rest. It'll be late when you get home."

I barely have time to feel a second's worth of hope.

"Don't be silly, girl!" Kweli waves a hand in her direction, dismissing her idea. "Of course we'll walk you home. Come on, get your things."

Davu shoots me a quick look of what may have been apology, but I'm too busy panicking to notice. *What if we meet someone Kweli knows and they say something? What if Davu's mother is home and she says something? What if Kweli turns me out on the streets tonight, after it's already dark—where will I sleep? What if Alasiri's here and is waiting to kill me when Kweli throws me out?* I have no answers. In a moment the three of us are standing in front of the metal door and Kweli is turning the key in the lock to let us out. In another moment he and Davu have crossed the threshold into the darkened street beyond and are waiting for me to follow them.

My hat is completely unnecessary because of the darkness, but I pull it low over my face and tuck my hands into the ends of my long sleeves, trying to cover up as much of my white skin as possible. Then I take a deep breath and follow them into the shadowy street.

The metal door closes with a *clank!* behind me and I jump a little, even though I'm the one who closed it.

"The way to my niece's house isn't difficult, boy. Repeat after me: five blocks straight ahead, left for three, take a right, then two more streets."

"Five blocks straight ahead, left for three, take a right, then two more streets," I repeat dutifully, glancing up and down the street for suspicious people, poachers, or *wagangas*.

"Very good, let's go." He holds out his free hand, the one that isn't holding his cane, to Davu. Davu takes Kweli's hand, and there is a brief pause where I can see her consider offering her other hand to me. I wait to see what she'll do. She doesn't hold her hand out to me. Instead, she puts it in her pocket.

I shrug as if it didn't matter to me one way or the other, but then I see that she has frozen awkwardly, emotions chasing themselves across her face too quickly for me to name them.

"Habo . . ." She trails off. Then, wordlessly, she pulls her hand out of her pocket. In it is my carving knife.

I should laugh. But there's something about knives that's really just not that funny to me right now. I look at her. She turns it in her hand and holds it out to me, hilt first.

"You should take this," she says softly.

"What's that?" asks Kweli, confused at the delay.

"Nothing, Great-Uncle," says Davu quickly. "I just had something that belonged to Habo in my pocket. We can go now."

I reach out and take the knife from her. The hilt is still warm from where it has spent the day nestled against her hip, and I wrap my fingers tightly around it. *What should I do with it?* Should I put it in my belt? My pocket? I flex my healing arm, remembering when I had to run away from Alasiri. A carving knife wouldn't have made a difference to the outcome of that day, but I lie to myself that it might have. I grip the knife in a solid hold and nod to Davu. We start walking.

We make it five blocks straight ahead, left for three, a right, and two more streets without incident. Even so, by the time we get to Davu's house, my palms are slippery with sweat and I'm having trouble making my breathing sound normal.

"Here we are," says Davu, and points a little ways down the street toward a large concrete house with a low wall surrounding the yard. There must be multiple families living in it. I notice construction materials stacked against the back wall. They must be making it bigger too, maybe to rent out more rooms.

"Lovely," says Kweli. "I suppose I should stop in and say hello to your mother and the boys."

Davu looks at me, at my barely contained anxiety, and then up the street at the clearly lit windows of her house. She winces slightly as she turns to Kweli.

"I don't think they're home yet, Great-Uncle. Perhaps next time?"

I let out a shuddering breath. *Thank you,* I mouth to her. But she refuses to meet my eyes.

"All right then, give her my love," says Kweli.

"Good night," says Davu.

"Good night, Davu. Thank you for visiting an old man," says Kweli.

"Good night," I mumble, but she has already turned away. She pauses at the door, not going in until we're out of sight.

"Well, that was a nice visit," says Kweli. He holds out his now-free hand to me, like family. I have to move the knife to my other hand and wipe the sweat off my palm in order to take it. The weight of my lie to Kweli is even heavier than my dread.

"*Ndiyo*," I echo, hollowly. "A nice visit."

"What did you think of Davu?" he asks, his cane swishing briskly over the sidewalk, his calloused hand holding mine with a surprisingly light touch. "A nice girl, isn't she?"

For a moment I struggle to put how I feel about Davu into words. Then I give up.

"*Ndiyo*," I agree. "A nice girl."

✳

My days fall into a pattern. Every day Kweli attacks a new stage of the large sculpture in the backyard and I run around like an ant, doing the housework, keeping his work area tidy, and hiding from the people passing by on the road outside our wall. Every evening Kweli asks me what I've learned. And every night, just as he is going to bed, Kweli hands me a new piece of wood and a carving assignment for the next day.

The dog and cat were the easiest. Since then, Kweli has

assigned me snakes, fish, people, goats, and automobiles. He has given me different knives to work with and different kinds of wood. Sometimes the wood is soft and the knife is sharp and the carving comes out as easily as scooping *ugali* off the bottom of a pan. Sometimes the knife is dull, or strangely shaped, and I have to wrestle the figure out of the block in a way that leaves my knuckle joints sore all night. Sometimes the wood is dry and filled with imperfections and I have to change my plan five or six times to account for them. Sometimes I don't finish in just one day, but those are evenings when I have many things to say I learned, and Kweli has never yelled at me for it.

Davu comes by about once a week, but she has always made sure to leave during broad daylight to prevent me having to escort her home. Other than Davu, no one else has come to the door except for people trying to beg, and I haven't opened the gate for them, pretending no one was home, so no one else has seen me. Davu has still not promised to be silent—she keeps telling me I should tell Kweli myself—but since she hasn't said anything yet to him about my odd looks, I think I'm safe for the moment.

I've managed to stay hidden better than I'd hoped: Kweli has invited me to town with him every Wednesday and Friday, but has so far not forced me to go with him when I make up excuses not to go. My excuses are terrible. I have a headache; I feel sick; I need to stay and clean up a mess I made just to have a mess to stay home and clean up. Each time I lie to Kweli, my belly twists with guilt, but I tell myself that's better than watching his face twist into hatred when he finds out I'm a lying *zeruzeru*. Each time, Kweli pauses for a moment, his head tipped toward me as if waiting for me to replace the excuse with the truth. But when I let the silence stretch, he simply nods and goes without me. He knows something isn't right, but he doesn't push me to tell him what that something is.

What he does push me to do is contact my family. But I've managed not to do that too. It's true that I think about them and my flight from Mwanza often, but these thoughts make me feel empty and angry. I don't want to walk out into the street to find Eshe and her phone and, even if I did, I don't know what I'd say to the people who couldn't protect me. Also, I'm hoping that as long as I don't have anyone else to rely on, Kweli won't send me away. I run my fingers along the thin scar on my forearm, pressing on it. It no longer hurts when I do this, but it helps to remind me why I can't get too comfortable, feel too safe. I throw myself into the daily work and my carvings and try to pretend that I never existed before arriving at the sculptor's house.

✳

Tonight marks a month since I tried to take a blind man's dinner: four weeks of safety, work, and good food; four weeks of spending time with Davu; four weeks of bad excuses that Kweli has accepted without comment. The September breeze whispers to me that this can't last, and deep down I know that's true. Every day for weeks I've braced myself for Kweli to finally say he has had enough help and send me on my way instead of giving me a new carving assignment, but so far that hasn't happened. I've found as many ways as I can to help Kweli around the house, doing all the things that need eyes. It makes me feel good to make his life easier. But, though he hasn't kicked me out, Kweli hasn't invited me to stay with him and become his apprentice, either. I try not to think about this too often.

Tonight is no different. As soon as my thoughts start to stray into dangerous territory, I discover I feel like a second helping of dinner and strike up a conversation while getting it.

"Your sculpture is coming along well, *Bwana*, don't you think?"

"I suppose."

"I think it looks good," I say, scooping more stew out of the pot and into my bowl. The tin ladle clanks against the side of the pot and Kweli stretches out his bowl. I put another ladle-full into his bowl, too. "What will it be when it's done?" I ask.

"What does it look like?"

I pause. Though no longer a long, scaly crocodile, I have trouble translating the ropy, knotted shapes of Kweli's sculpture into a word.

"I'm not sure." I discovered quickly that honesty is the best idea around Kweli. "There are so many twists in it; it still confuses me."

"Ha!" he says, and mumbles something that sounds like

"good eyes." For a moment I think that will be my only answer; it often is. But Kweli goes on: "It's 'Justice.'"

I scowl into the remains of my dinner. Sometimes I think
I'd be better off if Kweli didn't answer my questions. I have no
idea what he's talking about half of the time.

"What, boy? No answer? No impatient questions?"

I snort in response, sounding eerily like him.

"Justice," I mutter, but I think he hears me. I want to move
the conversation along to a more fruitful topic, but I know I
have to give some variety of apology. I heave a sigh and say,
"*Bwana*, I don't understand how you plan to carve justice, but
I will continue to watch how you do it. Maybe when you're
done, I'll know what you meant tonight." I leave a pause that
is only slightly shorter than what is polite, and then ask,
"What's my carving assignment tonight, *Bwana*?"

Kweli hands me a large block of wood and a knife. My
eyebrows shoot up in surprise. Kweli's assignments have always progressed in difficulty: The wood has become harder
and more temperamental, the knives duller and more oddly
shaped. But this is the buttery-textured wood I carved my
first dog from, and the knife is perfectly shaped and sized to
fit in my hand. I am so confused by the ease these materials
will lend me that I don't at once notice that Kweli has started
talking again.

"Sorry, *Bwana*! What did you say?"

"I just gave you your assignment, dreamer!"

I try to force my brain to remember the last sounds it
heard.

"A weevil? I am supposed to carve a weevil?" I think of the tiny bugs that burrow into the grain and float to the top when you boil it. I have no idea what they look like up close, but I could try to find one. I'm thinking hard about how to copy the exact shape of the little bug when Kweli corrects me.

"No, silly boy! Not a weevil! Hmph. I said: Your assignment is to carve Evil."

"Evil? How can I carve something that's not even real?"

"Evil isn't real? There's none of it in the world?" His questions snap in the darkeness like branches in a strom.

"No, that's not what I meant! Of course there's evil. Of course it's real, but . . . it doesn't have a body or a shape, like a goat or a truck does. How am I supposed to put something into wood that has no shape?"

Kweli stares off into the distance and I think I've won. But instead, he says, "This is the next step. You have shown me that you're a carver—even, sometimes, a good carver." I flush with the praise. "But you haven't sculpted anything yet.

"A sculptor," continues Kweli, "does not carve a thing, but a meaning. You've seen my sculptures. They aren't all pretty. Some of them are not even all that accurate, if you're expecting them to show you a cow or a girl. But each of them is the most accurate rendering I can manage of a thought or a feeling. This is the next stage. I need to see whether you are only a carver or whether you could be a sculptor."

As he gets up, he takes pity on my panic and adds, "The way we give shape to an idea, boy, is to show its shape in our life. Show me what you know of Evil. If you succeed, perhaps

I'll ask you to show me what you know of Love, or Happiness, or Pain. But for now, show me Evil."

And with that, he walks away, leaving me dumbfounded in the dark.

18.

THAT NIGHT, I have trouble falling asleep.
With this one assignment, Kweli will decide whether or not
I'm a sculptor. He may use it to decide whether or not I can
stay with him any longer. If I can impress him enough, maybe
he won't keep asking me to contact my family, won't even care
that I'm an albino. I want this normal, useful life to continue
so badly that the wanting is almost painful.

I roll toward the wall and see Kweli's face as he tells me to
carve the impossible. I turn to the ceiling and the weight of
what I have to prove with this block of wood pushes down on
me until I feel I can't breathe. I turn toward the room and its
emptiness mirrors what I feel capable of. Finally I turn onto
my face and try to smother my fears in the mattress.

A minute later I jolt up, gasping. It's no use. I have to find
some way to carve a physical image of Evil. Should I carve a
demon? I think of the Makonde masks in Kweli's storage hut.
They've always felt faintly evil to me. Should I make a mask?

I crawl off my pallet and across the moon-streaked floor to the bench where I left the wood and the knife. Not wanting to wake Kweli, I slink out of the house, into the night.

Stepping into the yard, my senses pop as the air opens up around me. I can only see gray shapes in the blackness, so I walk slowly, cautious of where I'm putting my feet, not wanting to step on things in the dark that could bite. When I reach a spot in the center of the swept yard untouched by shadows, I sit on the ground and hold the tools in my lap. I let the moonlight wash over me.

I sit and I think. Some distant part of me knows I'm going to regret this tomorrow when I'm tired and Kweli wants me to bound around like an antelope, doing errands, but I don't care. I need to figure out how to carve Evil.

It's as I sit there, waiting to know what to carve, that my eyes fall on the shine of the knife in the moonlight. And it hits me all in a rush. I do know Evil. My hands are shaking as I run them over the block of wood, tracing with my finger the lines my knife will carve.

Yes. It will fit there.

Yes. It could curve here.

Yes. I can do this.

When I pick up the knife and lay it gently against the side of the block, my hands no longer shake.

It takes me just under a week to finish my carving. I work

during lunches, every day when Kweli takes his naps, and late into the dry September nights when there is enough moon for me to see my fingers. I try to apply what I've learned from watching Kweli. That first night, I only carved the edges off the block, leaving a slab a little longer than my forearm and three times as wide in the rough outline of the shape I wanted to work with. Over the next few days I slowly whittled that blocky outline down, one layer of detail at a time. Today I finished it. I pull the knife down the long places to liberate the last curls of smoothness and dig the tip in firmly where I want texture and depth. I take a long look at it. Yes, it will do.

I glance over to the corner of the yard. Kweli is sunk deep in his own work, finishing "Justice," so I decide not to bother him now. I walk inside the house and set my statue down on my pallet. Tonight I'll give it to him and see what he thinks.

Realizing I'm thirsty after a morning of carving, I trot out the front of the house to get a drink of water from the tap.

"Who are you?" a shrill voice demands.

I freeze in my tracks, panic washing over me. I have walked out of the house without checking first and have walked straight into a woman who has come in looking for Kweli. The keys for the gate still sway from her fingers.

"Well? Who are you? I asked you a question, boy!" The woman is holding a large basket on her head with one hand, but now she plants the other deeply into the fat of her left hip and glares at me. The keys disappear entirely. I try to answer, but nothing comes out. I feel frozen in my body, unable to control it, like when you try to scream in a nightmare and can't. A distant part of my mind registers that Davu has just followed the woman through the door and is closing it behind her.

The woman looks past me and bellows into the house, "Uncle! What are you up to? What on earth are you doing with a mute *zeruzeru* in your house?"

And with that, I can almost hear the sound of my whole world crashing down around me. In my mind's eye I see myself being hated again, chased again, hunted again. I see my dream of staying here and becoming a sculptor wither like a seedling planted too late in the summer. I stare at the woman in despair, but she doesn't notice. She's too busy bellowing out questions that are destroying my life. Behind her I see Davu wince. Then Kweli appears in the door of the house.

"What's wrong, Chatha? Why all the shouting?"

"You tell me what's wrong!" Chatha booms, loudly enough that I'm sure the neighbors two streets over can hear her. "Why is this *zeruzeru* boy here? Are you picking up strays again?"

"Calling someone a stray is very unpleasant," says Kweli coldly. His lips have thinned, and the skin on his hand is tight where he's gripping his cane fiercely.

Chatha huffs in exasperation. "Unpleasant or not, the question stands! Who is this boy? Where is his family? What is he doing here with you?"

"Mother," Davu whispers to her, "you promised you wouldn't fight this time."

"Hush, Davu!" the big woman snaps, but Kweli's face clears

slightly.

"Is that you, Davu?"

"Ndiyo." Davu darts a look to her mother, then smiles at Kweli. "Hello, Great-Uncle. Mother and I brought you some fresh bread, and I found you a jar of honey in the grocery store."

At the mention of such civilized things as bread and honey, Kweli seems to collect himself. "Let's not talk in the yard like peddlers," he says. "Come in, Chatha, and let's have some tea while we talk. Habo, please go get some water."

Kweli and Chatha disappear into the house. Davu runs over to me and grabs my arm.

"I'm so sorry!" she whispers. "Mother decided at the last minute to come with me. I had no way to warn you."

I look at her with glassy eyes, not quite able to focus on either her face or her words. Her fingers are warm against my skin that has suddenly gone cold. That same far-away part of my mind that noticed her in the door earlier comments quietly that this is the first time Davu has touched me.

"Habo? The water?" Kweli's voice from inside the house breaks the spell on me and, mind whirling, I follow his instructions. Davu follows, but I'm too stunned to talk to her. Surely Kweli heard what Chatha said; she was yelling it loudly enough. Could it be that he doesn't know what the word *zeru-zeru* means? No, he lives in a huge city, not on some dusty little farm like my family used to. Why didn't he say anything?

Maybe I should just run away now, before he has a chance to throw me out.

But I don't. Instead, I let Davu guide me and the bucket of water around the house to the patio. Kweli and Chatha are sitting rigidly across from each other on stools by the fire. I see that Kweli has a pot on the fire, and I pour the water from the bucket into it. The metal is already hot, and the first water to touch it instantly hisses into steam. A hot billow clouds my face, but I pour the water in smoothly until the pot is nearly full. When Kweli hears the empty *thump* of the bucket on the ground, he reaches forward and drops in a handful of tea leaves and spices. Chatha watches this little ritual with hard eyes. You can see that holding her words in is a strain. But she's well-raised enough to wait for her uncle to start the conversation now that they're sitting down on his patio.

"So," says Kweli finally, stirring the tea leaves in the warming water with a long wooden spoon, "how is the family?"

"I'm well, Great-Uncle," says Davu, rolling over an uncarved log from Kweli's work area and sitting down on it. She pats the spot beside her for me. I sit, mechanically. "And my brothers are nothing but trouble, like always."

Kweli chuckles.

"They're fine, Uncle!" Chatha bursts out. "We're all fine. Now tell me about this boy. Where is he from? Why is he here?" She waves her big hands around as she asks these questions, seeming not to care that the gesture is lost on Kweli.

"Chatha, I'm surprised at you. You've seen me work with young people before."

"But always boys and girls we knew. Not mute albino strangers!"

"I'm not mute," I growl.

"Oh! He speaks!" She rolls her eyes as if this is some kind of miracle, crossing her arms tightly over her orange and red *khanga*. She glares at me. I glare back at her.

"He speaks," says Kweli flatly, still stirring the tea. "Sometimes quite a bit. Do you remember Ngonepe who worked with me a few years ago? There was a boy who hardly ever spoke. No, Habo here can be quite a talker when he is not stunned into silence by running into my niece at my door. Why, I am almost mute from the shock myself." He gives her a thin-lipped smile. "You haven't been by in weeks, Chatha."

"I was busy with getting some construction done in my house," says Chatha, smoothing her big hands over her sweat-wrinkled *khanga*. "*Ndiyo*, it's been a while. But now, today, I have come by to see my favorite uncle."

Kweli gives a dry laugh. Davu is perched nervously on the edge of her seat beside me like a bird, looking back and forth between Kweli and her mother.

"Chatha, I'm your only uncle."

Chatha's laugh transforms her face, twisting all the lines just slightly, changing them from scolding to mirth. I can suddenly see how she's related to Davu. When she's smiling, Chatha has a face I could almost trust. Almost. I go inside and find four cups for the tea.

"And that's the only reason you're my favorite, old man! You are far too much trouble." I hear from inside as I gather things to drink from.

"Too much trouble? I take care of myself. I'm no trouble

at all!"

I'm back outside with the cups in time to see the happy lines leave Chatha's face again. "That's exactly why are're too much trouble. You can't keep living here alone," she says.

Kweli stiffens on his stool, his face hardening into an ugly mask. He pulls the pot of tea off the fire with a calloused hand.

"The tea is ready," he says flatly.

"I'll serve, Great-Uncle," chirps Davu with false cheeriness. Pushing her sleeves up over her elbows and using the hem of her *khanga* to hold the edges of the pot without burning herself, she pours tea into each of our cups. Her hands shake slightly as she pours. I feel bad for her, but I'm grateful for the argument because no one is talking about me anymore.

For a few minutes everyone sips at their tea.

"What work have you been doing on your house, then?" asks Kweli. "A fancy new kitchen for you? A pool for the children?"

I think this is progress in the conversation until I see Davu shrink down beside me.

"I finished your rooms," says Chatha, lifting her chin.

"My what?"

"Your rooms. The workers finished building them last week, and I painted and decorated them for you. You have a bedroom and a bathroom at my house now."

I'm imagining what it would be like to have a bedroom and a bathroom to myself, and wondering what Chatha's house must look like on the inside, when Kweli answers.

"Absolutely not." The cold fury in Kweli's voice can't be

mistaken.

"Oh, Uncle!" Chatha is losing her patience. "What if you fell and hurt yourself? What if you became ill and no one was around? You can't even see and you've holed yourself up in this walled compound. It's dangerous for you to be alone!" She rubs her temples as if this whole conversation is giving her a headache. "I should make Davu talk sense into you! You listen to her better than you ever listen to me!"

"She needn't bother herself," says Kweli. "Now that Habo's here, he helps me with everything I need."

I look up in surprise. I didn't know that Kweli thought so highly of my help. It makes me feel proud, but I'm not so happy to be brought into this conversation. Chatha notices, of course. I'm getting the distinct impression that she is just as shrewd as her uncle. She opens her mouth to say something and then thinks better of it.

"Well." She narrows her eyes. "When he moves on, I want you to let us know right away, not wait a week and a half like you did when Ngonepe left."

"Hmph" is Kweli's only reply.

"And you, boy." Her sharp gaze swivels over to me. "Take good care of my difficult old uncle. The slightest problem at all, I want you to come get me. Is that clear? If he isn't doing as well as he is now the next time I visit, you'll have me to answer to."

The force of her gaze makes me dip my head. "I'll try, *Bibi*," I whisper.

Chatha fans herself with her hands, then sighs and heaves

herself to her feet. Davu shoots a concerned look at me, but jumps up and follows her mother.

"Very well. I'll leave you for today, Uncle, but please do think about what I've said." Chatha looks at Kweli, and for a moment I see what she sees: a stooped old man, leaning on a cane. Blind and alone. I can understand why she's trying to make him go live with her.

"Is there anything else you needed, Chatha?" Kweli replies.

Chatha sighs again and picks up the basket she came in with.

"Here's the bread I made you," says Chatha, unwrapping two great round loaves from her basket and setting them on the table. "And Davu's jar of honey. There's butter in the little box."

"You're going to make me fat," says Kweli, smiling for the first time in a while.

"Well, you and the boy both could use a few extra pounds. *Kwaheri*, Uncle."

"*Kwaheri*, Chatha. *Kwaheri*, Davu," says Kweli.

"I'll come again soon and see you," says Davu, but although her words are directed at Kweli, she's looking at me as she says this. I don't meet her eyes. Now that my secret is out, I don't think I'll be here when she comes back, no matter how happy Kweli is to have my help.

"*Kwaheri*, Davu. *Mama* Chatha," I mumble.

"*Kwaheri*," says Chatha to me, but Davu refuses to say good-bye.

With that, they're gone. I watch the bright print of Chatha's receding backside sway left and right, bracing myself for the inevitable: Kweli will have to talk to me now.

But again, he surprises me. Instead of turning to me and demanding the truth, Kweli simply rests a hand on my shoulder as we face out of the doorway together and sighs, "Well, well. A visit from Chatha is always an experience. Come, let's get dinner started."

My mind is such a muddle, I feel like I'm moving from instinct only: laying the fire, pouring the cornmeal and water into the pot for *ugali*, spreading the butter and the honey on two large slabs of bread. I carry the bread out to where Kweli is sitting on his stool by the fire, tending the *ugali*. I hand him his slice. For a moment we both sit there, chewing. When he finishes, Kweli tilts his head toward me and asks the question I've been dreading.

"So, is what Chatha said true?"

I choke on the last bite of my honey bread. I stall.

"About what, *Bwana*? She said many things."

"Don't be rude, boy! I've had enough of that for one day."

I duck my head in apology, even though he can't see it.

"*Ndiyo*," says a small voice I only partly recognize as my own. "It's the truth. I'll leave in the morning, if you like."

"No one said anything about leaving yet. You're one of these *zeruzeru*?"

"*Ndiyo*."

"And what does that mean?"

At this, my head snaps up so quickly I bite my tongue.

"What? You don't know what *zeruzeru* means? I thought everyone knew."

"There's no need to take that tone with me. What I know or don't know isn't the point. I'm curious to know what it means to *you*."

"Well . . ." I trail off, not sure what to say, how to start. How do you explain something like that?

"Yes?"

"Well. A *zeruzeru* is—I mean, I am—an albino. Someone with all the wrong colors. My skin is white, and my hair is yellow, and my eyes are a pale bluish color."

There is a pause.

"Let me feel your face," says Kweli. Surprised, I lean toward him and close my eyes. His sculptor's fingers brush over my head and face. I realize, crazy as it is, that Kweli is seeing me tonight for the first time in all our weeks together. Kweli finishes touching my face and drops his hands.

"What else?" Kweli asks.

"*Bwana?*"

"What else, boy? Your color can't be the only thing. What else does it mean?"

I'm not sure what he is asking, but answering Kweli's questions has become automatic and, before I realize it, I'm talking fast.

"It means that I burn in the sun when other people don't, which means that I couldn't do the farm work or play with the boys at school. It means that people stare at me everywhere I go. Even in my own home, sometimes Mother or one of my brothers will spin toward me in surprise when they see me out of the corner of their eyes, and then turn away. My eyes shake from side to side when I get tired, and I can't see well, and my father left us because of me, and then, in Mwanza, people tried to kill me like you'd kill an elephant for its tusks because they wanted to sell pieces of me to the *wagangas* to make good-luck talismans!"

I'm barely conscious of the fact that I'm on my feet, shouting at Kweli, as I continue. "I don't know why they think being an albino is lucky! It's awful! Normal people point at you when you arrive. They whisper when you leave. Everyone treats you differently, and you get hunted like an animal! That's not good luck! That's a curse! A curse! Do you want to know what I know of Evil? Do you want to see it? Here! Feel what it's like to be an albino!"

I realize that my voice is shrill and wild, but for the moment I'm beyond caring. I run into the house and roughly grab my statue from where I had placed it tenderly only an hour ago when it was all I cared about in the world. Now I grab it like a runaway puppy, march out to Kweli, and slam the statue into his lap.

Then I burst into tears.

I splay my fingers over my face and sob like a child, rocking slightly on my stool. Kweli reaches an arm out to me, but I jerk away. The anger pushes out through my eyes and runs like the lava of the Ol Doino Lengai volcano down my face, through my fingers, and into the dust of the courtyard. With each sob I feel the tearing pain of not fitting into my own village, my own family, since the day I was born. All the hard words I didn't realize I had committed to memory hurl themselves at me again. The feeling of being a stranger in my own skin, because of my skin, wrings my heart like laundry.

When I finish crying, my laundry-heart feels wrinkled and bruised, but clean.

I grind my fists into my eyes to squeeze out the last of the tears and then look at Kweli. He's sitting very still, holding my sculpture lightly, gently, not yet seeing it with his fingers, waiting for me to be done. It's only when I sniffle back the mucus in my nose and say, "Okay, *Bwana*. I'm all right now," that he slowly lets his fingers trace my statue.

He starts at the bottom, running his fingers up the spikes of tall carved grass, over the bloated bulge of the dead elephant, finding the missing face, the gaping holes where the tusks should be. His fingers find the man behind the elephant, looming up, dwarfing the corpse. He feels the twisted features of the snarling face, feels the way the man is leaning forward, one hand reaching out, grasping, the other holding a massive knife.

His fingers brush over the top of the head and the tip of the knife and find the line of people that make up the background of the statue. To Kweli's fingers they're just a line of people, but I know the faces on each one of them: Mother, a shadowy man who could be my father, Enzi, Chui, the three men who kicked us out of our house in Arusha, Asu. Together they form a wall behind the madman with the knife. But none of them is seeing him, because they have all turned their faces away. Kweli's fingers still, and he raises his head to me.

He says nothing, and I feel the need to end the silence, so I say the first thing that comes to my mind.

"It's not a pretty carving, *Bwana*."

"No," he answers softly. "No, it's not pretty. But then, I don't think that the experiences that shaped it were pretty."

"No."

Kweli runs his hands over the sculpture one more time and then hands it to me. I take it softly, sorry for my earlier treatment of it.

"It's not pretty," says Kweli as he puts it into my hands, "but it is good." My eyes are dancing with exhaustion and he is slightly fuzzy in my vision, but I can see that he's smiling. "Well, Habo, it seems you have the heart of a sculptor after all."

When I smile, the mask of dried tears covering my face cracks in a hundred places.

19.

LATER THAT SAME evening, as we're
wiping the remains of dinner out of our bowls with the still-
warm ashes of the fire, Kweli surprises me by revisiting a conversation that I thought was finished.

"You say that your skin is all white?" he asks.

"*Ndiyo.*"

"Hmm." He rolls the ash around and around in his bowl.
I can tell, even from all the way over here, that the bowl is
clean. I wait.

"The man with the knife, who was he?"

I look up at him, not sure what he's getting at.

"He's the hunter I told you about, the one that killed an
elephant for its ivory." I blush, remembering the half story I
told Kweli that first night. "He's also the one who tried to kill
me in Mwanza. He's the reason I ran away." I finally get up the
courage to ask the question that has been eating me out from
the inside, like termites in a tree. "*Bwana?*"

"Yes?"

"Are people going to try to kill me here like in Mwanza?"

Kweli turns his head toward me and considers my question.

"No, I don't think so," he says. "We don't do that thing here in Dar es Salaam."

That's the same thing that Davu told me, all those weeks ago. Maybe it's true.

"Are you sure?" I press. "You didn't even know what a *zeru-zeru* was."

"I knew the word. Just because I didn't know everything about the term doesn't mean I hadn't heard it before! In Mwenge, many of the shopkeepers have radios. I've heard the ministers of parliament talking about how the killings up in the Lake District have to stop. But," he adds, "that doesn't mean you shouldn't be cautious. This is a big city, and you're a country boy at heart. There are plenty of people who would kill you here, or rob you, or kidnap you, just like they would anyone else. Take me, for example. People try to take advantage of me because I'm blind and I have to be very careful sometimes not to let them. Even if no one is hunting you here, you still need to live thoughtfully."

I think about that, rubbing my hands absently over my face as I do. Just because no one is looking to hurt me doesn't mean that I won't be hurt. I don't know whether that's comforting or not, but I file Kweli's advice away. It's good advice.

"And the people in the background? Who are they?" Kweli asks, bringing the conversation back around to my statue.

I sigh. So much for being a boy of secrets.

"My family. And some people from Arusha."

"Why did you put them in a statue of Evil?"

Something in his tone makes me think this is important to him. I answer as truthfully as I can.

"None of my family was ever truly cruel to me," I explain. "Except maybe for my brother Chui." I think about all the times Chui teased me and then give a weak laugh. "Though, really, he's just a brother." Kweli stays quiet, waiting.

"They're part of Evil because they're looking away." I tick off each one on my fingers. "Chui taught the other children to tease me, and then looked away. My father saw I was different and looked away from my whole family. I think this is what made Mother look away from me all the times she did. The men from Arusha wouldn't help us stay in our home. My sister, Asu . . ." My voice breaks, but I force myself on. "My sister betrayed me."

"How did she betray you?"

"Alasiri told me he found out about where I was because Asu was talking about me to her friends at work. It's how he knew where to find me." The fear and anger of being attacked bubble up in me again, and I take a deep breath to steady myself. "None of them are evil people, but when evil things happened, they looked away and let them happen. I put them in the statue because that's Evil, too."

I finish speaking, and it's so quiet that I can hear the clank of dinner dishes from the house over the wall. Have I not answered Kweli's question? Is that why he's not talking? I try to think of something else to say, but I can't. So I sit in the gathering darkness and wait, knowing he'll talk when he's ready, or not at all.

I let my mind drift while I wait, listening to the layers of bug sounds, the soft hiss of the breeze through the tamarind tree leaves. I'm almost startled by Kweli's voice when it does come out of the darkness.

"And is this—this turning away, this hunting—is this why you've refused to go with me to the market?"

I feel my cheeks redden and I'm glad that Kweli can't see me.

"Ndiyo, Bwana."

Kweli nods. "I thought so."

"Bwana?"

"I knew you were ashamed to go out. I just wasn't sure why."

"It's just . . ." I struggle to put words to my fears. "It's just that everyone has seen me as less once they knew what I was. Alasiri wanted to kill me and take pieces of me to sell. I was afraid, Bwana." I need him to understand. "I was afraid that you'd want to get rid of me. Or that I'd meet up with someone who wanted to kill me." I pause, considering, then I take a deep breath and ask, "Do you want to get rid of me now, Bwana?"

Kweli's laugh is a hollow, tired laugh.

"No, Habo," he says quietly. "No. You are still welcome to stay for as long as you'd like. However!" He jabs a finger in my general direction. "There will be no more foolishness about your family. They need to know where you are and what you're doing. You can take a few days to think of what you will say, but you *will* let them know that you are all right. That is my one condition."

I can't believe it. He knows, and he's not throwing me out. I examine his face closely in the firelight, looking for the lie, looking for the hate. I don't find it. I remember Davu's story about him and Kebwe. *No one should be condemned because of an accident.* Now, finally, I understand what she was trying to tell me. The lump of fear that has been lodged in my heart since I met him crumbles slowly.

"*Ndiyo*," I say. "*Asante sana.*"

"*Karibu*," he replies. "And from now on, we will go into Mwenge together."

I swallow hard. Keeping my color from Kweli is no longer an issue, but I still don't feel comfortable parading around in public. *What if they laugh at me? What if they ignore me because I'm not worth talking to?* Even if no one here is going to try to kill me, there's still no guarantee that they'll accept me. I look up through my white eyelashes at Kweli, sitting there, saying nothing, supporting me and waiting.

I take a deep breath and make a decision. He has been nothing but good to me, and it's time to show him that I'm grateful for his kindness in a way that matters to him.

"*Sawa*," I say. "Tomorrow, we'll go into Mwenge together."

The next morning passes in a blur as we get ready to leave.

I'm torn between wanting this whole day to be over with quickly and dreading the moment when my chores end and we'll have to be on our way. I think about coming up with one of my excuses again—I do actually feel a headache coming on, after all, and I didn't sleep well last night—but I stick to my decision.

I layer on my second shirt for sun protection and put on my hat with its long tail. I pick up the bag with our lunch in it and drag my feet over to where Kweli is getting ready.

"Here," he says, and hands me a flat cardboard box filled with small sculptures padded in dried grass, old newspapers, and crumpled black plastic shopping bags. "Carry this. We'll drop these off at the shop when we go."

Kweli picks up a small purse, puts the drawstring around his neck, and tucks it inside his shirt. I balance the flat box on top of my floppy hat the best I can and follow Kweli out the door.

We don't retrace the path I took when I first came from the train station. Rather, to get to Mwenge, we follow Bagamoyo Road the other way until it turns into Old Bagamoyo Road. Walking slightly behind Kweli, I wonder what it would be like to walk up Bagamoyo Road blind. I look ahead carefully and, when I'm sure there's nothing threatening in the next stretch of sidewalk, I close my eyes and try to walk forward. Within five steps my mind has conjured all sorts of things about to hit me in the face and my eyes snap open. The road is as clear as before, and Kweli has gained distance on me, his stride not breaking as his stick skips over cracks in the cement. I can't imagine the bravery it takes to just go through one day not being able to see. I wipe the nervous sweat off my palms and jog to catch up to him.

As we walk past shops, houses, and *dala-dala* stands, people do double takes when they see me. With every person we pass I can feel the muscles in my shoulders tighten, and I wish I could tuck my head down like I used to so that I can't see them seeing me. But that would mean unbalancing my box, so I can't. My palms are sweating again as I imagine what they must be saying about us to one another. How, despite what Kweli said, they could be talking about what my death would be worth to them. Kweli, of course, simply walks on. I reconsider my earlier conclusion. Sometimes it would be just fine to be blind.

"Hey!" a man at a small roadside restaurant calls out to us. Kweli turns his head in the direction of the sound. I fight the urge to run.

"Who's that?" calls Kweli.

"Kweli! It's Chane. What are you doing on the road today? It's not your day to sell."

A smile breaks out on Kweli's face and he turns off the sidewalk toward the voice. I follow reluctantly, trying to stay out of sight behind him.

"Chane! Hello, old friend. How are you doing?" I fume quietly under my box, wanting to move on. I'm sure the fat lady behind the counter is staring at me.

"I'm well," replies Chane. "And who's this with you today?" I wince. So much for trying to hide.

"This is Habo. He's been helping me around the house these past few weeks."

"*Sawa,*" says Chane.

"And do you see?" asks Kweli. "Can you see that he's white?" There is real curiosity in Kweli's voice. I feel terribly awkward, but Chane doesn't seem bothered.

"*Ndiyo,* of course I can. He is quite white."

"He's a *zeruzeru,* an albino," says Kweli. I'm ready to have the earth swallow me up whole like a fish swallows a bug, but no, it leaves me there as they talk about me.

"Is he now? That's interesting."

"*Ndiyo.* Have you ever seen one before?"

"I know of a cab driver who is albino, and of course I've heard about the problems in the Lake District, but no, I've never met one before. Hello, boy. *Habari gani?*"

"*Nzuri,*" I mumble, embarrassed.

A bark of laughter from the other side of the restaurant interrupts our conversation. Three young men lounge by a small circular table covered in empty beer bottles. I wonder whether they've started drinking already or just never finished from last night.

"Hey, blind man! Look at us!"

I hear Chane grumble in anger, but Kweli just puts a hand on his arm.

"Let them be," he says. "They sound drunk."

The men don't like the fact that they're being ignored, and they start to yell out insults to Kweli. Then they see me and add in rude things about the way I look, too.

"Perhaps it would be better to talk another time," says Kweli to Chane. "I think we'll go to the market now."

Chane nods vigorously. "Yes, right. Go on. I'll make sure these idiots don't follow you."

"Come on, Habo," says Kweli.

"How could you just stand there and let them say those things?!" I explode at him once we're out of earshot.

"What were my options?"

"I . . . I don't know! But you didn't even get mad! They were saying awful things. Why didn't you get angry?"

"Why choose to be angry? It won't change them, and then I'm angry, which is no fun for me." Kweli chuckles. "Come on, let's go to Mwenge."

I wonder how Kweli can be so calm around rude strangers and get so angry when Chatha tries to help him. I sigh. I don't know if I'll ever understand him.

❋

The Mwenge Woodcarvers' Market is a square of buildings set off a roundabout in the road. I have no idea how Kweli crosses the four speeding lanes of traffic when he's alone. Even with my eyes wide open, I'm terrified we're going to be killed. Once we're safely across, though, there's no shortage of friendly voices to help guide Kweli to where he needs to go. A many-voiced chorus of *Habari gani, Kweli!* and *What are you doing here today, old friend?* and *Who is that with you?* greets us as we walk down a narrow alley of shops toward the dusty central rectangle of gray dirt and scraggly trees surrounded by the long, low buildings of the artists' market.

Kweli stops many times, introducing me to the other artists in the market: wood carvers, painters, and jewelry makers mostly, based on what I can see in their shops, though there are some potters and stone carvers, too. I'm polite and say hello, but I have trouble remembering all the names and faces. This is more people than I've met in over a month. They're all curious about me, but Kweli gives a quick explanation: "Habo's an albino. He's staying with me for now and helping me out. I hope you'll be good to him." And this seems to satisfy them.

"Everyone's very friendly," I murmur to Kweli as we head into the central square.

"Well, yes," answers Kweli. "Though we all compete with one another to catch the eyes of tourists, we share food and tea and help one another make change for the large bills the foreigners use to pay. It's a good community."

We walk down the aisle of open shop doors until we get to one on the far side of the square.

"This one is mine," says Kweli with a big smile. "Mine and some other carvers." I wonder how he knows this one is his. He must have been counting the steps from the curb or something. Interested, I peek inside.

Just like most of the other shop-cubbies in the market, Kweli's is a small room with many shelves on the walls and a clear area in front of it. The roof is corrugated metal, and the area out front is covered by a blue plastic tarp stretched between poles. The tarp is different; most of the other shops don't have one. When I ask about it, Kweli tells me this is important because, this way, when customers come, the room is cool and shaded and it makes them want to step in and look at the art.

"Especially Americans and Europeans," he says with a smile. "They're always eager to get out of the sun."

"Like me," I say.

Kweli pauses for a second and his smile falters.

"*Ndiyo.* Like you. Come on," he says, and walks into the shop.

When I walk in for the first time, the box still balanced on my head, I'm overwhelmed by the number of carvings in the room, but once I get over my surprise I realize that the space is actually quite organized. The bigger, more expensive pieces are by the door, and the smaller, less expensive pieces are at the back. When I ask Kweli about this, he explains that this way the customer has to walk past the bigger ones to get to the small ones.

"Who knows?" He winks at me. "Maybe they'll fall in love with a bigger one on their way to the small ones."

Huge Makonde masks glare down at me from the middle of the room as we walk into the shadowy shop. They're similar to the ones in the shed behind Kweli's house, and no matter how long I look at them, they still give me the chills. Kweli told me a little bit about their meaning when we were cleaning up around the shed a few days ago, how the Makonde people think that actual spirits live in the masks. I told him I didn't believe that spirits live in masks, but even so I don't go near the masks if I'm alone, or at night. I hurry past the middle of the store and join Kweli at the very back, where he's deep in conversation with a large woman with workman's hands.

Sensing that I'm beside him, Kweli says, "And this is Habo, the boy I was telling you about. He's becoming quite a carver himself."

"Hmph," says the woman. "Just what we need, another carver." Then she turns to me and her tone softens. "It's nice to meet you, Habo. I'm Zubeda, and I share this shop with Kweli and five others."

This is a surprise to me. "So many of you?" I ask.

"*Ndiyo*, seven. One for each day of the week," she answers. "That way we each take a day here, selling, and the rest of the week we can spend at home, working."

I can see the logic in that and I say so.

"It's a good system," she agrees. "Which reminds me, Kweli, I sold another one of your statues today. Do you want your part of the money now or later?"

"I'll take it now, if it's all the same to you," says Kweli. "And the boy has a box with some more little pieces of mine. You can put them anywhere you'd like."

As the two of them settle up, I wander around the store again, finally not worried about bumping anything with that great box on my head. The shop is narrow, and the aisles between the statues are even narrower, so I walk carefully. I don't want to damage anyone's work or offend Zubeda. Within a few minutes, Kweli and Zubeda walk out to join me where

I'm standing at the front of the shop.

Just then, a large group of tourists enters the market. So many white people at the same time! There must be over thirty of them. They start to flock and scatter like birds, picking through the art laid out before them. Vendors jump to their feet and start speaking to them in English, encouraging them to come in and buy from their shops. I suddenly see how rare it must be for any one shop to make a sale. With so many shops all selling the same thing . . . I look over at Kweli, understanding why he lives so simply.

Zubeda steps out into the central square and starts to talk to the tourists, trying to get them to come into our shop, but it doesn't work until one of them sees me.

"Oh!" he cries, and jabbers to his friends loudly over his shoulder.

About fifteen of them come over toward us in a group. I start to sweat, feeling cornered by the cluttered shop behind me. *What do they want with me?*

I back into the shop. The group follows me. I put a hand out onto a five-foot-tall statue of a giraffe to steady myself. A flash of bright light momentarily blinds me. I hold my hand over my face.

Suddenly, Zubeda is at my side.

"Smile!" she hisses at me in Kiswahili. She puts one arm around my shoulders and picks up a statue of a boy in the other. I smile.

The flashing camera lights go wild. Then Zubeda shepherds me out through them, dropping me by Kweli in the entryway.

She turns around and gets to work on the fifteen tourists now inside her shop. By the time she joins us ten minutes later, she has made three sales.

"I tell you, Kweli, this boy is good luck!" she crows as she waves to the tourists.

I don't know how to feel. Part of me wants to be sick all over Zubeda's feet. She's not the first to think I'm lucky, and the last time it nearly killed me.

Then again, as I see Zubeda counting out Kweli's share and handing it to him, I feel pretty good about myself. If those people hadn't been curious to see me, the shop wouldn't have made any money today. I kind of like that, instead of driving people away, my strange looks pulled people into Kweli's shop. It's a way that I, and only I, can give back to him for all the kindness he's shown me.

That said, my heart is pounding in my ears and the edges of my vision are light and fuzzy. I'm still not entirely sure I won't faint. I hate feeling trapped.

"Good," says Kweli. "That's over. Is that enough for you on your first day out?"

I am so grateful to him for understanding how overwhelmed I feel, my voice is shaky when I reply.

"*Ndiyo*. That's a good amount for today. I'm ready to go back to your compound if you are."

"*Sawa*," he says, and we go.

Within a week, I'm over my initial nervousness at leaving the compound and I no longer feel like I'm going to faint if people stare at me. I still don't like being cornered by a group, but now that I'm not afraid of people telling Kweli I'm an albino, I force myself to go out with him whenever he needs to run errands and when it's his day to sell at the market. *The quicker you learn to live in the city, the more likely it is that he'll let you stay with him,* I remind myself. So, day after day, I grit my teeth against the fear and walk out the big metal door in the wall with Kweli.

And, though I can't stop myself from looking over my shoulder for Alasiri or breaking into a sweat anytime I can't see at least a few ways to escape a room, I am slowly feeling more comfortable being out in the real world again. Even so, I still find ways to avoid calling my family. Having waited so long, it becomes more and more difficult to imagine what I'll say to them.

In this way, six more weeks pass and, with a roll of thunder, the short rains of November are upon us.

20.

THIS MORNING when I wake up with the first rays of light and start clattering around the kitchen getting breakfast together, Kweli doesn't join me right away. Oddly, he still hasn't gotten up by the time I've finished cooking our morning porridge.

"*Bwana!*" I call into the house, "*Bwana*, breakfast is ready!"

"You go ahead," answers Kweli. "I'm going to sleep a little longer today."

I'm puzzled by this response, but I don't pass up the opportunity for a little extra breakfast. Even so, I make sure I leave enough so that Kweli's bowl doesn't look *too* small. But when I'm finished eating and Kweli still hasn't come out, I begin to get concerned. I carry his bowl inside to his bed.

"Are you feeling all right, *Bwana*?"

"I think, Habo, that I will stay in bed today."

I set the bowl by the head of his bed, in easy reach in case he wants it.

"Are you sick, *Bwana*?" I squint in the dim indoors. "Should I go for the doctor?"

"No, no," comes the reply. "I just don't feel very well. I think it's something I ate yesterday not agreeing with me. A day of resting will be all that I need."

Something suddenly occurs to me. "But it's Friday!"

There is a low groan from the bed as Kweli processes this information.

"You'll have to go into Mwenge without me," he says finally. "I don't have the energy to go in myself, and it is not fair to the other artists if the shop isn't open at all. Can you do that?"

I look at him and think about saying no, but Kweli has spent so much of his time helping me that I pause. *Anyway, I reason, you've been out in the city for weeks and nothing has happened to you worse than some awkward stares and comments. Surely you can do this for Kweli.*

"*Ndiyo*," I say, and I see Kweli relax into the pillows. I'm glad that I made this choice. "That's no problem. I'll run the shop for the day as best I can, and I'll see you tonight in time to make dinner."

"Thank you, boy," he says, and drifts off to sleep.

I wake him once more before I leave to make him drink some water and show his hand where to find the extra water and food I've placed by his bed. As I walk out the door alone, I try to convince myself that we'll both be fine today.

I heft the crate of statues onto my head and follow the road into town. The early morning light is murky but the air is cool against my face. My hat is stacked on top of the crate and I have my sleeves and trouser legs rolled up because the sun isn't high yet. I like the way the dust covers my fish-meat-colored toes as I walk. I feel a twinge of unease deep in my stomach about heading into town alone, but I brush it away with the dust.

I get to Mwenge without incident, knowing the way by heart now, and I say hello to the other artists and answer their questions about why I'm coming alone and where Kweli is.

"He's taking a day to rest," I tell them. "He wasn't feeling well this morning, but I'll mind the shop today and he'll be better tomorrow. There's nothing to worry about." But rather than convince myself that he'll be feeling better by the time I get back, repeating that Kweli is okay over and over actually makes me afraid that, instead, he will worsen.

I open the shop with Kweli's rusty key and stretch the blue tarp between the poles. I unpack the statues from the box and put them out in front. Kweli always says to Zubeda, *Oh, put mine anywhere,* but I've noticed that the statues out front are more likely to be bought than the ones that someone has to go into the store to find. Also, the quality of what's in front is what will or will not pull someone into the store to look more. Whenever we're here alone, I always put Kweli's statues out in front.

The first day I came to the market with Kweli, I had trouble imagining that anyone would spend such a sum of money on a piece of wood, no matter how beautiful it was. But people did. Some bought Kweli's work because they fell in love with its smooth lines and deep meanings, others because they were fascinated by the idea of owning something made by a blind sculptor. When I grumbled about one customer who had said, "Oh, give me anything," after peppering Kweli with prying questions about being blind, Kweli had just smiled at me and shown me the roll of shillings in his hand. "I carve because I love it," he said. "I'm allowed to keep carving because I sell them, to whomever will buy. An obnoxious man's money buys me just as much food and materials as a pleasant man's. Remember, Habo, even a great artist has to eat."

Since then I've bitten my tongue whenever I've wanted to snap at a potential buyer and tried to imagine them as a large roll of shillings, or a pot of stew, or a piece of new wood.

The morning passes slowly, and I keep myself busy dusting the statues and tidying up so I don't dwell on worrying about Kweli. I wish I'd brought my own carving with me. Kweli has me carving Change right now, and it's a mess of unexpected angles and climbing vines. If I had it with me it'd be complicated enough to take my mind off things, but in my worry about Kweli I forgot it this morning. I can see in my head exactly where it must be on my mat, but that just makes me more annoyed, so I try not to think about it.

Whenever I hear someone's voice turn from a normal conversation into a high-pitched sales voice, I hurry out front because that means that a potential buyer has come to the market. I stand there and use the one bit of English, Spanish, French, German, Chinese, or Japanese that Kweli has taught me to memorize: *Hello good sir/madam, please come look in my shop. We have many nice things.* The rest of the transaction can be completed with smiles and fingers and numbers written down, but the greeting, Kweli says, must be in the person's home language. Sometimes it's difficult to guess which is the right language to use, so I cycle through whichever seem likely, one after another.

Though a few people stop by to stare at me, and one even goes so far as to walk around the shop and pick things up, no one buys anything from me all morning.

I eat my packed lunch in the blue-tinted shade of our awning, sweating in the November heat, worrying about how Kweli's doing and wondering how I'm going to spend the rest of the day. It's still many hours before sunset, when I can close up without it seeming like I'm not doing my job.

People wander in and out of the market, but no one comes into my shop. Is it because of me? I think about being more aggressive and talking to people, but I still have trouble calling that much attention to myself. Whenever more than a few people start to stare at me, I break into a cold sweat and want to find a place to hide. Maybe I should just go back to the compound. Kweli's an old man. Should I have gone and told Chatha right away instead of coming to the market and leaing him alone? I chew my lip and worry whether she will think I've broken my promise to keep Kweli well.

Then suddenly there's a change in the light, and I look up to see great dark clouds rolling in from the horizon. I've never been so glad to see rainy-season storm clouds in all my life.

Already the cry has gone up and everywhere people are scurrying around, packing up their wares and getting them under a roof before the storm hits. *Perfect!* If this storm is as bad as it looks, no one will think twice about my packing up. It has nothing to do with being an albino if I close the shop. It has everything to do with being a good businessman: Tourists do not shop in the rain, and only a poor seller leaves his wares out to be ruined in a downpour.

Stifling my grin of gratitude, I start bringing the statues in and lining them up inside the shop. It takes me a while because I have to be careful to leave at least enough room for the next carver to get in tomorrow morning, and by the time I'm hauling in the last big pieces by the door the rain has started to make big fat plopping sounds against the blue tarp. I look around the market. Most everyone has been able to move faster than me, and the majority of the shops are bolted up tightly. I'm tempted to leave the tarp up and just go, but that would be irresponsible. If it was ripped or blown away by a high wind, I'd never hear the end of it from Zubeda and, worse, Kweli would probably have to pay to replace it out of his earnings. I ignore the quickly emptying market and the curling, purple-gray sky and hurry to untie the tarp and bundle it inside. By the time I'm done folding it, it's raining heavily.

A crack of lightning makes me start, and I grimace ruefully. This will not be a pleasant walk home. If Kweli weren't sick, I'd stay here and wait it out, but I can't shake the feeling that he might need me, and so I lock the shop and head out into the pouring rain.

✻

Within seconds I'm soaked to the skin. I throw the piece of cardboard I was using as an umbrella by the side of the road; it's useless. When I get to the gate, I open it and slosh my way wetly through the front yard. Ahead of me I see the lights on in the house, which is nice, but unusual. When Kweli's home alone, he doesn't waste lamp oil. Which means that someone must be visiting. I feel better at once, glad that Davu, or maybe Chatha, has spent the day with him when he wasn't feeling well.

Since no one has called out to me, the storm must have covered the noise of my coming into the compound, and I decide to sneak around back instead of going through the front door to see if they're talking about me. It's a low impulse on my part, but it saves my life. Because when I sneak inside and peek around the doorway separating the kitchen alcove from the living space, I see that the person that Kweli is having tea with is not Chatha or Davu.

It's Alasiri.

✻

As quickly as it came, the November downpour ends. The high winds clear the last remaining clouds from the sky, and I'm trapped in the kitchen in the sudden silence left in the storm's wake.

He's here.

How is he here?

Is he here for me?

My thoughts tangle and jumble together in my dread.

Run! screams the voice in my head, and oh, do I want to run! Images flash through my memory, tinged gray and red: Alasiri digging his knife into the elephant's head, pulling its ears off. Alasiri staring me down, waving his knife and talking about my hair, my hands, my legs, like they weren't all attached to me. Escaping from Alasiri through the deserted streets of Mwanza. Alasiri, filling my vision as I run toward him, desperate to reach a train door that will mean my life one way or the other. The images swirl around me like a poisonous fog, and I have to shake my head to clear enough space to think.

Because I must think. I have to know why he's here, in Kweli's house. How he found me. Why Kweli, someone I've trusted completely, is calmly drinking tea with the man who is trying to kill me. I have to know these things in order to know what to do. And so, though my muscles are cramping and I'm sweating in terror, I lean forward, shielded by the counter, and listen.

". . . so, thanks to the new demand from China, the ivory trade is alive and well again," Alasiri is saying. "I'll provide you with the materials and arrange all of the transportation. All you would have to do is carve the pieces to the specifications from my buyers."

"I am afraid, young man"—the voice from the other room is Kweli's now—"that my answer is final. I will not do this thing for you."

"And I'm not sure, *Bwana*, that you understand just how much money I'm offering you. With very little effort on your part, we will both be rich very quickly."

"Kanu," says Kweli, "what money I do need I am happy to earn legally, even if that is the slow way."

This comment is greeted by a chuckle from Alasiri.

"Very well." I hear the scraping of a stool across the floor. "I can see you're decided."

"Yes, indeed."

"Then, since the rain has stopped, I will leave you to your evening plans, and I will go pursue mine. Shall I help you clear the tea things into the kitchen?"

My mind races. I'm completely exposed. There's no way that Alasiri wouldn't see me if he came into the kitchen. *Please, Kweli,* I beg in my mind, *please be too polite to let him clean up his own dishes!*

"No, no," I hear Kweli's voice say from the other room. "Just leave them there. I'll finish up my tea and put them away when I'm done. My assistant should be back soon anyway, and perhaps he would also like some. Go ahead and leave everything where it is."

"Very well," says Alasiri. "I'll just put down my cup."

Every muscle in my body tenses as I hear his footfalls cross the few steps between the table and the kitchen. My brilliant hiding place doesn't seem so brilliant anymore. I'm positive that he's going to see me and finish the job he started months ago, halfway across the country.

I look up and see a long-fingered hand with an expensive wristwatch and a finely tailored cuff reach over the half wall and set a tin cup down on the counter over my head. I wonder what—or who—had to die so that he could afford clothes like that.

I stop breathing and wait, the way a hare watches a hyena crouch when it's not yet sure if it has been seen. The hand pulls away, and I hear Alasiri's voice get fainter as he heads back toward Kweli.

"If you ever change your mind, *Bwana,* you can reach me by leaving a message for Kanu at Azize's guesthouse in Mikocheni. I'll get the message and come again."

Mikocheni! That's only one neighborhood over from Mwenge, where I was standing outside all day long, by myself, selling statues. Sweat is running down my forehead into my eyes even though the evening isn't hot, and it wraps me in the sticky-sweet smell of fear.

I hear the scrape of Kweli's stool and the tap of his cane finding the floor. Their voices get fainter as they both head out the front door toward the gate.

"Thank you, young man, but I do not think that is likely to happen. I wish you a good day."

"*Kwaheri,* then."

"*Kwaheri.*"

I slide to the floor in relief that I haven't been seen, my legs no longer able to support me. In the distance I hear the clanging of the metal door, and I allow myself to breathe again. But my breath comes in short, tight gasps.

Alasiri has again found my home. The wonderfully safe feeling I've treasured inside the high walls of Kweli's compound is gone, replaced by a feeling as narrow as the corn cave, pressing in on me. Whether or not it's to do business with Kweli, I'm sure that at some point Alasiri will return to try to make quick money with my death.

What do I do now?

He's here, in the city. He has developed a taste for fancy clothes. No matter what way I turn this about in my head, I can come to only one conlusion. Some day soon, Alasiri will come hunting me. Again.

When Kweli gets in from closing the gate, it's the sound of my panicked, gasping breaths that lead him to find me, curled in a ball on his kitchen floor.

21.

"SO YOU'RE TELLING me that this man who was just here, Kanu, is really Alasiri?"

I'm sitting across from Kweli, wrapped in blankets to stop my shivering, sipping tea that is still warm from when it was served to the man who tried to kill me.

"*Ndiyo*," I manage, between chattering teeth. "He was looking for me, and now he's found me. I just know it."

Kweli is silent for a moment while he considers this. My thoughts chase each other in circles, circles that make no sense. One minute I've resolved to be gone from the city by first light; the next I've decided never to leave the compound again. Why, *why* did Alasiri have to come here and ruin the best thing I've ever had? The unfairness makes me want to scream. But the part of me that feels hunted again doesn't want to make any noise at all. I stay silent.

Kweli sighs.

"I didn't like him when I thought he was simply a dealer

in illegal ivory. I like him even less now. I'm sorry for inviting him into my house! Imagine if you had been here!"

I have been imagining it. I've been trying to block those images out of my mind. But, as the hot tea fills my stomach and the blankets pull the dampness of my wet clothes away from me, I feel myself thawing inside, coming into myself again. I remember why I was so eager to get home in the first place.

"*Bwana*, how are you feeling?" I'm more than happy to change the subject of our conversation. I can't process this threat right now.

Kweli gives me a rueful smile. "I spent all morning in the outhouse. I don't know what it was that I ate, but it didn't agree with me."

"Well," I say, "I'm glad it wasn't anything more serious."

"Yes, yes, that's true," says Kweli. "But having to make tea and talk to that man who showed up at my door uninvited . . . well, I'm quite tired now."

I look more closely at Kweli in the lamplight. His cheeks seem a little sunken, and his hands are shaking slightly. I try to remember a time when I had diarrhea as a child.

The memory catches me by surprise, as do the feelings that come with it. I had been very young then, still too young to go to school, and I was very sick. Enzi and Chui had left for school. Asu, though she hesitated at the door and told me she'd hurry home, had left too. I had tossed and turned, shivering and sweating by turns on my pallet in the corner, not wanting to bother Mother because, even then, I had the sense that I was the reason for her sadness. Which is why I was surprised to wake up later and find that she had left her chores and was holding me as I slept.

I had startled awake and then relaxed again quickly, so happy to be in her arms that I pretended to fall asleep again so she wouldn't leave. And she didn't. She sat there, braced against the mud wall of our house, with my head and shoulders propped on her lap as she swabbed my forehead, neck, and shoulders with a damp cloth. She spooned salted honey-water into my mouth and she sang to me. Her songs weren't real, but just a one-sided conversation that she put into music. *This water will bring your fever down, rest now, rest now. Soon you'll feel better, little son. Sleep now, heal now.* Her voice wasn't very good, but I didn't care, and I still don't. When I woke up again it was Asu beside me and Mother was working, not looking at me, but I know I didn't dream it. Neither of us ever brought it up, but I held that moment close whenever Mother turned away from me in the years since.

Thinking about that day, I get up and find the honey jar that Chatha and Davu left with us. I pour a fresh cup of the nearly cool tea and stir a large spoonful of the honey into it along with a pinch of salt.

"Here, *Bwana,* drink this."

When Kweli has finished the tea with honey, I suggest he lie down. Soon he's asleep. This is good for Kweli, because I'm sure that liquids and rest are all he needs to make him feel better, but it's bad for me, because now I'm left with nothing to do but clean up the teacups and think about Alasiri.

I have to get out of here, I think as I rinse the cup he drank from. The scar on my arm stretches as I reach to place the cup on the sideboard, a flat pink line that whispers up at me about death.

For the past few months I feel like I've been looking over my shoulder, afraid. And now Alasiri has found me again. He must have asked around the market, found out about Kweli's albino apprentice. And even if he wasn't here for me, he's sure to try and find out more about Kweli and *then* he'll know I'm here.

I walk over to where I've been sleeping to pack my things, but I find that my hands aren't willing to move in the way that I tell them to. Instead, I find myself squatting there, staring at the woven blanket Kweli gave me for my bedroll, my carving knife with its sweat-soaked handle that fits my fingers perfectly, my fraying long-sleeve shirts and floppy hat. I sit and stare, *thinking* about packing them, but not doing it.

Why can't I make myself do it? I angrily reach up and brush the wetness off my face. *Alasiri has found your home,* I remind myself. *This is just like Mwanza.* I force myself to start rolling up my blanket. *Just like Mwanza, just like Mwanza* echoes in my head as my hands work. But by the time I'm done with the blanket, I've stopped again. Because this is *not* just like Mwanza. In Mwanza, I was hidden away and I couldn't do anything. I wasn't even really a person. Here, I've talked to people, worked in the market, helped Kweli.

I look over to where he's sleeping and see that his breathing is deep and even.

Yes, I've done things here that I couldn't do in Mwanza. I've been someone I couldn't have been in Mwanza. Been someone, period.

It doesn't matter, you have to leave. Is being someone worth dying for? asks the voice in my head.

To my surprise, the answer to that question is not as clear as it should be. Of course I don't want to die, but for the first time in my life, I *have* a life.

A clunk pulls me into the present. I look down to see what made the noise and find a piece of wood that I've knocked over resting against my foot.

I remember when Kweli gave it to me. It was weeks ago, just a few weeks after I had started to help him tend the shop at the market. It was a day in mid-October when I was having trouble getting my family off my mind and I had rattled around the shop like the seeds in a dried gourd, unable to sit quietly or do anything useful. Kweli had listened to me pace and mutter for a while, but then headed into the storage room behind the shop and returned with this piece of a branch. About as long as my arm and twice as thick, it was covered in an uneven bark. It was not a wood I had ever carved before. Kweli rested his hand lightly on my head.

"I bought this for you a little while ago, but it's a difficult wood to work with, and I've been saving it. I think that the challenge may be just what you need now."

"What kind of wood is this?" I had asked.

"It's ebony wood." I caught a flash of one of Kweli's smiles. "It reminded me of you."

I remember looking at the branch in my hands. It reminded him of me how? I'm dense? Rough? Ugly? Scarred? Rare? I gave up.

"How does the wood remind you of me, *Bwana*?"

Kweli chuckled. "You'll see" was all he had said, and he had gone off to tend to a customer. I had put the branch in my bag, determined to figure out its mystery some other time, but had brought it home and promptly forgotten about it because Davu had been waiting for us and I got distracted talking to her. Then, since I hadn't yet finished my "Change" sculpture, I continued to work on that, and by the time I was done, I had forgotten about the ebony.

Now, as I squat here in the dark trying to decide whether to leave or stay, I suddenly have to know why Kweli gave it to me.

I pick up my blade and gently shave away the gray-green bark. I give a small snort of annoyance when I see what's underneath. Of course it reminded him of me. The wood is white. I sigh against the disappointment of having become a white boy in Kweli's mind, too, and think about what I might carve with it. This was the first time Kweli gave wood without telling me what he wants. I think he wanted to see what I'd come up with myself.

For a while I do nothing but sit there, cradling the wood like a puppy in my arms, trying to force myself to think like a sculptor, but worrying instead about the problem of Alasiri. And then it comes to me. The last statue I had given Kweli was a picture of the evil I knew. Now it's time to balance that out with the good I know. Especially if I'm about to leave Kweli forever, I can at least do that much to show him his kindness wasn't wasted.

I heft the wood again and start to carve the outlines of my plan. I'm surprised by how hard the wood is. I remember Kweli's story of when he was a young man, telling me how he tried to force art out of the *mpingo* wood. Now I know what he means. I've never had to wrestle so hard with wood myself until now. It wrestles me back.

I'm digging into the white wood with the blade, unearthing the general shape of my statue, when my knife slips and pulls out a deep wedge. I look down at the chunk, baffled. The wood is no longer white.

I turn the ebony branch over in my hands, looking at it from all angles for the first time, and there, at the bottom where the branch was cut away from the tree, I can see the wood for what it really is. Once you get past a thin outer ring of whiteness, the wood is a deep, pure black all the way to the core.

It reminded me of you, Kweli had said.

I smile.

I lay my knife against the ebony branch and work until my head slumps onto the table and the knife slips out of my hand onto the floor. I don't even realize I've fallen asleep until I wake up the next morning with the sun shining in my eyes and a dent in my face from where it has pressed up against the black branch all night.

Rubbing gently at my cheek, I know what I have to do, I'm

just not brave enough to do it.

❋

I'm stirring the porridge, which I've made thinner than usual so that it'll be easier for Kweli to eat, when he shuffles out of the house and joins me by the fire. He sits heavily on his stool, still tired from being ill yesterday, but his cheeks are no longer sunken.

"Good morning, *Bwana*."

"Good morning, Habo. Thank you for all your help yesterday." His tone is stiff. He seems uncomfortable.

"*Karibu*," I say. "It wasn't a problem."

"I don't . . ." Kweli pauses, struggling to finish his sentence. I stir the porridge and wait. "I don't like having to get help from people," Kweli finally admits.

I think about it, think about how cranky Kweli gets when Chatha tries to do too much for him.

"I understand," I say, wanting to show him I do. "My sister used to do everything for me: make sure I dressed right and stayed out of the sun; made sure I had only easy chores and bigger food servings. She'd even fight with my brothers for me." Chui's sullenness toward me suddenly makes more sense as I say this.

"Sounds like you had two mothers," Kweli says with a smile.

"*Ndiyo*. I liked it as a kid. It made me feel safe. But I never realized how good it feels to take care of myself until I came here." I think for a minute. "I wouldn't ever want to go back to having someone do everything for me. It's like . . . I don't know."

"It's the best way to remind others, and yourself, that you are not a child or an invalid."

"Exactly!" I say.

"You do understand." Kweli smiles. I see the tight lines around his mouth relax again. "Perhaps that's why it's not as difficult for me to accept help from you. Either way, though, *asante*. It was nice to not be sick alone."

"*Karibu*," I say again, and hand him his breakfast.

For a few minutes we sit there quietly, eating and listening to the mumble and whir of the city waking up outside the walls. Enjoying the light breeze while it lasts.

Then Kweli says, "We need to talk about my visitor from yesterday."

The thin porridge turns into a brick in my belly.

"*Ndiyo*." I sigh. "We do."

"With this man, this Alasiri, loose in the city," Kweli goes on, "I don't think you should go anywhere alone."

"Should I stay here, inside the compound?"

"What do you think?" asks Kweli, the early morning light glinting off the white in his hair, reminding me how old he is.

"I don't know," I say. "I'm afraid if I go out into the city again, Alasiri will find me. I don't know if it's safe for me to go to the Mwenge market anymore if he's staying in Mikocheni."

"No," Kweli agrees. "It's not worth your life."

I don't say anything to this, because what my life is worth

is the very question I've been turning over and over in my head. I've been told that I'm priceless. I've been told that I'm worthless. Which, if either, is true?

"Then again," I go on, "now that he knows where you live, he could come back any time. It would be easy for him to find out you have an albino boy living with you. We haven't made any secret of that for a while."

"Then we mustn't leave you here alone, either."

I pause, not sure how to say what I know I have to say.

"*Bwana*, I don't think I can stay here with you very much longer. I mean . . . I want to, but I don't think I should. Especially if he has his knife." I sigh and then finish. "If I stay here, neither of us is safe."

"You should call your family," Kweli growls, but without much force. I've been putting him off for so long that I don't think he really expects me to say yes anymore.

"That won't help," I say. "Besides, why worry them? I'll call them when Alasiri isn't a danger to me anymore."

"Let me think more about the problem." Kweli sighs. "There must be some way we can keep you safe."

I doubt I'll ever be safe. But it makes me feel warm inside that, even when given the best reasons in the world, Kweli has not chosen to send me away.

"Perhaps, *Bwana*," I say. "Perhaps."

✳

For the rest of the day, every time I hear the slightest noise from the street, I feel all the old fear wash up inside me like an electric tide, but this time I refuse to let it close over me. *You need to stop this*, I tell myself sternly, and I force myself to practice being calm, even as I count the things around me that could be used as weapons if I have to fight for my life.

The ugali pan is heavy and hot.

A statue could be thrown or used as a club.

The lit firewood could burn and bruise.

The day passes slowly, since Kweli is too tired to work. He sits at his workbench quietly, working on a small project. He finished "Justice" weeks ago, and it was instantly bought by a judge for his office. However, now he's not working on the next big statue he started, "Resentment." I'm slightly curious to know what it is he's working on, but I don't go over to see what it is.

Since Kweli doesn't have any chores for me, I make good progress on my statue. The wood is hard, but I don't take any shortcuts to make it easier to carve. Instead, I use all the nervous energy I'm feeling and go about carving it the slow way, waiting to make sure that Kweli is completely better before I discuss my crazy idea with him.

I struggle with my carving, using the muscles in my arms and shoulders to pull off the extra wood. The shape of a young woman lifts up out of the branch. My knuckles ache as I force detail into the hard wood. She balances a tall jug of water on her head. The material of her *khanga* curves, showing she's walking. I rub my eyes. They have to be clear for me to finish her. She turns around slightly as she walks, reaching one arm behind her, as if she's waiting for a small boy to catch up.

As evening falls, I finish my statue. Asu smiles back up at me from my hands.

I look up and see that Kweli is putting a pot of water on the fire for *ugali* and realize that he must be done, too. I walk over to the fire to help him prepare the dinner.

"Oh, hello, Habo," says Kweli. "How was your day?"

I'm proud of how my statue turned out, because the wood was so difficult to work with, but I don't want it to seem like I'm bragging, so I just say, "I worked on a statue all day, *Bwana,* like you did. It's done now."

"Ahhh," says Kweli, nodding his head in understanding, "Yes, it can sometimes be like that. The whole world fades away and there is nothing but you and the dream you're putting into the wood."

I smile. That's a nice way to put it.

"*Ndiyo.*" I stir the cornmeal, slapping it against the sides of the pot, waiting for the *ugali* to get to the right consistency. "It was like that."

Kweli sniffs the air appreciatively. "It smells like the *ugali* is done, too."

For a few minutes the final clatter of getting the bowls and serving out the stiff cooked cornmeal wedges and vegetables is enough to claim our attention. But once we've settled down with our bowls, Kweli asks to feel the statue I've carved. I get up and fetch it for him.

"Go ahead and eat," he says, and takes it from me.

As Kweli runs his fingers over my statue, seeing it, I pinch off pieces of the cornmeal and chew them slowly, giving him time to think.

Finally Kweli looks up and asks, "What have you carved?"

I know better than to say it's my sister. That would've been my answer when I was only a boy carving things in easy wood. But Kweli has given me ebony to work with, and he said that I had the heart of a sculptor.

"It's 'Love,' *Bwana*."

"It's very simple."

I am not sure if that's an insult or a compliment, so I just explain the best I can.

"When you're small, small things are big. Asu always showed me that I mattered to her as much as the rest of my family. Waiting for me to catch up when she walked to and from the river told me that I was just as good as my other brothers." I shrug my shoulders even though he can't see me. "She always loved me."

"It's quite good," he says, handing her back to me. "The next time I go to the market, I'll see if I can sell it." I snap my head up and look at him. Kweli has never offered to sell one of my pieces before. A deep feeling of pride swells inside my chest. And yet, for some reason, I hesitate to say yes. I run my hand over Asu's carved face.

Into the silence, Kweli adds, "Even sculptors have to eat, Habo," and I know he's right.

"*Ndiyo. Asante sana* for being willing to sell my work with yours."

"*Karibu.*"

We sit there in silence for a few moments while I mull over Kweli's offer, wondering whether this means he might be willing to become his official apprentice, when Kweli clears his throat. I glance up and study his face. He seems embarrassed! I've never seen Kweli look anything but confident, sometimes even bossy.

"Yes, *Bwana*?" I manage, trying not to laugh.

"Hrm. Yes, well, I have a carving to show you, too."

Now it's my turn to be surprised. I squint across the darkening yard. "Resentment" still hulks, unfinished, in the far darkness. This must be one of Kweli's little statues, maybe the one I saw him working on today.

"*Sawa*," I say.

"Here." Kweli thrusts something toward me. I reach out reflexively and take it, feeling the weight of it before I can see its shape. It's the head and shoulders of a person, slightly longer than my hand, and I turn and hold it up to the fire to get a better look. For a moment, I don't realize what I'm seeing. And then I do.

When I was eight years old, I climbed the wild mango tree at the edge of the schoolyard. When I was more than twice my height off the ground, I fell and landed on my back. For a moment that seemed like forever I lay there, stunned, without the ability to pull air into my lungs. That feeling is the closest thing I've felt to how I feel now, looking at Kweli's statue.

Because his statue is me.

My eyes look out from either side of my nose, my mouth is open like I'm about to say something. My left ear is just a little lower than my right. It's the face that has stared at me from every puddle, car bumper, and windowpane my entire life.

But I am black.

Carved into *mpingo*, I can see the way I would look if I wasn't an albino. I've grown so used to the deep luster of Kweli's Makonde carvings that I had stopped noticing it as a color. But now I see. Put into blackwood, I'm like any other African boy. Holding my head in my hands, I understand that this is why Kweli had trouble understanding what I meant when I said I was an albino. Because, in his mind, this is what I look like.

I look at Kweli, who is still sitting on his stool stiffly, like he doesn't know what to do with his arms or knees.

"*Asante*," I whisper.

Kweli nods, not saying anything, and then gets up to put the dishes away.

I turn the statue over in my hands again. The boy stares back at me. There is nothing wrong with him. There is no reason he should have to hide, no reason he should be forced from his home.

I don't want to die. I won't be afraid anymore. I refuse to run.

I make my decision. Tomorrow morning, at first light, I'm going to go into the city and tell my story to the police and get Alasiri thrown into jail forever.

I get up and follow Kweli inside to tell him what I've decided to do.

22.

I GO TO BED convinced my decision is a good one. However, the longer I'm awake this morning, the more I question it. Who am I to walk up to a magistrate or a policeman? Will they even believe me? Or, like the police in Mwanza that did nothing about Charlie Ngeleja's murder, even if they do believe me, will they care?

I chew the inside of my cheek as I work. By the time we're heading out the door, I can taste blood.

"Ready?" asks Kweli. He had been delighted last night when I shared my plan with him. *Your safety is the most important thing,* he had said, over and over. He had even seemed slightly annoyed that he hadn't thought of it first, certain that the police could help us. That they would be willing to help us.

I'm not. The idea of going to the police terrifies me. The idea of meeting Alasiri again terrifies me. But the idea of losing Kweli, losing myself, terrifies me more than both of them combined.

"*Ndiyo*," I say. "Let's go."

We walk down the street to the *dala-dala* stand, just like we've done many times before, but somehow now it feels different. It's not just knowing that I'm again going toward Alasiri in order to try to get away from him. It's also because I've seen the way Kweli sees me, and I can't quite shake that image. Could I learn to see myself that way, too?

We get onto the *dala-dala* going into the center of town.

"Where should we go?" I ask.

"We should go to the central police station," Kweli answers. "I've never been there myself, but I think that will be the right place to go."

"Why not our local station?"

"Well, this is a big problem. I think we should go to the biggest police station, don't you?"

"I suppose," I say, feeling small.

I sit quietly beside him, watching the high walls and tall buildings whisk by my window. Soon the traffic is so bad, we're at a standstill. *Traffic is always bad in Dar es Salaam*, Kweli tells me. I mumble agreement and keep staring out the window.

I'm unsure if going to the central police station is the best idea, but I resolve not to back down. This is finally my chance to tell the truth and have it matter.

A while later, the *dala-dala* driver tells us we've arrived at Sokoine Drive. We get down carefully.

"Well, Habo?" asks Kweli. "Do you see the police station?"

I look up and down the road. This place feels familiar to me, and for a moment I can't place why. Then I see the looming hulk of the train station and I remember. This is where I began my journey in Dar es Salaam. I take a deep breath.

"I'm not sure, *Bwana*. Let's walk down the road a little and see if we can find it. The *dala-dala* driver said this was the right place."

"*Sawa*," says Kweli, and puts his hand on my shoulder. I know it's only because we're in an unfamiliar place that he needs the extra guidance, but having Kweli need me makes me braver.

"Let's start this way," I say, and head down the street to our left. Within half a block, we've found it. The tall white building is labeled in big letters even I can see, and there are policemen standing around outside. There's no way to be confused about what it is. My palms begin to sweat.

You can do this, I tell myself.

"*Bwana*, I think I've found it."

"Excellent!" Kweli has none of my misgivings. "Let's go in and see who we can talk to about your story."

I take a deep breath and lead Kweli toward the big painted doors. Walking through them, we step together into a shadowy, tiled entryway. There's a man in a khaki uniform sitting at a table to one side. He doesn't look up when we enter.

"Well?" prompts Kweli when I pause inside the door.

"There is a policeman at a table," I tell him. My voice carries in the open space. I shuffle forward, Kweli still attached to my shoulder.

"Excuse me?"

"Yes?" The man sounds annoyed.

"I . . . I . . ." *Get a hold of yourself! Do it!* "I have some information about a criminal who's in the city right now," I say.

The man gives me a long, cold stare and then runs his eyes over Kweli, too, taking in everything about us. Our inexpensive clothes. My white skin. Kweli's cane and unfocused eyes.

"What kind of information?" he asks.

"I—"

"We would really be more comfortable giving the information to a detective or a supervisor," Kweli cuts in smoothly over me. "I don't want to talk about what we know in an entryway."

The man glares at Kweli, but after a brief hesitation, gets up from the table.

"One moment," he says. I wait with Kweli, shuffling from one foot to the other, feeling braver by the minute. We haven't been thrown out on the street yet. A few minutes later, he comes back and says, "Follow me."

The policeman leads us down a passageway with many doors in it. He stops at one about halfway down and opens it for us. There isn't much in the room. A fat, cranky-looking man sits behind a scarred metal desk with a computer and a small lamp on it. A bookshelf and a single chair are the only other furniture. Everywhere there are piles of paper. I think it's to make the man look busy rather than because he's actually busy. The top papers on the pile by the window are yellow and curling up at the edges from being in the sun so long.

"Here they are," our policeman says to the man sitting be-hind the desk, then turns and walks away. He doesn't intro-duce the man, and I'm left wondering who it is we've just been led in to see. He must be a detective or a supervisor, though. His shoulder has three eight-pointed silver stars pinned on the khaki fabric. The policeman in the front hall only had one star.

"Well?" bellows the man. The buttons of his shirt strain across his belly when he talks. "Don't just stand there! Come in, sit down, and say what it is you have to say."

At his brash manner all my confidence vanishes. I remem-ber how no one cared about Charlie's murder and wonder why I thought it would make a difference for me to come here. I swallow and lead Kweli to the one chair in the room. I stand in front of the big man's desk, wiping my sweaty palms on the sides of my pants. There's a ripped map of the city on the wall by the window. I tell myself that the little holes in it are all crimes this man has solved to give myself the courage to start talking.

"My name is Habo," I say. I flick a glance up at the man, whose eyes keep floating over to his computer screen as he listens. I talk a little bit louder. "I would like to report a crimi-nal who is in the city right now. His name is Alasiri. He tried to kill me when we lived in Mwanza."

The man starts typing something on his computer. He talks to me sideways, over his shoulder.

"That's not my jurisdiction. That has to do with the police in Mwanza."

"But . . ." I say, trailing off. Auntie said the police in Mwanza wouldn't do anything. I'm beginning to wonder whether this is true of all the police everywhere. Thankfully, Kweli comes to my rescue again.

"This man is not in Mwanza now," Kweli says calmly. "He is here, in your jurisdiction. He was at my house yesterday."

The man holds up a finger—*wait*—and keeps typing.

"One moment," he mumbles.

For a few minutes, Kweli and I can do nothing but wait for the man to finish typing. In a way, I'm glad. It gives me a chance to think about what I can say to get this policeman to help us.

Yes, the crime I'm reporting happened in Mwanza, but I need to get rid of Alasiri *here*. I rack my brain, thinking of what I can say that will get him put in jail. Then it comes to me: Alasiri is also doing illegal things here in the city. I clear my throat. The man behind the desk looks up at me, annoyed. I don't wait for him to say anything, though, I just plunge forward.

"Alasiri is also doing illegal things here in Dar es Salaam. I met him when my family was crossing the Serengeti. I saw him take ivory tusks from an elephant there and then drive them to Mwanza province to sell. Yesterday he tried to get Kweli"—I wave a hand in his direction—"to carve tusks that he has brought into the city and plans to sell to China."

I finally have the man's attention. He takes out a notepad and starts scribbling furiously.

"That," he says, his shoulders rounding as he hunches over

his desk, "is very interesting. Was he working alone when he went poaching in the national park?"

"No, there were three other men with him, but I didn't get their names."

The man reaches into his desk drawer and takes out a sheaf of pictures. He pushes a handful across the desk to me.

"Were they any of these men?"

I have to hold the pictures up very close to my face in order to be sure. The big man curls his lip disgustedly when he sees this, but he doesn't say anything. I glance over at Kweli, re- membering the statue he made for me last night. *You have no reason to be ashamed,* I remind myself. *Just do what you came here for.*

I page through the photos slowly. Finally I pull a picture of a short man with a narrow, unpleasant face from the stack, put it on top, and hand all the pictures back to the policeman. I point.

"This one might have been there, but I'm not sure."

The policeman scribbles down more information, copy- ing the number printed on the bottom of the picture into his notebook. He's taking me very seriously now, and I feel my confidence pick up. After a moment he says, "Is there any- thing else?"

"*Ndiyo.*" I swallow, determined to make it clear to him that Alasiri has done something far worse than kill elephants. "When I was living in Mwanza, Alasiri was contacted by a *wa- ganga* who wanted to buy albino body parts. He came after me, broke into my auntie's home, and tried to kill me with a knife. I ran away, but he chased me . . ." I trail off because the man is no longer writing.

His eyes flicker to the corner of his desk. I see a small bundle sitting on the base of the desk lamp. It's wrapped in a piece of animal skin and tied with strips of red thread. I can't tell from here what animal the skin came from, but it's definitely a pouch of luck medicine. Seeing that my gaze has followed his, the policeman closes his meaty fist over the little pouch and pulls it into a desk drawer, out of sight.

My hands have started to sweat again. I look at the man, doing the best I can to focus on him as my eyes shake. He meets my eyes for a moment, then looks away. *He's ashamed,* I think. But knowing this doesn't make things better. I understand now why Auntie didn't think the police would do anything: If even the police believe in the magic of the *wagangas,* or are afraid of it, then of course they won't do anything. This big man in front of me, this policeman who could do so much good, is afraid of the *wagangas* just like I am.

I sigh.

He caps his pen. "Do you have anything else to say about the ivory?" he asks.

"No," I say.

The man turns to Kweli. "And you, *Bwana*? Will you make a statement about this man Alasiri and what he asked you to do?"

"Of course," says Kweli.

As Kweli describes his visit with Alasiri, I sink into myself, trying not to let my frustration pull me away from my main problem. Yes, this man cares more about ivory than my attempted murder, but if I want to keep my life as a carver here with Kweli, I need to find a way to get Alasiri thrown in prison. I decide not to leave until this sweaty, paunchy man assures me that this will happen.

"Habo?" Kweli's soft voice breaks into my thoughts.

"Yes, *Bwana*? I'm sorry, I wasn't paying attention."

"Habo, this man has asked me to describe Alasiri for the report. Could you do it?"

Now it makes sense to me why Alasiri went to so much trouble to try to convince Kweli to carve for him. Especially using a fake name, a blind man could never betray him to the police. He must have thought he was perfectly safe coming to Kweli and laying out his whole plan. After all, what description of him could Kweli give? The sound of his voice?

I turn back to the policeman.

"*Ndiyo*, I can describe him for your report. Alasiri is tall; a little bit handsome. He has medium-dark skin and a long face, with clear brown eyes set wide apart. Yesterday when we saw him he had short hair, no beard, and was wearing a new dress shirt and a fancy gold watch."

The man writes all this down.

"Thank you for your report, both of you. I will pass this description along to the police in Mikocheni, where you said he was staying, and the surrounding areas, and we'll see if we can catch him."

"And when you do catch him, what will happen then?" Kweli asks.

"Well." The man leans forward in his chair and scratches one ear. "We would bring him in, of course, and try to put him on trial, but—"

"But what?" I interrupt.

"Well, the testimony of a thirteen-year-old boy and a blind man . . . my apologies, but it might not be enough to convict him if he can afford a good lawyer."

I'm not happy with this. I know that Alasiri has come into money from the clothes he was wearing. I can't have him know that Kweli and I turned him in and not go to jail. It would be like inviting him to our house to attack us.

An idea occurs to me.

For a moment, I hesitate, frightened by the perfect craziness of what I'm about to suggest. Then I think about my carvings, about the bust that Kweli carved of me, about Davu, my first real friend, about the artisans in the market who have quietly accepted me as one of their own, and I take a deep breath.

"What kind of evidence would you need to guarantee a conviction?" Kweli is asking.

"What if," I break in, not waiting for the policeman to answer, "what if you personally, or one of your policemen, saw Alasiri walk into Kweli's home and give him some ivory to carve? Would that be enough to get him the maximum sentence?"

The man blinks at me in surprise.

"Well, yes," he says. "But I wasn't there yesterday." His eyebrows knot together angrily. "If you're implying that I falsify my report, young man—"

"No, no!" I say quickly. "That's not it at all. What I mean is, what if we could get him to come back and you could be there watching?"

"Now Habo, wait a moment," starts Kweli, holding up a hand toward me, but I'm too excited by my plan to slow down now.

"No, *Bwana,* think about it! Do you remember the last thing he said? Alasiri told you that if you changed your mind, you should leave a message for him!" I've started to pace in front of the policeman's desk as I talk. "You could leave a message, saying that you do want to do this and that he should bring the ivory to you in your home. But when he comes, there could be policemen hiding somewhere in the house and they could hear him tell you to carve it and then come out and see him with the ivory in his hands and they could arrest him." I am breathless with excitement. "What do you think?"

There is a pause as both men consider my idea. Finally: "I suppose that could work," says the man behind the desk.

I feel ready to jump up and down, shouting, but Kweli is shaking his head.

"If we do this thing for you," Kweli says, "what protections can you give us?"

"What do you mean?" asks the policeman.

"Well," says Kweli, "if we're going to use my house as a trap, then this criminal will absolutely know for certain that it was us who turned him in. What if you don't manage to capture him? Or what if he escapes? Or is released from prison? What will your department do to ensure our safety?"

"Hmmm." The man behind the desk strokes the sides of his face, considering. "Well, yes, I think we could do quite a bit to guarantee your safety." He ticks off the points on his fingers. "First, we'll keep an officer assigned to your house until this man is captured. If he escapes, we'll do the same. As for when he's released from prison, well, I can guarantee you that, if we can catch him in the act of trafficking illegal ivory, that will not be for a very long time. Our government is very committed to cracking down on the killing of protected species."

He says this with a smile, and though Kweli is nodding, I want to scream at the man. Why is he so proud of himself? He's happy about cracking down on the killing of elephants, but he doesn't care about the killing of people like me? Faintly I hear Kweli agreeing to the plan, but I am again sunk inside, angry and disappointed.

There is a flurry of paperwork that Kweli has to ask someone to read to us, and then we are outside the police station, on our way home to set a trap for a poacher.

23.

"I THINK," says Kweli when we're on the *dala-dala* headed for home, "that until we have a policeman safely hidden away in the house, you should stay with Chatha. If this man Alasiri comes back to my house to try to convince me again to work for him, I don't want you to be there."

I frown, not liking the thought of Kweli alone with Alasiri, but I eventually realize he's right: Alasiri has no reason to harm Kweli, and he still has a strong reason to harm me.

"*Sawa,*" I say. "That makes sense." I don't really feel like talking, still angry at the officer.

Kweli lets me stew for a few minutes longer, and then, facing straight ahead, he asks quietly, "Is there anything else you'd like to talk about?"

"All he cared about was the ivory!" I explode. "Well, what about me? What about my life? Doesn't that matter to anybody?"

"Of course it does," says Kweli. "It matters to you. It

matters to me."

His soft words make me feel bad for yelling. I heave a big sigh and face out the bus window again.

"I just hoped . . ." I say, more quietly this time. "I just wanted to have my story matter." I struggle for the words to go with what I want to say. "I wanted to be able to see justice. I wanted . . . I don't know what I wanted exactly."

Kweli waits.

"I wanted . . ." I can hear the tears roughening my voice but I refuse to let them out. I will not shame myself in public. "I wanted to matter more than the ivory." Kweli reaches over and pulls me into his chest. I swallow hard against the feelings crowding my throat. I expect Kweli to comfort me with hollow words, to tell me that I do matter more than ivory, of course I do, how could I even think that I didn't. But he doesn't.

Instead he says, "*Ndiyo*, of course you want that. You must never stop wanting that." He takes a deep breath and hugs me a little tighter. "I'm sorry that you learned today that not everyone will agree this is true, but you must never stop wanting it to be. There are people who aren't ready yet to see your worth, whole cities of them, whole countries of them, perhaps, but someday they will."

"When?" I ask brokenly.

"I don't know," says Kweli. "Some of us already do. Some may never. The most important person to see it is you."

I nod into his chest. This is exactly what I've been thinking about for the past few days. Kweli pushes me out to arm's length and rummages around in his pockets. I sit back against the seat and huff out a deep breath to steady myself.

Kweli pulls a bill out of his pocket. "Think of it this way," he says. "What's this?"

"Money," I say.

"It's a piece of paper," Kweli corrects. "What's it worth?"

I squint at the bill. It's orange, and I can vaguely make out a shape in the middle that might be a drawing of a lion.

"Two thousand shillings," I say.

Kweli reaches into his pocket again and pulls out a scrap of paper. He holds it up beside the bill. "What's this worth?"

"Nothing," I say. "That's just a piece of paper."

"Really? Tell me: Why is this piece of paper"—he flutters the money in my face—"worth two thousand shillings, and this isn't worth anything?"

It's such a stupid question, it takes me a minute to come up with an answer.

"Well . . . no reason really, I guess, but everyone knows that money is worth something. You could walk into any store and they would take it. It just *is*."

"It's worth something because everyone agrees it is worth something?"

"That's right."

"And otherwise it's just a piece of paper?"

"I suppose."

"Exactly," he says, smiling at me. "Everything only has the value we give it."

That's a big thought. Kweli lets it sink in a minute.

"So you're saying," I think out loud, "that people like me aren't valued right because we don't look like normal people?"

"Often that's true," says Kweli. "It's like you're a piece of paper money no one has seen before. People look at your color, at your features, and they aren't sure how to value you."

I take a deep breath. "I like that," I say, smiling. "A new piece of money."

Kweli smiles. "As long as you know your worth, other people will catch on eventually. You're a good person, Habo. A smart boy with a good heart. I've learned your worth. Davu and Chatha and the other artists in the market are learning it, too."

I take a deep breath. He's right. People here have treated me differently, but only when I stopped hiding in the shadows and let them really see me.

"Thank you, *Bwana*," I say. "I'll try to remember this."

Kweli reaches out and squeezes my shoulder one more time. Then he gets up and asks the *dala-dala* driver to let us out one stop early.

We get off and Kweli turns his face towards the setting sun.

"Come on," he says, feeling his way forward with his stick. "Let's go to Chatha's house."

When we get to Chatha's, I feel around the doorframe for a bell. Kweli said that Chatha married well and has a fancy modern house, but I don't find the button with my fingers and the afternoon shadows make it hard for me to see, so I give up and knock loudly.

"*Hodi hodi!*" I yell at the door. "*Mama* Chatha!"

Kweli smiles beside me. "I like the old ways better, too," he whispers.

I hear footsteps inside the house, coming closer. The door cracks open and a suspicious eye appears in the crack.

"What do you want?" asks Davu. Then, seeing us, the eye widens with surprise. "Oh, Habo! Great-Uncle! It's you."

There's a brief scraping sound as Davu unlatches the door and opens it for us. She's wearing a pretty yellow and green *khanga,* and now she has a big smile on her face. Chatha comes up behind her.

"Hello, Uncle," says Chatha. "Come in, come in."

"Hello, Davu. Hello, Chatha," Kweli echoes as we both shuffle into the hallway. "Habo and I have a favor to ask you."

After being led to a large living room and given tea, Davu and Chatha listen with great interest to Kweli's retelling of the past two days, and I have to tell the rest of my story to Chatha. They exclaim in alarm over Alasiri's reappearance in my life, and applaud our decision to go to the police. Chatha is not at all pleased when she hears about my plan, however.

"You're tempting this man into your house? Are you mad?" Chatha is waving her hands around in the air. Kweli isn't benefiting from that display of her anger, but he can certainly hear the tone in her voice as she shouts at him.

"It's a little risky, I admit," concedes Kweli. "But getting him arrested on strong evidence is the best strategy to keep us both safe in the future."

Chatha looks at me with narrowed eyes, and I imagine her weighing her uncle's safety against my own. I glance away, embarrassed that, in my attempt to stay here, I've brought danger to Kweli.

"And," continues Kweli, "this is the reason we've walked across town to see you. Until we have a policeman hiding at my house, I don't want Habo to come back to the compound. Now that Alasiri knows where it is, he could return at any time. It was sheer luck that he didn't see Habo the first time he came."

"Of course he should stay here," says Chatha definitively. I glance up, surprised. I didn't think she liked me, but looking at her now I see no dislike, only a fierceness that is directed at protecting me. Chatha heaves herself to her feet and stands behind me, one meaty hand pressing onto each of my shoulders, holding me down as if I was going to run out into danger that very moment. Davu winks at me from across the table, grinning. I give her a shaky smile back. "Habo will stay here with us," Chatha continues, "but I'm not about to let you go home alone with this crazed poacher-murderer on the loose!"

"Chatha, I have lived alone for many years and managed to survive all kinds of things you know nothing about."

"Nonsense! You're not spending tonight alone!" Chatha's

voice is climbing.

Davu winces, and I can see this turning into a classic Cha-tha-Kweli fight. I hurry to break in.

"*Bwana!*"

"What is it, Habo?" Kweli's face is twisted into a scowl, his white eyebrows low over his sightless eyes.

"Please, *Bwana*. You brought me here to be safer. I need to know that you'll be safe, too. Please let someone stay with you tonight."

Stubbornness and fondness chase each other across Kwe-li's face. Then he huffs out a loud breath and crosses his arms over his chest.

"Very well," he grumbles.

Davu's mouth drops open in surprise, and I feel Chatha's hands go very still on my shoulders.

"Well," Chatha says. Her voice is quiet again and a little shaky. "Well, good."

"So?" asks Kweli. "Who's the lucky winner? Who gets to spend the night with a cranky old blind man?"

I look around the room, unsure of who will be sent to keep him company. I'm clearly not allowed to, and Davu isn't a bet-ter choice. Chatha removes the doubt by declaring, "My hus-band will go with you. I'll feel better if you have another man around until the police show up. We'll be safe enough here. Yes, my husband will stay with you tonight."

Kweli gives Chatha a sly smile. "I knew, if I lived long enough, I'd finally find a use for that man!"

There is a split second of shocked silence, and then

everyone bursts out laughing.

Covered by the noise, Chatha leans forward and whispers in my ear: "*Asante sana*, Habo." She squeezes my shoulders to punctuate her words. I guess I can be a little useful even to Chatha.

"*Karibu sana*," I whisper back.

Her hands smell like pepper and limes. The weight of them feels good.

※

Later that evening, after a shared dinner around a big dining room table and some time for Chatha's husband to pack a bag for overnight, Kweli heads home, leaving me with Chatha, Davu, and Davu's three younger brothers.

I can't stop marveling at Davu's house. It's so grand: two stories tall, with big rooms, electricity, water taps in the bathrooms and kitchen, even an air-conditioning unit in Chatha's bedroom. It's by far the fanciest house I have ever been in. And, it turns out they don't share it with any other families. After helping Davu wash the dishes with a slippery liquid detergent and stack them in a side rack to dry, we head into the living room to sit on couches and watch her color television.

"Why are you so quiet?" asks Davu.

In reality I'm thinking about how rich Davu and her family are and remembering the one-room, dirt-floored house I grew up in. I run my fingers along the seam of the pattern on the couch and shrug my shoulders, not looking at her.

"Well, it's annoying," says Davu. "You should stop."

She walks over to the TV and starts turning the dial to get different channels. I'm fascinated in spite of myself. I've seen TVs in shops and through the glass windows of wealthy houses before, but I've never actually known someone who's owned one. I lean forward, watching the sound and color blink from one topic to another. There are funny moving drawings in very bright colors with squeaky voices, shows where people are winning prizes and money, shows with people sitting around talking, news, and—

"Wait!" I say, reaching out toward the TV. "What was that?"

"What?" asks Davu.

"What was that? What was on the channel you just switched from?"

Davu clicks back and makes a face. "Politics? You want to watch a report on parliament?"

"Wait," I mumble. "Leave it there for a minute."

Davu makes a disgusted noise but leaves the TV on the channel I asked for. I'm leaning off the very edge of my seat, tense, eager.

"Really, Habo! This is so boring. Why are we watching this?"

"Just wait . . . There!"

I jump off the couch and touch my finger to the screen. The camera obediently zooms in on the minister of parliament I was pointing to as it's her turn to talk. And there she is, her face filling my screen: the lady albino MP that Auntie told me about.

"Oh!" is all I hear behind me from Davu, but I don't turn

around because I'm so absorbed in staring at this woman on TV, looking at her features, hearing her voice. She is wrapped in a tan and red *khanga*, with a head scarf of the same fabric. She's wearing glasses. Her face looks like mine. Her eyes look like mine.

"Look," I whisper to Davu. "Look."

"She's just like you," murmurs Davu.

My heart explodes with happiness.

When Chatha comes downstairs, Davu pounces on her.

"Mama! Mama! We found a woman on TV, in the parliament, who's just like Habo. Come see!" And she pulls her over to where we were both crouching on the floor with our faces close to the screen.

"Get away from there!" says Chatha crossly. "You'll ruin your eyes."

Too late, I think, but I obediently scuttle backward onto the couch.

"She's not on right now," I say to Chatha, "because someone else is talking. Oh, and there's another one, too: a man. I just saw him when Davu went to get you."

"Mm-hmm," says Chatha, and I'm afraid she'll leave. For some reason it's really important to me that everyone see them. And then the woman is on the screen again, and Chatha leans forward and squints at her. *"Ndiyo,"* she says. And my heart soars.

Yes means this is real.

It's too late to go anywhere that evening, but Chatha promises Davu and me, as she forces us to go to bed, that tomorrow she'll take us to the National Central Library, where we can find out more about my MPs.

I lie on the soft bed in the room Chatha built for Kweli. It's small and clean and has it's own bathroom, and is so new it still smells like wet paint. I can understand why Kweli won't give up his freedom, even for all this luxury, but tonight I'm happy to enjoy it in his place. I sigh, contentedly, and stare at the ceiling.

I am a Tanzanian, I think. *I am an albino. I could work in parliament if I wanted to.*

And with these happy thoughts chasing one another around in my head, I fall asleep.

24.

THE NEXT MORNING I'm awake
with the first light. I get up and use the shiny tiled bathroom
with the hot and cold water taps on the sink, and then sit down
in the kitchen to wait for everybody else to wake up. I'm alive
with excitement. Today, Chatha promised, we're goimng to the
library and find out more. I have never in my life wanted so
much to know more than I do.

I kick the leg of the kitchen table with my bare foot softly,
impatient. I'm also slightly embarrassed, because when we go
to the library it will become very clear to everyone that I'm
no good at reading. But I want to know so badly that I hardly
even care about this. I'll blame my bad eyes, like always, and
I'll get someone to read the important things to me.

How will you know what's important if you can't read it? asks
an ugly voice in my head, but I ignore it.

I'm saved from thinking by a commotion from upstairs.
Within minutes Davu and her brothers come rampaging

into the kitchen. The seven-year-old and Davu pour cold cereal into bowls for all of us. The two youngest, four-year-old twins, come running at me. They remind me of Kito and I hug them tightly. I had originally expected the children to be afraid of me, but like their parents, sister, and great-uncle, they treated me normally.

The cold cereal tastes strange to me. It's very sweet and sits in a big puddle of milk. It doesn't fill your insides the way hot porridge or *ugali* does. But I don't want to complain. I eat the rich-people's breakfast and wash out my bowl in the sink with the wet detergent again, like the others.

It's a day off school, so it takes a while to get all the children dressed and out the door and over to a neighbor who is willing to watch them, but then Chatha, Davu, and I are on our way.

We don't take a *dala-dala,* but instead the three of us pile into a private taxi. I run my hands over the black plastic seats, hardly able to believe all the new things I'm getting to do in just two days.

Enjoy it while you can, whispers that same ugly voice in my head, *this may be the last time you go anywhere. Remember, Alasiri is in the city, hunting you.*

I swallow against the sudden tightness in my throat and sink down lower in my seat, farther from the window.

"National Central Library, Bibi Titi Mohamed Road," says Chatha, and the taxi weaves off into the Dar es Salaam traffic, taking me to my answers.

We pull up outside a soaring white building that looks like

it was built in layers. We climb the many steps to the front
door and walk inside. For a moment, I'm not sure what to
make of the space. There are study tables and large open
spaces, and people crowding both. The hurricane-glass windows are open to allow a breeze to come through the building,
and there are electric fans and bright lights hanging from the
white ceilings high above, making it easy to see. And everywhere: books! Shelves and shelves of books lining the walls.
So many books. I had no idea there were this many books in
all Tanzania, let alone in one library in Dar es Salaam. I turn
in slow circles, taking it all in.

"Habo!" Davu's voice breaks my spell. I see that she and
Chatha are across the foyer, in front of the membership reg-
istration desk. I hurry to catch up with them. I get there just
in time to see Chatha hand over some money.

"What's she doing?" I whisper to Davu.

"She's paying for us to have a day membership."

"How much does that cost?"

"One thousand shillings each," she answers. "Why are we
whispering?"

Just then, Chatha turns around. In her pudgy fingers she
holds two slips of paper.

"Now," says Chatha. "I have to run a few errands. Here are
your day passes." She hands them to us. "Stay in the building, don't go anywhere with strangers, and I'll be back in four
hours. Okay?"

"*Sawa*," says Davu, snatching her pass and twirling it
around in her fingers. I look up at Chatha, up the mountain

of well-fed, well-dressed woman to her round face. I look past the scowl and meet her eyes, wide-set and kind no matter how hard she tries to mask it, and think about how she has taken time out of her day, paid for a taxi, and now paid for two day memberships at the library, just because she knows it's important to me to find out more about something.

"*Asante sana,*" I say, still whispering out of habit.

Chatha smiles at me in a way that scrunches up her entire face. "*Karibu sana,* Habo. Go on."

"*Kwaheri,* Mama!" Davu waves and then grabs my hand and leads me away into the middle of the library.

We spend the first few hours of our time talking to people in reference, finding books about albinism and newspaper articles about my ministers of parliament. When Davu discovers that I'm bad at reading, she can't believe it.

"How did you not learn to read? Didn't you go to school?"

"I went to school," I mumble, looking away from her.

"And they didn't teach you to read?" she asks.

"They taught us to read," I say. "But they made me sit at the back and I couldn't see, so I never learned very well."

Davu is quiet for a moment. I sneak a peek at her face. Her eyes are clear, considering. Her mouth is a serious line across her face. I look away, ashamed.

"Oh, this is ridiculous," Davu huffs. She stuffs the newspapers and a large book we found under her arm, grabs my elbow, and hauls me toward one of the reference desks. "Excuse me!" she calls to the man working there. "I need a magnifying glass. Can you get me one, please?"

The man blinks at her in surprise for a moment and then smiles, promising to look for one for her. Davu and I stand there, waiting for him, Davu muttering to herself under her breath the whole time. I'm no longer entirely sure who or what she's angry at, so I just keep my head down and try to think about how to get away from Davu and the man at the desk. I had thought it might be awkward for Chatha and Davu to know that I can't really read, but I had no idea Davu would make such a big deal out of it. No one else has ever cared that I'm no good at reading. I scuff my feet against the floor.

"Can we go now?" I ask.

"No," says Davu, still looking after where the man has gone. She holds out the mess of newspapers to me. "Here, do something with these."

So I do. I carefully re-fold the newspapers and make them into an easy-to-carry packet while we wait. I tuck them into the large book.

Finally, the man shows up again, holding a square of plastic with a bulge in the middle.

"Here you go," he says, handing it to her.

"*Asante*," says Davu. "I'll bring it back soon." And grabbing me by the arm again, she grabs the big book with our newspapers in it and marches off in a new direction.

After a short walk, we arrive in a section of the library that looks different. The walls are painted a light green, all the furniture is low to the ground, and all the books are slim and brightly colored.

"This," says Davu, "is the children's room."

I flush bright red. I'm not a child! Why did Davu bring me here? Just because my reading isn't good doesn't mean that I'm stupid.

"I don't want to read anything in here," I say.

"We don't have to stay long," Davu says over her shoulder, already scanning the shelves. "I'm just looking for a simple book to see if you can read it using this." She waves the magnifying glass at me. I cross my arms and stand by the wall, wishing I could disappear. All the little kids in the room are staring at me. I pretend to be very interested in the shelf in front of me.

"Now." Davu is suddenly at my elbow. "Come over to a table and let's have a look at these."

I sigh and follow her. Maybe if I'm really nice and do everything she wants, she'll lose interest quickly in this project and we can go read the books we found about albinos. I sit in one of the small chairs at the table. Davu plops down beside me, a pile of thin books in her arms. She sets the big book off to one side and hands me one of the thin books and the square of plastic.

"What do you want me to do with this?" I ask.

"Hold it in front of the book and see if that makes it easier for you to see."

Scowling, I hold the square of plastic over one of the colorful children's books Davu has brought me. To my great surprise, the tiny text on the page leaps toward me, becoming as easy to see as the Vodafone and Airtel signs on the bus ride from Arusha.

I must have gasped because Davu giggles beside me. "Better?" she asks.

"I can see," I say, squinting at the page. "I can see the words."

"I thought so," Davu crows. "You just need glasses! Some of the boys in my class have glasses, you know. They're smart. You'll look good in glasses."

I pick at my fingers, not sure what to make of all this attention and the talk of glasses. Shyly, I hold the square of plastic up to my face and bend over the children's book again, trying to quietly sound out the sentence in my mind. A brown finger, magnified to the size of a sausage, pushes onto the page in front of me. I jump, surprised, but Davu is reading the words to me, moving her finger with the sounds. I put the plastic back up to my eye and follow along with her giant sausage finger.

"Rat was the only one who knew how to make fire." I read shakily, with bumps and stops, like a handcart pushed over a rutted road, but I don't stop. "Rat liked all the animals, but Elephant was his best friend."

Even though Elephant first steals Rat's food, he learns the true value of friendship in the end. I look at Davu, bending over the table, completely unashamed at reading a children's picture book. *I have a friend*, I think. This makes me very happy. Together, we finish the story.

"Hooray, you did it!" she says, way too loudly. "Let's pick

out another few for you to take home."

"We can take them home?"

"Ndiyo," says Davu. "Our day passes allow us each to take out two books for two weeks. We'll have to return the magnifying glass, of course, but I'll ask Mother to buy you one on the way home. That way you can practice your reading while you wait for it to be safe to go to Kweli's."

That reminds me why I'm here. I suddenly feel queasy and the room sways slightly around me. I grip the little table in front of me to steady myself and take a few deep breaths.

There's no other way, I tell myself. *You have to either face the danger of setting a trap for the lion or be hunted by him for the rest of your life.*

"Can we go look at the newspapers now?" I ask.

"Of course." Davu shoves all the little kid books onto a cart in the corner. Then, taking two skinny books from the shelf at random, she grabs my hand and we head out into the main library. Davu is practically skipping as we walk. Her eyes are bright, and her braids bounce around her face. I follow her quietly, gripping the heavy books and the folded newspapers under my free arm, the magnifying glass safe in my pocket.

We find a free table in a corner and spread the newspapers out around us. Slowly, Davu and I wade through them. There are some talking about the inauguration of the albino MPs we saw on the television. The woman was appointed, but the man was elected. Both of them had received death threats. The woman MP has adopted two albino girls who were attacked with machetes near Mwanza. I shiver. And then there's no escaping the horror.

Albino girl killed for body parts.

Africans with albinism hunted; Limbs sold on black market.

Tanzania's first elected albino MP fears for life.

Seven new albino killings in Tanzania and Burundi.

Life of fear for Tanzania's albinos.

Article after article tell about mutilations and murders.

You're next, the hideous little voice whispers in my head. *Tomorrow these headlines could be about you.*

I stare at the newspapers spread out on the table in front of me. Names, dates, descriptions, pictures. I feel cold and numb. A warm hand on my arm pulls me back into reality.

I look over at Davu and see tears streaming down her face. She squeezes my arm softly.

"Let's read this for a while instead," she says, and pushes the *A* volume of the encyclopedia she found over the open newspapers in front of us.

"*Sawa,*" I manage, and open the book.

We look up *albino* together, though Davu does most of the reading because the print is so small.

"I think this basically means that you're white because your skin doesn't have any color," she says, frowning to figure out the big words.

"That's a stupid book," I say, because really, even I could figure that out.

"If you're going to be difficult, I just won't read to you anymore." Davu scowls at me.

"No, no, sorry!" I say. "Please, keep reading." Her braids

whisk forward, covering her face as she bends over the page.

"It's a 'genetic condition' . . . whatever that means," she mumbles to herself. "Oh, here's something that's nice and simple." She looks up. "You got this from your parents."

"But my parents are black."

"Well, this book says that both of your parents had to have the thing that made you this way. If only one of them had it, you wouldn't be albino . . . It also says here that this means that some kids in the same family will have it and others won't."

Davu goes on, but I'm not really listening to her anymore. I'm stuck on what she just said. Both of my parents had to be albino-makers. So my father left for no reason. It was his fault as much as Mother's. I miss her suddenly, thinking of the hollow-eyed nights she spent trying to keep the farm without him. I know I've been putting Kweli off, refusing to call home, but maybe I'll do it soon. I'd like to tell Mother what I just learned.

"Are you even paying attention?" Davu sighs. I jerk around to face her. There is a wry smile on her face.

"Sorry," I mumble. "It's a lot to think about."

Her expression softens. "That's enough of the encyclopedia anyway," she says, shoving it to one side. "All those big words were giving me a headache. Let's look at some more newspapers."

She leans back from the table so I can't see the pages, and flips through them quickly, her eyes darting back and forth across the page. She tosses most of them over to the far side of the table, keeping only a few. Finally, she takes the small pile and sets it in front of me.

"Here," she says. "Read these."

Tanzania jails 'albino trafficker.'

Albino trials begin in Tanzania.

Albino killers get death penalty.

Davu makes me read the large print of the headlines, sounding out the words for me if I have trouble getting them right away. The pile she won't let me read is a lot bigger but, even so, I can't help but smile. It's been a long time since anyone has made this much of a fuss over me. In a sudden pang, I miss Asu terribly. She would love this whole library, this whole experience.

"Read this one too," says Davu, handing me another newspaper.

"*Sawa*," I say, and hunch over the table, sounding out the words that leap at me under the magnifying glass.

We spend another hour finding things in the book areas. Then Davu remembers something that gets her really excited.

"The computer room!" she squeaks, grabbing my arm and pulling me inside. "Just wait till you see what we can find on the Internet!"

Apparently Davu learned how to search the Internet in computer class. I think about my one-room school where we sat on the floor in my little village and cannot imagine what Davu's school must be like if they have a room set aside only for computers. It must be like this library.

Neither of us has any money, so we wait along the sides

of the room and check when each person gets up. After a few tries, we find someone who still has time left on the clock. I pull up a second chair and let Davu show me what she knows about computers. She even makes the print really big so our reading lessons can continue.

On the Internet, Davu finds nice pictures of people like me that I stare at for a long time, wondering about who those people are and what their story is. We also find horrible pictures about the killings that we click past quickly, but not quickly enough to stop the little voice from remining me that Alasiri is in Dar es Salaam. We find out that Tanzania has an official Albino Society, and that there are organizations in the city that are dedicated to protecting and educating people like me. We find out that I should be wearing something called sunscreen, because I will probably get skin cancer if I don't. The pictures for that are awful and make me feel queasy again. I don't know how I'm going to afford it since it's really only sold to foreigners, but Davu assures me we'll find a way. We find more news stories about my MPs, campaigning for albino rights, insisting that the killings stop. While we're at it we find information on prison sentences for poaching elephants and trading in illegal ivory too.

It's so much for me to take in all in one go. But Davu is frantically scribbling notes, so I know that I'll be able to think about this more later. When our time expires on the computer, Davu looks at the clock.

"Oh no!" she squeaks. "Mother's going to kill us!"

We head to the checkout station where Chatha is indeed

waiting for us, arms crossed tightly. We make meek apologies and then use our day memberships to check out the two simple books for me, and two other books about albinism that Davu found for us to read when we get home. We pile into the taxi, and I look over my shoulder one last time at the library.

I wonder how much a full membership costs and how many carvings I would need to sell to get one.

When we get to Davu's house, we get another surprise. There, waiting for us in the living room, are Kweli and Davu's father. Over an afternoon together and dinner, the men catch us up on all the developments in the plan. The policeman has arrived. The message has been sent. A reply has been received. Alasiri's trap is set to be sprung tonight.

25.

I'M SHAKING as I walk with Kweli. Ahead of me the night-dark street stretches like a tunnel with no ending, and I feel like I'm a boat, cut away from the shore, floating, floating, sinking in the ocean of the city. Alasiri isn't due to arrive until after midnight, but my mind conjures him leaping from every doorway we pass. The deep shadows between buildings and the faint flicker of a streetlight off their grayed-out fronts remind me of the tall rock formations in Mwanza and how I had to duck between them, fleeing for my life. Without meaning to I start slinking along in the shadows, making myself more obvious in an attempt to disappear. When we pass under a streetlamp, my clear arm hairs shine up at me like silver.

I'm beginning to wonder whether I should have stayed at Chatha's, or at least let her husband come with us. Everyone tried to convince me to stay there and just let everything be taken care of, but I told them this matters too much to me, and Kweli said he didn't want to be fussed over any more. If I want to sleep soundly for the rest of my life, I need to watch them take Alasiri away with my own eyes. I swallow hard against the bile rising in my throat.

"So, Habo, did you have a nice day without me?" Kweli's voice interrupts my frightened thoughts.

"*Ndiyo, Bwana*," I say, without thinking. Then, realizing how that might sound like a criticism, I hurry to explain. "Davu took me to the library and we found books about albinism and newspapers about the albino MPs. I saw them on the TV at Davu's house. They look just like me."

"Hmm," responds Kweli mildly.

"It's really interesting, *Bwana*. There's so much information out there that I never knew. Davu used the computer and showed me pictures in color. It's like a TV, but you control what you see and how long you see it for." I pause, realizing that my comparison of a computer to a television will not be something that Kweli can understand at all. I cast around in my head for an example that would make sense to a blind man. "Looking at a television is like . . . drinking water straight from the tap. You capture a little of it, but a lot more rushes past you. Going to a book or a computer is like getting handed a glass of water. It stays put and you can sip it at your own pace."

Kweli smiles at me. "Very nice, Habo. I'm glad you had a good time. Perhaps, when this is all done, you can read me some of these books."

"Well . . ."

Kweli cocks his head at me quizzically. I sigh. It seems everyone's going to find out about my reading ability today.

"It may be a while before I can do that, *Bwana*. Because my eyes are so bad, I'm not very good at reading."

"How did you manage today?"

I groan. "Davu made me hold a magnifying glass up to my face and sound things out slowly. Then she ended up reading most everything to me anyway."

Kweli laughs. "That sounds like Davu." We walk for a block without saying anything. Then he says, "But you said that, with the magnifying glass, you were able to read?"

"*Ndiyo*. Chatha bought me one on the way home from the library."

"Well, that means that you can learn."

I shrug. "Davu thinks I should get glasses."

"Fine," says Kweli. "Do whatever you have to, but learn to read. Believe me, Habo, it's not good to go through life as a man who cannot read."

There is real pain in Kweli's voice. I consider for a moment, then make a decision.

"*Bwana*, I promise I'll learn to read, whatever it takes, and then I'll read you whatever books you want."

Kweli chuckles beside me in the darkness. "*Asante*, Habo. That would be nice. Now, you go hide somewhere safe while I talk to the policeman in the house. We'll wait in the main room for our visitor and you can come out at the end after he's been arrested and see for yourself."

I blink and look up in surprise. Our conversation has made

the streets between Chatha's house and the compound melt away, and now we're in front of the metal door in Kweli's wall. Kweli turns his key and we head inside together, closing it behind us.

Chatting with Kweli has kept my mind off of this evening, but now my concerns swamp me.

"Be careful, *Bwana*" is all I can manage, and then Kweli is walking calmly into the dark house to wait for Alasiri.

Now, where's the best place to stay out of the way? I think to myself as I walk around the side of the house to the back yard. I look around. The yard stretches before me, ghostly in the moonlight. I examine my options. The back table, the tree, the shed. The back table is too exposed. The tree might be safest, but it's too far away for me to hear anything. That leaves the art shed: close enough to hear what's going on in the house, but well hidden from view.

I head towards it, then hesitate. The door to the art shed yawns darkly and I feel a trickle of fear trace along my spine. I decide the tree is a better bet after all and am just turning around when I hear a soft clattering sound, as if someone has bumped into one of Kweli's statues.

I whip around, squinting into the formless dark of the shed. *It's probably just the policeman,* I tell myself. *You never told Kweli where you were going to hide. The policeman probably chose to go in the art shed for the same reasons you were going to.* I decide I'd feel much safer waiting with the policeman than sitting in the tree alone. I retrace my steps.

"*Hujambo,*" I call softly into the the shed.

There's a beat of silence. Then, a quiet "Who's there?" echoes out of the shed at me. The voice sounds confused.

"I'm Habo. I'm Kweli's assistant."

I hear the scuff of feet coming toward me. The voice sounds familiar, but with the slight echo of the shed I can't quite place it. Is he the policeman from the lobby?

"Did you bring everything you need for tonight?" I say, to fill the silence.

A man steps out of the shed into the moonlight. A tall, thin, slightly handsome man. A man not wearing a policeman's uniform.

"Why yes, I have," says Alasiri, a baffled look on his face. "But I'm wondering why on earth you, of all people, are so keen to help me."

I freeze where I'm standing. No, this isn't right. He's not supposed to be here until after midnight. He's not supposed to be in the shed. *Where is the policeman?*

I stumble backward, away from him. *What do I do?*

"Don't come any closer!" I say, trying to buy myself time to think.

Obligingly, Alasiri stops about two meters away from me, hands on hips, considering me. He looks truly surprised to see me and I realize that he didn't know that I was living here after all.

I force myself to think. Alasiri's here to conduct business with Kweli. But now Alasiri has seen me and knows that I can identify him to the police. He might not go through with the deal if there are witnesses. A cold sweat starts to run between my shoulder blades.

"Why are you here?" I blurt out, thinking about the shed in particular. Alasiri takes it as a more general question.

"That," says Alasiri, "is really none of your business. A better question is, why are *you* here?" There's genuine puzzlement in his voice.

I remind myself that Alasiri doesn't know anything about me or my life here or my involvement with Kweli or the police or that, somewhere in the compound, there's a policeman. There has to be some way that I can make this all work out. *Did I tell him something that has already given the trap away?* I think quickly through what's been said so far. No, I don't think so, though he must be suspicious. I decide to try and make the trap work anyway and hope like I've never hoped before that the policeman is within earshot.

"I told you already," I say, putting anger in my voice to cover the fear that would otherwise be there, "I work for Kweli. He said he was expecting a delivery of . . ." I pause just long enough for Alasiri to think I don't want to tell him about the ivory ". . . carving materials tonight. I was going to the shed to make some room for it." As I say this, the noises in the shed suddenly make sense. That must be what Alasiri was doing, putting the ivory in the shed. Or . . . was he hiding the body of the policeman, knocked out or, worse, dead? What if Alasiri got here first and there's no one here to help us? Black dots begin to dance along the edges of my vision and I feel dizzy with fright.

Alasiri's eyes have narrowed. "Interesting," he says. "You're not running away. Why aren't you running away from me, Dhahabo?"

My heart is hammering in my chest. *Where's his knife? Does he have it with him right now?* I squint through the moonlight at him, but I can't tell if the sheath is attached to his side or not.

Alasiri sees me looking. A slow smile creeps across his face and he reaches around to his hip and pulls his knife out of his belt, the same hunting knife that has haunted my dreams.

"Ah, you remembered," he says, and starts to walk slowly toward me.

My breathing hitches in my chest and my eyes dart around the yard as I back away from the glinting blade.

What can I use against him? Because of Kweli's blindness I've memorized the exact locations of all the hatchets and carving tools, and I know I could find them in the dark. That's no good, though. I'm used to using a knife on wood, Alasiri is used to using it to kill and dismember. It would be no competition at all.

My heart is leaping around in my chest like a bird caught in a basket. I can't win against him on strength. I'm going to have to outsmart him somehow. *What can I use against him?* How is Alasiri weak? I think hard. He's superstitious. He's overconfident. He's greedy.

A terrible plan occurs to me. The question I asked myself only three days ago echoes at me eerily: *Is this worth dying for?* Now is the time to answer that for sure.

"What are you going to do?" I ask loudly. And now I do let

the fear show in my voice along with the anger. I let the sound carry. *Surely I'm being loud enough? Kweli! Can you hear me?*

"I think you know," he says. "I'm going to finish what I started in Mwanza. I'm not going to let you report me to the police, and I like to finish what I start."

"No," I shout. "I wouldn't let you kill me in Mwanza, and I'm not going to let you kill me here, either."

"Habo? What's going on?" Kweli appears at the back door of the house. This is a key part of my idea. The only way I get to stay alive is if I can make Alasiri think he can have both me and the ivory. I start yelling at Kweli, telling him things he already knows, hoping he understands I'm changing the plan.

"Kweli! This man is not Kanu! His real name is Alasiri. He's the one who tried to kill me in Mwanza!" I haven't taken my eyes off of Alasiri, who has paused, knife held loosely and at the ready in his hand, looking between us. *Please don't go after Kweli.* I hope beyond hope that I haven't just doomed both of us. *Where's the policeman?* My brilliant plan is nothing but a death sentence if he's not there to save us in the end.

Since Kweli has not turned on any lamps, the moonlight is still the only thing lighting us in shades of inky blue and gray. My skin glows like a beacon.

"Kweli!" I say, filling my voice with all the fear I've been keeping bottled up. "Don't let him kill me! Don't do his carvings if he kills me!"

Please, Kweli! Please understand what I'm trying to tell you.

"Of course not!" barks Kweli. "I don't know who you are," he says to the yard at large, "but if you hurt Habo in any way,

I will absolutely not work for you."

I hold my breath, watching Alasiri, trying to look small and vulnerable, praying he takes the bait. When I see that hateful smile stretch across his face, I know he has. I see his muscles tense up a moment before he springs at me.

It is the hardest thing I have ever done not to dodge his grab. *This matters more!* I tell myself fiercely. And, pretending to stumble in the darkness, I let myself be caught.

With a jolt, Alasiri's body hits mine. His hands wrap around me. In a moment, he has turned me around, one of his arms twisting my own up against my shoulder blade, the other holding the knife against my throat. I cry out.

"Habo?" asks Kweli worriedly. He takes a step toward the sounds, one hand outstretched.

"Don't come any closer," says Alasiri. He puts his face down beside mine and whispers softly to me. "Go ahead, Dhahabo, tell him why he shouldn't."

"He has a knife at my throat," I manage to squeak. I'm on my tiptoes, trying to lessen the pressure on my twisted arm and I don't need to fake the terror in my voice. The heat of Alasiri's body sears through my sweat-soaked shirt. His knife is a line of ice just above my collarbone.

"So, *Bwana*," says Alasiri silkily, "I have an even better idea than our original deal. You will carve for me, free of charge, and in exchange I will not kill your assistant."

"*Bwana*, he has me! Please, please, say yes," I rasp. The pressure against my throat is making it hard for me to breathe.

Kweli cocks his head sideways at me, a line appearing

between his eyebrows. *Don't call the policeman out, Kweli. We haven't gotten him to confess to anything yet.*

"I don't like this," says Kweli. I'm not sure whether this is addressed to me or to Alasiri, but Alasiri takes it as being addressed to him. He gives a short laugh.

"No one asked you to like it, old man. But you'll do it anyway."

"And just what is it you expect me to do?" asks Kweli. Through the thick fog of terror wrapping around me, I feel a small glow of triumph. Kweli understood. He's playing along. That means that the policeman must be somewhere nearby.

Doesn't it?

Alasiri, thinking he's won, takes the knife away to gesture at Kweli with it as he speaks. Though he still holds my twisted left arm, I sink down from my tiptoes, gasping with relief at the removal of the knife.

"I," says Alasiri, "have just put twelve ivory tusks of varying sizes in your shed. You will carve these for me. The larger ones should be inlaid with animal motifs; the smaller ones can be cut and made into stand-alone statues. You have just one week to do this. Until then, Habo will stay with me. In a week's time, you will drop the carvings off, packed in boxes, in an abandoned warehouse that I'll tell you how to find. You will leave them there and walk away. If you bring anyone with you, or if anyone goes into that warehouse at any time in the upcoming week except you, Habo will die. I will leave the pieces for you that I have no use for." I don't need to fake the shiver that racks me when he says this.

"What if I refuse?" asks Kweli.

"Then I will kill you both now and take my ivory some-where else for carving," replies Alasiri. "There are plenty of people eager for the money. You were perfect, but there are others who can do what I need."

"And what are you going to do with Habo for the week? No, you'll leave him here."

"Oh, I think not. And have you hide him away somewhere? I don't trust you not to protect the ghost boy. I'll be taking him with me, for safekeeping."

There is absolutely no doubt in my mind that, if we really were to go through with his plan, Alasiri would get his ivory and kill me afterward anyway. Possibly Kweli, too. There's no way he would leave witnesses who know his real name and can describe him to the police. What he doesn't know is that he has just confessed to them. I hope.

Okay, I think, *where is that policeman now?*

"No!" shouts Kweli.

Taking this as my cue, I shove back against Alasiri, hard. My arm screams in pain because of the way he's still holding my wrist against my shoulder blade, but my movement sends him off balance, and the two of us land in the dirt. His grip on my arm doesn't loosen, but the impact sends his knife flying.

Alasiri growls indistinctly, trying to choke me with his free hand. But I'm no longer vulnerable, no longer weak. I writhe and scream at him like a wild animal, throwing my head hard against his face, kicking him with my legs.

I hear Kweli bellow and look up in time to see his walking

stick come whistling toward us. I duck out of the way and am gratified to hear Alasiri curse when Kweli's stick crunches into his shoulder. Instead of choking me, his other arm is now trying to fend off Kweli.

A strong white light pierces the darkness, blinding me. The click of a gun causes us all to freeze.

"Thank you both," says a deep voice from behind the light. I blink at it, unable to see the face of the policeman holding the flashlight. "That confession will do nicely. Now, you, let go of the boy or be shot."

About time you showed up, I think angrily.

As soon as I feel Alasiri's grip slacken on my wrist, I twist away from him, scramble to my feet, and run to Kweli. He wraps his arms around me, and I finally let everything out by sobbing into his chest.

"You were very brave," he whispers. His strong hands squeeze my shoulder in a hard hug. "But don't you ever put yourself into that kind of danger again. Do you hear me?"

"*Sawa,*" I manage, and hug him back.

The policeman, a wide-shouldered man with a shaved head, comes up beside us, pushing a handcuffed Alasiri ahead of him. Kweli releases me and I turn around to face them.

"Go ahead and turn on some lights," says the policeman. "I'm radioing the car to take him in." He grabs Alasiri by the shoulder and starts to steer him around to the front of the the house.

Alasiri glares at me through eyes that are starting to blacken with bruises along the temple and snarls, "You just wait until I get out. Spend the rest of your life afraid, looking over your shoulder. Because one day, I'll come get you."

I feel cold at his words but the policeman saves me the trouble of responding.

"Your lawyer will love that," he says drily. The muscles of his arms strain against his khaki shirt as he pushes Alasiri toward the gate. "Don't worry, boy; when you add up the sentences for poaching, smuggling, assault, attempted kidnapping, and attempted murder, there's no way that he'll be coming out again as long as you're alive."

I find myself able to relax when he says this. He listed my attempted murder as a crime along with poaching. Not everyone thinks my life is worth less than ivory.

I nod at the policeman and offer him a shaky smile.

Kweli and I follow the policeman out to the front gate, Kweli simply to keep me company, me because I need to see this all the way to the end. I flex my sprained shoulder, touch the hairline scar fading on my forearm. *Forever,* I think. *Forever is worth it.*

I stand in the doorway with Kweli, watching them shove Alasiri roughly into the barred police wagon and drive away. I shiver and am turning away to go back inside when the headlights of the police car pick out the lone figure of a woman standing across the street, watching us. I squint in the quick flash of light, trying to make out her features. Then, for the second time tonight, I freeze.

Because there, facing me, her eyes going wide and standing so still she could be her own statue, is Asu.

26

26.

THERE IS A SHORT silence when neither of us moves. Then she's clutching me, and my hands are fisted in the material of her *khanga*, trying to pull her closer.

"Habo!" she's saying, over and over, touching my hair, touching my face.

"Asu!"

For a few moments there is nothing more to say than that.

Then she pushes my shoulders away and looks me in the eyes.

"What are you doing here? How could you think of leaving us like that? Why haven't you contacted us to tell us you're okay?" She grabs my arms and shakes me. Tears stream down her face, but she's no longer sad. She's angry. "Do you know what we thought when we came home and Kito was hysterical about a man with a knife and your blood was all over the floor? Did you even think about what that would do to us? How worried we would be?"

I'm shocked. Asu has never yelled at me like this before. And now I'm angry, too. I've had an awful night. I've just escaped a horrible death at the hands of a criminal and I'm no longer a toddler that she can shake for misbehaving. I jerk out of her grasp and yell right back.

"Well what did you want me to do? Just go home and pretend like nothing had happened? Just walk into that little corn-cave-trap again that Alasiri found me in the first time?" I point toward the retreating red lights of the police car. "That same one that *you* told him where to find me in?"

The color drains out of her face as I shout those words. Immediately I regret them.

"I—I'm sorry," I stammer. "I didn't mean it like that."

"You think I told him where to find you?" Her voice is a whisper.

"He said you did. He said you told your friends at work about me, and Mrs. Msembo overheard you and called him."

"Oh my god," she whispers. She steps away to arm's length and covers her mouth with her hands, making it hard to hear her. "I did tell them about you. Once. Only once. Halima and Aisha . . . We were comparing our brothers and sisters . . . I . . ." She seems to struggle for a minute, then changes what she was going to say. "He found you because of me?"

Her question hangs between us. In the silence, my eyes adjust to the low light of the streetlamp and register the details of her appearance that tell me more about the hardships she has suffered than she will ever tell me. Her cheeks have sunk in: She has gone without enough food for many days. There are new lines beside her eyes and dark circles under them: She has not been sleeping well for worry. Her *khanga* is dusty and stained along the hem: She has traveled a lot, probably sleeping on the streets to save money.

"I don't know," I reply. I say it just to make her feel better, but once the words have left my mouth, I realize they're true. I don't know if it's Asu's fault. Yes, she may have talked about me at work, but Alasiri had a good idea where we were staying from having dropped us off in town. Back when Mother thought he might be a good match for Asu, she was telling him all kinds of things about us. It would have been a short search for him to ask around the Kirumba fish market for people who had family visiting from Arusha. And I remember the crazy *waganga*'s interest in me before we even got to Mwanza. Alasiri knew too much about me long before Asu ever said anything to her friends over lunch in Mrs. Msembo's house.

I hear Davu's words again: *No one should be condemned because of an accident.*

"I'm sorry," I whisper. "It's not your fault."

"Is that why you didn't come wake me when you came to get your clothes?" She hugs her arms around herself as if she's cold. "You must hate me now."

I reach out and grab her hand.

"No! No, that's not it at all. I . . . I knew that if I stayed, or if any of you came with me, you'd be in danger because of me. I couldn't let that happen. I'm sorry you were sad, Asu. I hoped . . ." I trail off, remembering what I had hoped. "I hoped that you'd think I was dead and forget about me. Then you wouldn't need to be worried anymore."

There are tears streaming down Asu's face again, and she reaches up her free hand to me.

"*Punguani* . . . How was I going to think you were dead when you came back to get your clothes and the money?" she asks, shaking her head. I realize how silly it is that I swore Kito to secrecy. She's right: It must have been pretty obvious I was alive. Asu goes on: "And how could you ever think that I'd be happier if you were dead? I wouldn't trade all the worry in the world for your death."

"I won't forget again," I say, and finally she smiles.

"Boy, are you going to introduce me properly to this sister of yours or just keep talking in the middle of the street?"

In the shock of finding Asu, I've completely forgotten Kweli for a moment. I smile and turn around to introduce them.

"Asu, meet Kweli. He's a wonderful sculptor who is teaching me to carve. Just don't ever try to steal his dinner!"

Kweli barks a laugh. Asu steps forward and bows her head. "*Shikamu, Bwana.*"

"*Marahaba*, Habo's sister." He smiles. "I am very old, girl," says Kweli, "and very wise." Asu looks confused by this little speech, but I start to laugh quietly. I know Kweli well enough now to see the moods behind his odd words. "And one of the things I have learned in all this time are the five secrets to a happy life. The first is: No stories without food."

My laugh is no longer so quiet. Asu looks puzzled, but she's smiling now, too.

"What are the other four, *Bwana*?" I ask. I have a feeling

that Kweli is making this up on the spot.

"That is the only one that matters just now." Kweli scowls. Now I'm nearly positive he's making this up. "Come, let's go get something to eat. There is a little restaurant just up the road that's open until midnight and does a lovely fried green banana stew."

"Oh, you're too kind . . ." starts Asu, but I grab her hand and smile, squeezing her fingers to tell her it's all right.

"That sounds fine, *Bwana*," I say. "Let's go."

We walk to the restaurant through the dark streets together, all three of us holding hands like family, and I ask Asu how she knew where to look for me in Dar es Salaam.

"I didn't! When you disappeared, we searched and searched in Mwanza, but couldn't find you. They remembered you at the train station, so we knew you had left the city but we had no idea where you were going." Her voice is sad now, but she goes on, squeezing my hand tightly. "I felt so terrible, I couldn't do anything. I sat around the house, unable to work, unable to care about anything but the feeling that we'd lost you. And then little Kito finally came and told me not to be sad, that you were going to Dar es Salaam."

She glares at me when she says this and I feel a twinge of guilt about not telling my family where I was going and swearing Kito to secrecy.

"But even then we didn't know how far you'd gotten, whether you'd even made it and, if you had, how to find you in the city." She shakes her head, remembering. "We were sick with worry. We worked extra jobs for months trying to raise enough money to follow you." She looks away. "I was supposed to wait for Uncle Adin to come with me, but it was taking too long. I was afraid you'd get hurt, or killed. Afraid you'd run out of money and have to beg in a city where you didn't know anyone. A few days ago, when there was finally enough money for one with a little left over, I snuck off alone."

I'm shocked to hear this, since Asu was the one who had made such a fuss about us traveling to Mwanza in the first place without Enzi for protection. But looking at her, I can see that she wasn't thinking about herself when she made that decision. I feel small for yelling at her and I slip my arm around her and give her a little hug. She squeezes me back.

"Once I got here," she continues, "I felt lost. The city is so big!"

I nod. I had felt exactly the same way when I stepped off the train. Asu squares her shoulders.

"I knew right away that I would get lost if I just ran out into the city; that I needed a plan. So I sat down to think. We had figured out how much food and money you had taken and I realized that you'd run out of food pretty quickly. So, instead of asking around the guesthouses, I started going in circles around the train station, asking everywhere that sold food if they had seen an albino boy."

I'm impressed by Asu's plan. But I didn't stop anywhere to buy food, so I'm still not sure how she found me.

"I've never been so glad before that you were different," she says, laughing a little. "No one had sold you food, but a few people remembered seeing you, even though it was months ago. I walked in circles all day, asking everyone I met. A few people knew about albinos, but when I found who they were talking about, none of them were you. By the end of yesterday I hadn't gotten anywhere."

"I found somewhere to sleep and then got up the next day and kept going. The city was so big I started to give up hope that I would ever see you again," she says softly. "Then, this morning, I was talking to a bunch of food stall vendors in a central square of the city and they told me there was an organization that helped people like you. They told me where to go to find it. I thought maybe you would have gone there, so I went looking for them."

I wish I had thought of that. I had no idea there would be an organization that would help me just because I'm albino. *But then,* I think to myself, *you would never have met Kweli.* I decide I'm okay with the way things turned out. But I also want to find out more about this organization Asu is talking about.

"As I worked north through the city, on my way to the organization's headquarters, I kept asking along the way if anyone had seen an albino. It slowed me down and I wasn't really expecting them to say *yes* anymore but then, out of nowhere, a candy vendor in Mwenge told me he had seen an albino boy working at the woodcarvers' market. I decided to go there first, just in case."

Asu's smile widens. "And I'm so glad I did. I walked into the market and asked my question and suddenly, everyone was talking at once! Yes, they said, they knew an albino. Yes, he was a boy about thirteen years old, about so tall. Yes, he had arrived only recently."

There are tears standing in her eyes. "It hurt to hope, but I asked them where I could find you. They told me you were living with a blind sculptor and told me the address. I got a little lost," she admits, "but then finally, I found the house.

"Suddenly, I'm terrified again, because there are police cars in front of the house with their lights on and all I can think is, *No! Don't have him be hurt just when I've found him!*" Asu looks down at me hollowly, caught up in the fear. "And then my heart stops because I see them leading Alasiri out of the gate."

She closes her eyes, as if it's painful to talk. I wince, imagining how that must have looked, how she must have felt.

"I thought he had found you first and killed you. I stood there in shock as they put him in the car and drove away, terrified to ask the policemen if he had murdered you. And then, I look up, and there you are, standing right in front of me, healthy and whole."

Her voice breaks as she says this, and she pulls me into a tight hug. I hug her back, overwhelmed.

A giant voice startles us.

"Kweli! You crazy old man! What are you doing out this late?"

"Coming to see you, of course, my beautiful Uxuri," says Kweli with a smile, and he steers us toward a counter with stools in front of it and a large woman in an electric yellow *khanga* behind it, laughing at Kweli.

Asu and I sit on the stools in front of the serving counter

and let Kweli take the lead in ordering our late dinner. He and I have come here twice before, on days when we have sold lots of statues, and Kweli always flirts with the big woman who cooks here. She laughs him off every time, but I've noticed there are always more pieces of meat or vegetables in his bowl than there are in mine. Perhaps that's another one of his five secrets to a happy life: *Always flirt with women who serve food.* I grin. I'll ask him later.

Kweli puts on his usual show. Asu looks embarrassed, but I pay close attention to his technique. I can learn more than sculpting from this cranky old man, that's for sure. We pay and then hunch happily at the counter with our bowls.

"Ai!" Kweli suddenly exclaims. "My stew is too hot to eat! Girl, will you switch with me?"

"Of course, *Bwana.*" Asu hands her bowl over. For a moment I'm confused, because I can see the sheets of steam rising off of the new bowl that Kweli is happily sipping. But then I look over and see Asu lift a large piece of fried green banana into her mouth with her skinny fingers and I smile. Yes, there is a great deal more than sculpting I can learn from him.

"So," says Kweli between sips of stew. "Now that we have food, it's a better time for stories. Go ahead, Habo."

I set my bowl on the counter, and tell Asu all about how I ran away, and took the train, and wandered through the streets of Dar es Salaam until I got so hungry I tried to sneak away with an old man's dinner. Kweli interjects annoyingly with reminders not to skimp on the description of how cleverly he caught me, how handily he beat me. I scowl at him even though he can't see it. Asu covers her mouth with her hand, amused by our bickering. I continue my story, telling her about learning to carve.

"I carved you, you know," I tell her.

"Really?" she asks, her eyes shiny with curiosity. "I'd like to see that!"

"You can when we get home." I smile at her. "You look great in it."

For a moment she looks at me blankly. I realize I used the word *home* to describe Kweli's compound instead of anywhere that Asu considers home. When I think about it, it may be the first time I've said it out loud around Kweli, too. I wince and race on, hoping to cover the awkward silence.

"So, Kweli has let me stay with him and is teaching me to carve. But when I found out that Alasiri was trying to get Kweli to carve ivory for him, we went to the police and figured out a way to trap him and send him to jail. And that's my story," I say, picking up my bowl of stew.

"So," Asu says, pushing a high note into her voice that tells me she's choosing to be cheerful even when she doesn't feel like it. "You ran away from home to go to the big city and became an apprentice to a great sculptor! Who would have thought it?"

I choke on my stew. The topic of formal apprenticeship is one I haven't brought up, but now Asu has said it and there's no unsaying it. I dart a glance at Kweli. His face is still and unreadable.

"Well, I'm not really Kweli's apprentice. I would have to be much better than I am now—isn't that right, *Bwana*?"

I hope he will tell me that someday I will be good enough. That someday I can be his apprentice. It almost hurts to hope so hard. But Kweli says none of thse things. Instead, his smile blazes out like full sun on a still lake.

"Silly boy, you already are," he says.

I think my face may break from smiling.

"Thank you, *Bwana*," I manage. "I'll work hard."

"Hmph," he says. Then he turns to Asu. "And you, girl? What's the end of your story? You ran away from home to the big city and found your brother. What will you do now?"

"I . . . don't know," she says. "I didn't think beyond finding Habo, I suppose. I never dreamed I'd find him." Her eyes are soft, but she's biting her lower lip the way she does when she's feeling stressed. "Especially not to find him happy and healthy and managing just fine without me." She gives me a smile that is slightly sad, then turns to Kweli. "I don't know what I'll do now."

I realize that, far from being able to take care of me, Asu needs someone to take care of her right now. I think of the money that I still have saved and realize that I can be the one to help her this time.

"You sound just like your brother!" Kweli sighs. "My goodness, does no one in your family plan things out ahead of time?"

I laugh sheepishly then turn back to Asu.

"Will you go back to Mwanza?" I ask.

"I hate to go without you."

"You know I can't live there."

"No," she agrees. "It's not safe. Mwanza is no place for an albino. But I don't know what other choices I have." Asu looks down. Her hands, where they're resting in her lap, begin to pick at a rip in her *khanga*. "I don't have any money left, and I don't know anyone in the city."

Kweli clears his throat. "Well, you know Habo. And now you know me. I can offer you a few options. Even paying for carving materials and school supplies, Habo will soon start earning money from his sculptures."

"School supplies?!" I exclaim. "I don't want to go to school here!"

"If you are staying with me, that is not an option," says Kweli. "No boy who can see will be unable to read if I have anything to say about it! When the new school year starts in January, you're going back to school. Until then, you can work on your reading."

I scowl at him, but of course he doesn't benefit from the full weight of my displeasure.

Kweli waves away my objections with one calloused hand and continues: "As I was saying, he will start to earn money, and we can find you a job, too. Once you both have a little saved up, you can buy another train ticket if you want, or set yourself up in town here. Until then, I'm sure that my niece will pounce on the opportunity to help you." Kweli gives a mischievous smile. "Chatha loves it when I pick up strays."

I groan, thinking of Chatha's reaction when she first found me living with her uncle.

Kweli laughs at my response. "Besides," he says. His smile is truly devious now. "I hear she has a spare bedroom."

I decide to be very far away when that conversation happens between Kweli and Chatha.

"Thank you, *Bwana!*" Asu looks overwhelmed. "It would be good to have work. I wouldn't want to be an imposition."

"*Ndiyo*," says Kweli, "it's good to be independent. I agree."

"*Asante*," says Asu again.

"Excellent!" Kweli pushes himself to his feet, dusts off his hands, and grabs his walking stick. "That's settled then. Now, if everyone's done, let's go home. I, for one, am so tired after tonight's excitement that I think I will sleep for a week."

I pick up our three bowls and hand them to the restaurant lady with our thanks.

"Oh, but we have to let the rest of the family know you're safe!" exclaims Asu.

"What?"

"The rest of the family: Mother, Auntie, Chui, everyone! I haven't had enough money to call them, but there's so much to tell them! Alasiri's going to jail! You're safe!"

Kweli tips his head toward me, his brows drawn together. "Now there's a good idea," he mutters.

I feel torn: Part of me wants nothing more than to talk to them all again—Mother, to tell her it's not her fault I was born the way I am; Auntie, to apologize for taking her money and thank her for telling me about the albino MPs; Chui, because he cried for me—but another part of me is still angry at them.

"They're probably glad I'm gone," I grumble.

"How can you say that?" snaps Asu. "Were you there to see? Mother took a double shift at the factory while I searched for you in Mwanza. She worked eighteen hours a day, and Chui dropped out of school, all to raise money quickly so someone could come after you."

I feel ashamed.

"I'm sorry," I manage. "It's just . . . they always treated me so differently. It felt like I was such a burden. That everyone was always mad at me."

"Habo." Asu sighs. "You're family. Even if they didn't love having you around all the time, they still love *you*."

I stare at her for a long moment, looking at her gaunt face, weighing the truth in her words. Could it be true that, in spite of everyone's feelings about me, they loved me somehow? I think of the times Mother held me when she thought no one was looking, and how Chui talked to me about his dreams when we were driving across the Serengeti. The tightness I've always carried around inside my ribs loosens like a coil of wire unspooling. It's a good feeling.

"*Sawa*," I say at last. "Let's go talk to them."

"Finally," Kweli humphs. He reaches out and rests a hand on my shoulder, squeezing slightly. "I'm glad you are finally doing this, Habo. I had no peace thinking that your family didn't know you were safe."

I nod, and since his hand is on the base of my neck, Kweli feels this and smiles.

"So," he says, "one last delay." He pulls a handful of small bills out of the pouch around his neck and hands them to Asu to count. "I don't know what it costs to call Mwanza province, but that should cover it. Let's go find Eshe. We'll tell her it's an emergency and give her a little extra because of the hour."

"*Ndiyo*," I say. "*Asante*."

"*Asante sana*," echoes Asu when she sees the money in her hand.

"*Karibu*," says Kweli, and he turns, leading us to Eshe's house. After a few steps, I slip my hand into Asu's again. She smiles down at me. Her dark brown eyes sparkle from her earlier tears.

"It is hard to believe I found you," she murmurs.

"I know," I say. Then I turn and smile at her. "I'll have to do a new carving for Kweli called 'Happiness.' But he'll have to give me a very big piece of wood first."

Asu laughs and squeezes my hand.

We find Eshe's house and explain the call we want to make. She takes our money and helps us talk to the operator to find the number of the store up the road from Auntie's house. When it's ringing, Eshe passes the phone to me.

For a moment I hesitate, but then I remember an impossible promise I made to a little boy more than three months ago.

"Hello?" asks a stranger's voice, heavy with sleep.

"Hello," I say, grinning. "My name is Habo. I'm calling from Dar es Salaam. I need to speak to Kito."

AUTHOR'S NOTE

Although *Golden Boy* is a work of fiction, the situations portrayed in it are real, and there are a few things that I have taken directly from reality.

The first are the materials that Habo and Davu read together in the library. The children's book they read aloud is a real book, *True Friends: A tale from Tanzania* by John Kilaka. All of the newspaper headlines they read came from real newspapers. The second, sadly, are the stories of the people with albinism in *Golden Boy* who have last names. The two ministers of parliament are real, and so is Charlie Ngeleja. He died in Mwanza the way Auntie describes to Habo's family. Charlie's is just one story, but there are too many like his.

When I came across a news story in 2009 that told about the kidnapping, mutilation, and murder of African albinos for use as good-luck talismans, I was upset that I had never heard about the tragedy before. I started looking for books on the subject and found none. The most I could find were a few articles from international newspapers and a documentary produced by Al Jazeera English: *Africa Uncovered: Murder & Myth*. This haunting documentary touched a nerve and sent me down the path of writing *Golden Boy*.

Albinism, a genetic condition where the skin has no melanin, is five times as common in sub-Saharan Africa as it is in Europe, but not nearly as accepted. People with albinism suffer from poor vision and are very susceptible to skin conditions. Because of their impaired vision, people with albinism in Africa are often sent to schools for the blind. Even if they are allowed to attend regular school, they are often made to sit at the back of classrooms, where they can't see the board. This leads to the under-education of adults with albinism and a misperception in society that they are stupid or somehow less capable of higher thought than others.

Because of the lack of pigment in their skin, people with albinism burn easily and frequently in the sun. In developing countries, where sunscreen is generally priced for foreigners, mothers often have to take on a second job simply to cover the cost of sunscreen and protective clothing for a child with albinism. Even so, people with albinism rarely know to use enough and get skin cancer at young ages. The average life expectancy in Tanzania for a person with albinism is between thirty-five and forty years of age, mostly as a result of skin cancer.

Today in parts of Africa, especially in northern Tanzania, people with albinism are sought out, maimed, and killed because of a belief that their body parts are lucky, or that the death of an albino will lift a curse. In certain regions, it is believed that albino hair woven into nets will catch fish; in others it is believed that albino legs will cause a mine to produce gold. Though the specifics vary, the basic belief is widespread. Under the Same Sun, a nonprofit organization that works to rescue people with albinism from attacks and help them get access to a real education, reported on June 14, 2012, that so far in Tanzania, seventy-one people with albinism have been murdered, an additional twenty-eight have survived attacks with severe mutilations, and there have been nineteen grave robberies.

Though children with albinism were always considered unlucky and frequently killed at birth, as were twins and people with deformities, the hunting of people with albinism is not some long-held tradition. Rather, the superstitions about albino body parts have only gained popularity in the last fifteen years or so. The use of human body parts for witchcraft purposes goes through cycles: At one point in time, the heads of bald men were seen as lucky; at another, the bodies of very old women. However, no trend has been as extensive or lethal as the current one: the targeting of albinos.

Tanzania stands at the center of this trend, both in horror and in reasons to hope. The vast majority of the killings in all of East Africa have occurred in Tanzania, predominantly in the northern districts around Lake Victoria. However, Tanzania is also leading the way in albino advocacy, including allowing people with albinism to serve in the parliament and publicize this issue. One of the albino ministers of parliament, Al-Shymaa Kway-Geer, was appointed to her post by the Tanzanian government. The other, Salum Khalfani Bar'wani, even more wonderfully, was elected. These brave leaders are bringing the albino crisis into the news and into political discussion. They are working with international organizations and, most importantly, are serving as role models. Their visibility and work is vital. It inspires people with albinism to become more active in lobbying for equal rights and shows those in the mainstream that if you allow a person with albinism to benefit from education, they can succeed at the highest level.

I traveled to Tanzania in the summer of 2011 to finalize research for Golden Boy. Not only did this allow me to do some key fact-checking (turns out, for example, that the train leaves Mwanza at six a.m., not six p.m. like the railway website says!) but it also allowed me to meet with the staff of Under the Same Sun. UTSS moves people with albinism who have been attacked to safe houses, provides them with glasses and sun protection, and pays for their schooling. They also work on initiatives to help people understand albinism. Their informational campaigns teach that albinos are people just like anyone else, that albinism is a condition inherited from both the mother and the father, and that albinos have no magical powers and should be treated with respect and human dignity.

If you are interested in engaging with this issue, there are multiple things you can do. You can collect vision aids (glasses, magnifying glasses) and sun protection (sunscreen, wide-brimmed hats, long-sleeved sun-proof clothing) and send them to organizations that will distribute them to people with albinism in Africa. You can raise money for advocacy groups that promote the humanity of people with albinism in government circles. You can also do some of your own advocacy by writing letters to members of the government, encouraging them to pay attention to this human rights crisis. Last, but definitely not least, you can choose to treat those who look different from you as if they were just as smart and as important as you are. Positive changes in the attitude of the world only happen one interaction at a time, one person at a time.

Be that one person.

Tara Sullivan
AUGUST 15, 2012
MALDEN, MASSACHUSETTS

KISWAHILI WORDS & PHRASES

A

adin slender (name of uncle)

aisha life (name of girl who works with Asu)

alasiri afternoon (name of poacher)

asante thank you

asubuhi morning (name of eldest sister)

B

bibi ma'am; respectful term for a woman

bongo flava Tanzainan hip-hop music. Lyrics usually address social and political issues such as poverty and corruption.

bwana mister; sir

C

chane dependable (name of Kweli's friend)

chatha ending (name of Kweli's niece)

chui leopard (name of second brother)

chuijoya paper leopard; coward

D

dala-dala minivan used as local bus

davu beginning (name of Chatha's daughter)

dhahabo gold (name of main character)

E

enzi powerful (name of eldest brother)

eshe life (name of woman with phone)

H

habari gani? "what's the news?"

halima gentle (name of girl who works with Asu)

hodi hodi "hello-hello": phrase used instead of knocking to enter a house

hujambo "hello": literally, "how are you?"

K

karibu welcome / you're welcome

K, CONT.

khanga traditional clothing

kito jewel (name of youngest cousin)

kondo war (name of cousin)

kwaheri good-bye

kweli truth (name of sculptor)

M

manyara a region in Tanzania; type of wood used in fencing

marahaba response to "shikamu." Literarlly, "I'm delighted."

mbili two

mkunga midwife

mmoja one

mpingo East African blackwood tree

mtoto boy

N

nane eight

ndiyo yes

neema prosperous (name of aunt)

ngonepe repose (name of Kweli's former apprentice)

ni to be

nne four

nzuri good

P

pepo ghost

pili second born (name of cousin)

punguani idiot

R

raziya agreeable; good-natured (name of mother)

S

sabahani excuse me

safari journey

saba seven

sana very much

sawa okay

sita six

shikamu polite way to greet elders. Literally "I hold your feet."

T

tano five

tatu three

thelathini thirty

V

ugali thick cornmeal porridge

uxuri beauty (name of woman in restaurant)

W

waganga witch doctor
waganga wa jadi users of
magic & advisors to chiefs
(inherited position)
waganga wa kienyeji roadside
charlatans; similar in activities
to waganga wa jadi, but not a
prestigious or inherited position
waganga wa tiba asili
traditional healers

Y

yeye he

Z

zeruzeru albino; literally
"zero-zero"
zubeda the best one (name
of carver)

RESOURCES

To find out more about the issues raised in *Golden Boy*, including more information on the current upsurge in ivory poaching and specific things that you can do to help people with albinism in Africa, please visit my webpage, www.sullivanstories.com.

DOCUMENTARIES

Please be warned: The images found in the following videos are quite graphic.

- ***Africa Uncovered: Murder & Myth***,
  Al Jazeera English documentary, July 28, 2008,
  http://www.youtube.com/watch?v=W23rqCzVYzM (Part 1);
  http://www.youtube.com/watch?v=IsfWvnE4njs (Part 2)
- ***Deadly Hunt: Albinos in Tanzania***,
  United Nations video report, October 19, 2009,
  http://www.youtube.com/watch?NR=1&feature=endscreen&v=zd
  7RRr5Eubg
- ***White and Black: Crimes of Colour***,
  Under the Same Sun documentary, 2010.
- **"Zeru, Zeru: Being Albino in Tanzania,"**
  a photojournalism piece by Franck Vogel, Visura Magazine.com,
  http://www.visuramagazine.com/franck-vogel-zeru-zeru#.
  UCwqe46PdRk

NONPROFIT ORGANIZATIONS WORKING IN THE FIELD

Please be warned: The images found on the following sites are quite graphic.

- **Under the Same Sun:** www.underthesamesun.com
  A Canadian charity founded in 2008, UTSS focuses on the education and support of students. UTSS educates the general populace to value people with albinism and works to ensure that people with albinism have access to education themselves. They provide student scholarships, school supplies, and lifesaving sunscreen and hats.
- **Asante Mariamu:** www.asante-mariamu.org
  Named after Mariamu Staford, the Tanzanian woman with albinism who survived an attack and the loss of her arms in 2008, Asante Mariamu runs "SunDrives," raising funds for lifesaving sun protection clothing, sunglasses, and sunscreen. It also supports a dermatology clinic for people with albinism in Malawi and works to bring international attention to this crisis.
- **The Salif Keita Global Foundation Inc.:** www.salifkeita.us
  A nonprofit organization founded by Malian musician and singer Salif Keita, himself a person with albinism, SKGF brings media attention to the global plight of people with albinism, engages in advocacy for their rights and social integration, and raises funds to provide them with free health care, support groups, and educational services in the United States, Africa, and around the world.

ACKNOWLEDGMENTS

First and foremost, thanks are due to my wonderful husband, Nick Boivin. Thank you for encouraging me to chase the dream of becoming an author, badgering me to keep going through the rough spots, and cheering my every success. Thank you for doing the laundry and walking the dog when I needed time to write. I noticed and was grateful. And I didn't really want that blue sweater you put through the dryer, anyway.

To my family: Thank you for reading to me incessantly as a child and for always being excited when I wrote. To Mom, for going into innumerable bookstores in the United States and Ireland every summer and buying hundreds of books (staggered in difficulty to grow with my reading ability) that you boxed up and shipped to wherever we were living . . . and then proceeded to read with me every night. To Dad, for using whatever squeaky voices were required for the complete experience of *Calvin & Hobbes*, and then traveling with me to Tanzania and reading every single draft of my book when I got around to writing one myself. To my brother, Mark, for letting me read to you and pass on all that fun, even when you got all grown up.

I am grateful to the staff of both the Canadian and Tanzanian branches of Under the Same Sun, an organization doing a remarkable job of helping people with albinism in Tanzania, for sharing their time and expertise with me. Special thanks to Vicky Ntetema, a woman fearlessly working for the human rights of people with albinism in Africa in spite of the ongoing threat to her personal safety, who took hours out of her busy day to tell me her story and give me an understanding of both the problem and the work being done for a solution.

A big thank-you also to my terrific writers' groups, and to Carol McIntosh and Josie Doak, my insightful beta readers. To Susan Weber, Kim Girard, Carol Gray, and John Englander, who were there as I bungled through a first draft. To Katie Slivensky, Lisa Palin, Lauren Barrett, Julia Maranan, and Annie McGough: Thank you for being with me through the slow and terrifying process of turning that first draft into a published novel.

To the PEN New England Susan P. Bloom Discovery Award selection committee, for discovering *Golden Boy* and helping me catch the eye of my amazing agent, Caryn Wiseman. To Caryn, for that magical sentence "I'd love to see the full manuscript," and all your tireless work since then to ensure that I got only the best out of being a debut author. And to Kate Ritchey, Cindy Howle, Ryan Thomann, Cecilia Yung and all the marvelous people at G. P. Putnam's Sons who have taken my story and, with boundless enthusiasm, turned it into a beautiful book.

Finally, and most especially, to my phenomenal editor, Stacey Barney, for falling in love with Habo and having the vision to see this novel in the one you saw. I am continuously amazed at the care you take in bettering my writing. You pushed *Golden Boy* far beyond what I was originally able to imagine, and I know I couldn't have gotten to this point without your guidance. I consider myself immeasurably blessed to have had you edit my first book. Thank you.